HAVANA HEAT

ANASTASIA AMOR

BRODT PUBLISHING

ACKNOWLEDGEMENTS

The wonderful people I met in Cuba were key in the writing of this book as were Jane, Kristen and my psychic friends. Special thanks to Bruce for his edits.

By ANASTASIA AMOR

ADIE STURM MYSTERIES

Corpse for Cozumel
Days of the Dead
The Curse of the Carnaval
Dead Delicious

PARANORMAL FANTASY ROMANCE SERIES

Havana Heat

EROTIC ROMANCE

Exploring Irresistible

Praise for ANASTASIA AMOR

A CORPSE FOR COZUMEL! "The suspense starts in the first few pages and continues until the very end…strong, sexy characters and intense sexual tension keep you wanting more…great read that's hard to put down."
—— Two Lips Reviews

"I had no idea who the murderer was until the end …...expanse of detail of the locations … a vivid world for all who read her work." —Enchanting Reviews

"…hot sexy men... thrilling suspense… keep looking over your shoulder. You won't guess who the killer is until it's too late." —Night Owl Romance Reviews

DAYS OF THE DEAD! "…murder, hot romance, intrigue, and suspense… a modern-day, sexy Agatha Christie...charming and quite captivating…put together well!" —*4 Stars!* ReviewYourBook

"…Funny or maybe just weird situations abound. This is a fun read, and will be very welcomed by fans of the series."—Long And Short Reviews

THE CURSE OF THE CARNAVAL…Epic Nominee

DEAD DELICIOUS: ADIE STURM MYSTERY…Global Nominee
—Highly recommended!
"…*Dead Delicious* made me a huge Adie Sturm fan… Adie Sturm is…strong, sexy, and independent… I absolutely loved this book … the colorful band of tour group members who will have you laughing one minute and tearing your hair out the next. …fun, fast-paced, drop dead sexy, and keeps your pulse racing in more ways than one. *Anastasia Amor is truly the queen of steamy mysteries.*"
—Natalie G. Owens, *An Eternity of Roses*

EXPLORING IRRESISTIBLE—"*5.0 out of 5 stars Irresistible in every way!* Exploring Irresistible is as decadent as fine dark chocolate and tropical drinks…vivid descriptions put me right there…sensuous romance at it's best. … burning adventure of passion and erotic fantasy." —Michelle Stinson Ross

HAVANA HEAT

5 Stars!

"Havana Heat is a sensory experience. It's a sultry pleasure trip that rouses all the senses and won't let go. I think that the best attribute of this novel is its ability to surprise and engage. Every chapter, every scene, thrusts you in a different world, a varied experience that transports you utterly into magical realms and otherworldly adventures. The story has many threads woven into the plot but they are seamlessly pulled into the finish line and tied together. The paranormal aspect is highly original and captivating. Havana Heat makes you breathless. It will take you to Cuba with a one-way ticket and refuse to let you leave. I wanted to be there with Reese and Anise, Francisco and Sylvie. Your heartstrings will be pulled quite ruthlessly and in some poignant parts, you won't be able to stop a tear or two from falling. Fast paced and drop dead sexy, Amor's writing style hits all the right spots for me. You're going to love this, and trust me, the romance on these pages is something you won't soon forget." ——Natalie G. Owens, *An Eternity of Roses*

"Twists and turns in this tropical romance make it a paranormal reading adventure that will keep you on your toes until the last word!"
——Barbara Huffert, *Linked*

1

Skeletal fingers rapped sharply on the glass.

Dream fragments scattered. Muffled by the rush of the ocean, the curtain rod rattled as a cool wind forced its way in.

"I have come for you."

Unsure, I sat up. My skin prickled. Someone was here. I could sense him. In the shadows of the room, my eyes searched. Slivers of moonlight danced on the floor. His voice echoed in my brain. Where was this man whose whisper sent shudders down my spine?

It's only a dream," my Logical Voice said softly. You're tired. The trip from Toronto was much too long. Shut the patio doors and go back to sleep.

Tossing the thin cotton sheet aside, I slid over the edge of the bed and onto the floor. The tiles felt cool on my feet. At the door, I paused. Over the dark canopy of the sky, gray clouds coasted like ghost ships shifting in synchronicity. As I hugged my chest for warmth, I had my first glimpse of the Cuban shoreline.

About a hundred meters from the hotel, white caps shimmered and crashed down before racing back, disappearing into the frothy foam. The waves captivated. The hypnotic rhythm drew me into a trancelike state. When rain rode in with the wind, I tore my eyes away from the view and closed the door, latching it shut.

Rain in the tropics is unpredictable. It can come in softly, rolling in like an English morning mist, but other times it's as wild and erratic as a tormented soul searching for redemption. This night was one where nature's mood was as strange as my own.

As I swung around, an odd sensation overcame me. I froze.

A husky voice whispered, "Don't despair. I am here to take you back."

From behind, strong arms wrapped round and pulled me close. A tender kiss brushed the nape of my neck. My body responded involuntarily. A flash of heat fired my core.

A stranger…or was he? I *knew* those hands. Lightly, they swept over my bare shoulders to the small of my waist. Warm breath tickled my ear, igniting flames that surged like wildfire into every part of my body. A teasing tongue feathered down the curve of my neck. Yet, curiosity combated pleasure. I turned.

But where there should have been a man there was nothing. A whiff of spice lingered in the air.

For a moment I stood still, waiting for him to return, but when a fresh breeze chilled my body I grabbed the silk robe I'd thrown on the wicker chair and pulled it on. Tentatively, I slipped my fingers underneath to touch my bare shoulder where his lips had singed my skin. He had been here in this room, as surely as I breathed.

On the bedside table my cell flashed red. I clicked the center. The time read six-o-six.

***

A few hours later…

It was overcast. Cool after last night's rain. I drew my cardigan in closer doing up the first few buttons. A courtesy shuttle was provided for the tourists staying at the Hotel Caribe. Twice a day it left for Havana.

Like Noah's ark, the tourists boarded in pairs; students, middle-aged couples, retirees and finally two young men, a lanky geek with glasses and his bald friend.

As the bus pulled into the street, I took out a paperback with the intention of reading. Flashes of palm trees scattered in the grassy fields distracted me. It would have eased my curiosity to see more but the long driveways meandering away from the public road kept the beachfront hotels hidden.

2

My stomach grumbled, telling me I should have eaten yet food wasn't on my mind. The spirit in my room was. Its presence didn't surprise me. Voices and visions had always been part of my life. A hidden part. Only my mom knew and she was long dead. As for my sisters, I'd lost contact years ago. My secret was mine alone.

Spirits didn't bother me but this time it was personal. Ghosts are attracted to someone with a sixth sense. And then there was the fact that I was alone.

I had no regrets about my separation. The last thing I wanted was a man controlling my life again. For years, Henry had preferred to isolate himself in the basement reading. Our once active sex life was a distant memory. And then there were the verbal slurs. One day I decided I'd had enough.

Ten years of combat duty in a core area school and the added stress of the break-up prompted a quick escape. Cuba was perfect. With any luck I'd find out something about my grandmother and take all the photos I needed.

Outside, the traffic whirled by in a fifties time warp. Studebakers and Chevys were glamorously pleasing in an array of pastels and two-tones. Chrome wheels and decorative doohickeys glimmered brightly in the sunlight. The wheels of the antique vehicles shot up showers of brown mud as they sank into potholes filled with last night's rain. With a smile plastered on my lips I felt happier than I had in a long time.

A sudden grind of brakes brought the bus to a halt. The driver let on a slender Cuban girl. When she got off further down the road, one of the single guys, the bald troll, perked up like a dog in heat and sprinted after her. From the window I could see a field and a dirt trail but nothing else.

From what I knew, he would offer her the required amount and she'd take it. Money exchanged for beauty. Girls came cheap here. Prostitution was the ticket to a good life. The smartest ones hooked a tourist permanently.

Along the road the driver stopped periodically to pick up locals and let them off until we entered Havana, where the bus pulled into a paved lot on a hill and parked. Having a terrible sense of direction, I played it safe by following the tourists from the bus in the direction of the harbor.

Sunlight hit the azure waters dotted with sail boats. It was time

3

to get to work. From my oversized bag I dug out my new Nikon. It was the best digital camera I'd ever owned and a ticket to a new life.

A fisherman casting out over the railing was perfectly framed. With the wide angle lens, I captured the statue of a Cuban liberator at the edge of a broad sidewalk bordering the sea with a fort in the background. Through the lens, the Spanish fort from across the bay; appeared like a hazy fantasy castle.

A park was ahead. Broad-leafed trees shaded a well-manicured lawn. A stone statue of a lion spouted water into a tiny pool. Through the foliage, I spotted a carousel loaded with children riding painted horses, while young mothers stood below waving.

Across the street, a turquoise apartment building caught my eye. Paint peeled in irregular strips across the three storey structure. Peach buildings neighbored the residence on either side. Smiling in satisfaction, I took it in through the camera lens. It was beautiful in its neglect. Much like Italy. Yet as a photographer I knew it needed something. When I saw a boy and girl of about eight run into the narrow street in front of an old man on a rickety bike, I raised my camera. It should have been perfectly framed but somehow, it wasn't. Out in the street, I tried again, this time zooming in.

A motor roared. With a step backwards my heel caught on the cobblestone. The bike swerved wildly and I hit the ground. My head spun like a rollercoaster out of control.

"Are you alright?" a deep voice shouted from above. Black sunglasses covered his eyes. Generous lips turned down at the corners. "You okay?"

When the man kneeled, a whiff of spice assailed my senses. I'd swear it was the same scent that lingered in my hotel room. With the helmet off, unruly sun-streaked hair fell over a high forehead. The lean, hard-muscled body in a black t-shirt was a real eye-opener. Jeans and sturdy leather boots gave him a tough look yet I didn't take him for a biker.

Sunglasses removed, I looked up into eyes as green as a jungle lagoon.

"Miss?"

I shook my head. Words stuck in my throat.

The stranger pulled me up. A jolt shot through my body. I

tried to resist but his grip was vice-like.

"Can you walk?"

The powerful current from his hands caught me off guard.

"Do you speak English? German…Deutsch?"

Confused, my pulse raced erratically. My Logical Voice warned, "Slow down, girl. So what if he's big and slick? You don't need him."

But my Hormone Voice was in heat. "A real woman needs a man."

"Shut up!" I muttered under my breath. Sex only confused things.

Lifting me up as easily as an insignificant sack of potatoes, the stranger strode over to the sidewalk where he gently deposited me on a bench.

As I looked up into those mesmerizing eyes, I rambled distractedly, "I could have walked."

"I'm sorry for knocking you down. The truck blocked my view. I really didn't see you."

"I know. It's my fault. I was taking a photo."

"You did this for a picture?" He slumped down on the bench, his lips thinning. His brow furrowed. "Do you know how close I was to seriously injuring you?"

I wasn't listening. Strange vibrations tapped my senses. I stared, trying to figure it out.

"Do you realize how dangerous that was?"

Every instinct told me there was a connection between us.

"I almost killed you when you ran out into the street. I'm sorry for hurting you but you have to see how stupid that was."

Whatever fascination I'd felt initially was beginning to curdle like stale milk. Crazy voices in my brain were bad enough. Sure, I'd made a mistake but I didn't need the lecture. "See that road?" I pointed to the narrow street with the two-story buildings in rainbow colors. The children were still playing as if nothing had happened. The old man leaned on his bike looking at us. "It was perfect for the photo." Suddenly remembering my camera, I picked up the Nixon and examined the lens.

"Never mind that."

"This camera is important."

The man's voice suddenly softened. "I'm more concerned

about you. Please, let me have a look." His hand skimmed the back of my head.

I winced at his touch, not so much from pain but from the energy that came from his fingers.

"There's definitely a bump. Hurt bad?"

"Not enough to be sent to a Cuban hospital."

The stranger didn't give up. He stuck three fingers up before my eyes. "How many?"

"I don't need a test."

"Stubborn, aren't you? Woman, this is for your own good."

"Isn't that what they always say before something nasty happens?"

His answering smile was magnetic. "How many fingers do you see?"

I looked at the long shapely fingers before my face. "Three. You see, it's as I said before. Nothing's wrong. I'm fine. No concussion."

His eyes shot to the motorcycle. "Wait here. I'll be right back." In a few strides he reached his motorcycle and shoved it over to the side of the road, then grabbed a water bottle from a saddle bag. In the crowd he stood taller than most of the locals and tourists. I tried not to stare but as he examined the motorcycle from all angles, my eyes skimmed the black jeans snugly fitting in the right places. The lust factor went up a notch. He was as delicious as chocolate.

I should give him some slack. The accident was my fault. Of course, he would be ticked off.

Then reality struck me like a brick. He was eye candy and I looked like a wasted hooker. Quickly, I wiped under each eye for smudged mascara and fluffed my hair before straightening the skirt of my dress.

Meanwhile, the hottie was doing his male thing checking out his macho machine. Finally satisfied his bike was intact and in good running order, he returned to the bench with his leg dragging ever so slightly. He passed me a water bottle.

I frowned.

He grinned. "It's okay. I just opened it. You won't catch anything.

After I had a drink I shot him a look. "Are you okay?"

When he didn't answer right away I repeated, "Your leg?"

"I am more concerned about you."

"You're the one who's limping."

His eyes glimmered with something I couldn't read. "Nothing to worry about. If you think you're okay, I'll go. I'm running late."

I clasped his forearm to stop him. Electric sparks flew to my fingertips. "Would you like a doctor? I don't know the city but surely there's a clinic." My words escaped in a hushed whisper.

"I'm good," he said curtly.

Whether it was his tone or his action, there was no mistaking the message. Once on my feet, I snatched up my camera and purse. "Good bye, and again, I'm really sorry for spoiling your day."

Conscious of the wall he had inserted between us, I swung around and headed down the street. I wandered off into the crowd, not quite sure what my destination was, and passed a stall with pottery displayed. My mind was not on the clay pieces. As I massaged my temples, I thought of the stranger. He had secrets. I sensed it. Although my best move would be to stay away, a part of me wanted to touch him, run my fingers down the length of his body, and press my lips on his.

As I reached the second vendor, I felt those enigmatic eyes searing a hole in my back. I couldn't resist. I had to look back. The black-clad figure still stood where I'd left him—one hand leaning on the motorcycle watching me.

2

Sizzling with heat, the curvaceous body in the floaty yellow dress was a mesmerizing sight. With each step, her hips swung as if she were dancing a slow suggestive salsa. And that sweet female scent. A breath of it made him weak in the knees. Yet it was more than that. A gold hazy light surrounded her body. He wasn't sure what the aura meant but it was definitely arousing.

This woman was *déjà vu*. He had seen her before but where? Yet how could that be? He wouldn't have forgotten those icy blue eyes. Reese shook his head to clear it.

He was running late. They would be expecting him. Women took too much time and energy. Both of which he had none.

Swinging his leg over the motorcycle, he revved the engine and pulled out onto the cobble-stoned street. The pain would have to wait. Delores had said her family needed help and what kind of a doctor would he be if he didn't come through for them?

At the corner, he veered off down a road, drove a hundred meters and then slowed down before he stopped at his destination. The seventeenth century Spanish style building was brightly painted terra cotta. Attractive but for the rivers of flaking paint and laundry hung randomly on black wrought-iron balconies.

Reese pulled in and parked his motorcycle, his eyes wandering above the worn wooden doorframe where *Viva la revolución* was scrawled in black paint. With a creak, the rickety wood door opened and Reese headed up a narrow stairway. A tiny window high in the stairwell shed a glimmer of light on the specks of dust flying about. From one of the apartments, the stale smell of cigar smoke pressed heavily in the air.

As he reached the sixth floor, a sharp pain tore into his leg. He grimaced, pressing his hand on the spot. A trickle of blood ran down his calf splattering his shoe. "Shit," he muttered, wiping it off with a tissue.

Number sixty-six was embossed on a walnut grained door. Tucking the tissue back into his pocket, he rapped briskly and waited. Footsteps tapped lightly and the door opened.

The brunette in a low-cut cotton blouse and short skirt could bring traffic to a halt. Black stilettos made her legs look long and touchable. But it was the coal black eyes in the flawless ivory face that made him stare.

"Welcome!" Her even smile was a dentist's dream. "Delores assured me you would visit. In the e-mail my aunt mentioned your medical expertise. That is reassuring. I have been worried ever since my daughter's temperature rose." She pushed her hand up into the thick dark hair pinned in a loose bun. "Our doctor has been unsure of what to do." Taking his arm, the young woman led the way to a bedroom in the back.

A pretty girl of about fifteen lay on a single bed, a sheet drawn up to a floral t-shirt. Her face shone with sweat.

From out of his medical bag, Reese took a small thermometer. "How long has she had this fever?"

"Two days, doctor, but it's been off and on for months. I have tried various herbal remedies and they have helped yet her body still succumbs to the fever."

"Don't worry, Señora. I'll check her out carefully." Inserting the tip of the device into the girl's ear, he waited. When it beeped he studied the reading and turned to the woman. "I can see why your doctor was puzzled. It's a low grade fever." He felt below the girl's jaw. "Swollen glands." From out of his medical bag, he scooped up a tongue depressor and instructed, "*Chica,* this won't hurt. Just need to take a look. *Digame,* ah-hh."

The girl glared. Reese didn't know what to make of it. There was so much hostility in those eyes. Had they exchanged words before he came? He lifted a questioning eyebrow to the mother.

The corners of the woman's lips curled down as she stared angrily back at her daughter.

Reluctantly, the girl opened her mouth. Inserting a tongue

depressor, Reese checked inside wondering what had her knickers in a twist. He supposed it was teenage rebellion. He got that. Besides, he'd been a bit of a bullet before he'd gotten his act together.

"Will she be alright, doctor?" A thin veneer of social correctness covered the mother's displeasure.

"Yes. I'll give you antibiotics for her." Reese felt like he had stepped into a war just before the attack. Around the girl, a red aura flamed brightly. The anger had nothing to do with the fever. There was a gulf between mother and daughter. He set a bottle of pills on the bedside table. "These will do the trick. Make sure they are taken with plenty of water." He smiled reassuringly and dug into his bag once more to retrieve a small bottle filled with a red liquid. "Throat spray for the pain. Your daughter should be much better in a couple of days." Getting on his feet, he winced.

Dark eyes swept down his body. "Are you alright?"

"It's nothing to be concerned about."

The Latina stared silently a moment and then said, "Thank you, *doctor*. Delores told me what an exalted pediatrician you are in your country. It is so kind of you to come by. Now twice there has been this fever." Another view of pearly whites and she purred softly, her eyes heavy-lidded. "Lola is my name."

"Reese." He was aware of the come-on. This wasn't what he expected. "I'm glad I could be of assistance." He tried to look professional but Lola's beauty was disconcerting.

After pouring a glass of water, Lola gave her daughter a pill. She set the empty glass on the night table, pulled the sheet up to the girl's chin and turned to the door, waiting for Reese to leave.

"My English is good. Is it not?" she remarked casually, once they were out in the hallway.

"Yes, it's excellent."

"Thank you. I studied at the university here. English is required in the hotel I work." Coffee eyes under smoky lashes met his. "I would like to pay you for your trouble."

Reese shook his head. "No, it's not necessary. Delores and my mom are best friends. I was happy to come and help if I could."

She motioned to the living room. "Please sit. At least let me offer you a drink." She hurried into the kitchen before he could refuse.

A French provincial couch in a gray silk print and a high-backed chair in matching upholstery faced an oak coffee table. Flower pots filled with blooming tropical plants took up the rest of the space.

He sat down on the couch. In front of him on the table, a stack of cards caught his eye. They were larger and longer than regular playing cards. Reese took them and flipped through. Many were picture cards, the lettering in Spanish.

"The tarot," Lola said, carrying in two mugs filled with beer. "Are you interested in your fortune?"

He shook his head but she ignored him. "Shuffle and count out twenty-one," she instructed.

Something about her manner made him curious enough to pick up the cards. The pack was thick, almost twice that of playing cards. The shuffling went slowly.

"Have you been practicing medicine long?" Lola asked, when he started to count.

Not sure on his counting, he muttered distractedly, "Four years as a pediatrician but I worked in a general practice as well."

"Delores said you were exceptional."

"Mm-mm. Perhaps she exaggerates." Reese took a chance and counted out another eleven before setting the stack down. "Now what?"

"You are very intelligent," she said, laying out the picture cards on the table. Her finger nails were long and gold, curving at the ends. "Most people would have counted wrong with a distraction."

"So what does it mean?" Reese eyed the first card. A King sitting on a shell-shaped throne.

Lola pointed. "A very important card. Rare. It represents you. The King of Cups. You are kind and generous. In control of your emotions. You don't like drama." She picked up her beer. "This beer is special. I made it myself. *Salud!*"

Reese followed her lead and clicked her glass. "*Salud!*" he said, tipping back the beer. "It's good. Different. What is your special ingredient?

"A herb called calamus."

"What is its purpose?"

She smiled mysteriously. "It has many."

Reese laughed. "Alright. I'll Google it later. Now you have me curious. What about the fortune?"

"See, you do want to know, don't you? Drink and I will continue." Leaning forward, she gazed up at him in such a way it allowed a perfect view of cleavage only partially concealed by a scoop-necked white blouse. "You meet your soul mate. She is waiting for you." A long gold fingernail pointed at a Queen in a long dress sitting on a throne near the shoreline. In her hands she held a gold cup with an ornate lid. "It is love. She contains it in the cup."

Reese downed the beer. "And the rest?"

"Pain in the past. Challenges in the future. Together you will be with her and then apart." Lola eyes narrowed. "There are obstacles to this love."

A smile played on his lips. "Nothing but love in these cards?"

"Adventure, journeys, traps." She pointed to a card with a hand holding a sword upright. "The Ace of Swords. You see, there is power with change. And mental clarity." She glanced at the cards nearby. "Eventually you will have a breakthrough." Lola stroked his forearm. "Don't worry. You will make the right decision."

Feeling slightly uncomfortable, Reese surveyed the room. "You like it here?"

"This is a small apartment. It will do for now. I have one room for my daughter and a second bedroom I share with my sister." Over the rim of the glass, her eyes sent a message. "She's away."

Reese's glance fixed itself on her breasts. It had been a long time since he'd spent time with a woman and this one was particularly enticing. He picked up his mug and tilted it back, unsure as how to proceed.

Unexpectedly, Lola brought her hands up to her hair, and undid a clasp at the back of her head, letting down shiny black locks. Like a frisky filly she shook her mane, until it settled in disarray on the curve of her shoulders. "Oh, I think I've caught my necklace in my hair. Can you help me?" With a twist, she lifted her hair and presented her back to him.

"I'm not good with this."

"See the larger loop? Press down."

Finding a gold oval with a tiny button, he squeezed and the

necklace slipped through his fingers.

But Lola was prepared. Quickly, she caught it and held the necklace up. The medallion flickered with the light. A long Madonna-like face stared back.

"Who is she?"

"Watch. She smiles."

The heavy round medallion had uneven edges. Lola spun the coin, sing-songing, "See her smile. Look at her sparkle. See her smile."

"She is a saint?"

Lola's voice was melodically pleasing to the ear. "Look. See how she sparkles?"

Reese peered at the gleaming medallion again thinking his imagination was playing tricks on him. It was almost as if the medallion was sending him a message. He tried to look away but the saint's sparkle held him in her grip.

From a distance he heard Lola speak. "Reese, what is your last name?"

He was feeling so mellow it was difficult to get the words out. "Lyon, Reese...Lyon." It wasn't exactly clear why he was still here. Reese knew he should be going yet Lola's dark liquid pools kept drawing him in. A part of him said to hell with convention. What was wrong with having sex with this damn attractive woman?

His eyes wandered back to the coffee table. On it was a statue of a woman in onyx holding a sword. Distractedly, he picked it up. An odd feeling overcame him. He sensed danger.

"Put it down," Lola said sharply, eyes narrowing.

The words took him aback. When he slowly returned the figure to the table, he had a faint feeling of relief. He looked at Lola. Her face was close yet far away. "Another saint?"

"It is the same one." Dark eyes glinted. "Santa Barbara Benedita."

Odd how he'd thought a moment ago that Lola looked so Spanish but now he saw something else in her blood lines. That slight flare of the nostrils and the plumped lips. They wouldn't have cosmetic fillers here. Was she a quadroon? The mixture of black and white made for an extremely sexy woman.

"I'm sorry. I was rude, Reese. We treasure our saints. They are part of our belief system."

"Catholic or," he considered, "Voodoo?"

She shook her head dismissively. "Neither. Santeria. We don't speak of it much to outsiders."

"And I am one of those."

Lola smiled. "For now you are, but we could become closer and I might be persuaded to tell you more. How do you like that idea, Reese? I guarantee a pleasurable experience."

It would be a diversion from his mixed up life, wouldn't it? Possibly she felt the same way. Unfortunately, accepting sex would amount to payment for a service. No, that would be wrong. Something else bothered him as well. It was like a dark cloud had settled around him. Had he taken on some negative energy? This same feeling had come over him before Lisa's death.

Drinking deeply of the beer, he finished it, set the glass on the table and stood. "*Gracias* for the beer, Señora. I must go."

"Lola to you, Reese. My name is Lola Rios Cadena," she corrected with a wicked smile.

"Cadena. Just like Delores?"

"Spanish women don't need to change their name when they marry." She looked away. "But in my case, I was never married. I am free to do as I please." Her gaze returned to him as she slowly skimmed her hands over his chest. "I think you want to stay," she purred.

The stirring of his body agreed but he shook his head reluctantly. His brain was in a cloud, his thoughts disjointed.

"You look rather tired," she said, wetting her lips with the tip of her tongue. "I think I could help you to relax."

His mind flashed to the blonde and the hazy gold energy that had surrounded her body. She was the woman he had always imagined he'd encounter and today he had. He could kick himself for stupidly walking away.

Lola stroked his thigh, a seductive smile on her lips. She was lovely. All thoughts of the blonde vanished.

With one gold fingernail, Lola undid her top button. And then another until the blouse slipped off her shoulders. Her breasts were full and high in a black push-up bra. Looking directly into his eyes, Lola unclasped the front-closure. In a daze, he brought his hand forward to caress one peak and then the other, fingertips lightly skimming the perked hard buds.

With a power he wouldn't have guessed, Lola took control, shoving him back on the couch.

"I want you now, Reese," she whispered, straddling him.

It was almost agonizing to wait for her to undo his belt and slip down the zipper of his jeans.

***

Back on his motorcycle, Reese headed into the old town. The ragged buildings and cobblestone streets had their own charm. He could grow to love this place. Once he drove around the square in front of the cathedral, a change came over him. He felt lightheaded. Obviously the accident had taken a greater toll on him than he'd realized, or was it Lola? She was more than what she seemed. A puzzle with many pieces.

Reese frowned. From the color of the sky, it would rain soon. It would be wise to find somewhere to rest and take the pressure off his leg. A few drinks would go down good.

On a side street off of the square, Reese noticed a yellow building with the word *Mojito* etched on a wooden sign. A hole-in-the-wall bar. Not one of the famous Hemingway tourist traps. It wouldn't be busy. Climbing off the bike made him wince. He had banged it good.

A black cat lay stretched out on the doorstep of the yellow building. It opened one golden eye and he could have sworn the cat grinned. Stooping down, he scratched the feline's head until it started to purr and roll on its back offering a fluffy white stomach for scratching. Obliging with a quick rub, Reese smiled. From the sheen of his fur he guessed the little guy had an owner. With another quick scratch, he stepped over the cat. *"Adios,* puss," he said, before heading inside.

For a moment he waited for his eyes to adjust to the dim light. A glance around told him the interior was as clean as it was sparse with white stucco walls and a ceiling trimmed with heavy oak beams. The focus of the room was a curved bar. A few square tables and chairs were scattered around randomly. With the exception of a couple quietly conversing at a table in the corner partially hidden by a potted palm, the place was empty.

Behind the bar, a black man in his early forties, six two at the very least, with a wide frame that carried a lot of weight, paused in the steady motion of wiping the counter. The bartender looked up. A pair of brilliant blue eyes in a dusky face took him by surprise.

"*Hola, señor.* Something to drink?" His kinky gray hair spoke of his African roots yet the narrow hooked nose was pure Conquistador.

"Scotch?"

The bartender shook his head. Swiveling around, he snatched up a bottle of dark liquor labeled Bacardi in one hand and a bottle of Smirnoff vodka in the other. "I have these."

"Rum would be fine." The shelf held numerous bottles of rum in shades of dark to white. Off to the far left, Reese saw a bottle he was unfamiliar with. He peered at the name, intrigued. He had always wondered about Absinthe. "Is that the real thing?" he said, indicating with a jerk of his chin.

"It is. My Russian friend gave it to me."

"Russians are still here?"

Jorge nodded. "A big population of Chinese also. Those are the languages we learn in school. Not many know English." He set the bottle in front of Reese.

The doctor picked it up and examined the label. "From Czechoslovakia?"

"It's the real thing. It has the wormword."

"In that case, I'll try it."

Jorge shrugged. "Sorry, no sugar cube. If you want it fancy with the spoon you're in the wrong bar."

On the counter in front of him, the bartender set down the bottle and a glass in which he poured the greenish-hued liquid. "It's strong," he warned. "Two shots and my customer had trouble finding his way home. You want water?"

Reese shook his head. "Straight." He downed the liqueur and the bartender refilled his glass. With the second one, he savored the taste. A little bitter but smoothly abundant with spicy flavors, something like licorice. Some thought Absinthe had the power to invoke visions. Even if the myth behind it wasn't true, he had to admit it had quite the kick. Eighty percent alcohol should be strong enough to kill any pain.

"You are enjoying Havana, Señor?"

"Yes. It's an interesting city."

"An inspiring city. The history, the music, and my friend, you cannot forget the beautiful women."

Reese nodded. Lola was lovely and passionate.

The blue eyes regarded him seriously. "Do you need a woman, *señor?* I have a friend who is *muy guapa.* Um, yes, in English, I think you say pretty? And she is a bargain. Doesn't ask for much." The bartender rinsed a beer glass in his sink. "Tonight Sofia is at home. Fifty pesos for her and twenty for the *casa.*"

Seeing Reese's puzzled look, he explained, "We always charge for the house. It's her father's."

"You mean her father wouldn't mind?"

"No, not at all. The family needs the money. The women have a responsibility to help." With a shrug of his shoulders he said, "Of course there will be a charge for the taxi unless you have your own transportation?"

"Yes, I do actually, but, no thanks. Although," seeing the bartender frown, he added, "I'm sure she is a wonderful girl but no."

"You might change your mind. She has," he made a swirling motion with his hands, "a good figure." Not hearing a response, he added, "Or is a woman not to your liking?" He lifted an eyebrow. "Perhaps, you are not that way inclined?"

"What?"

"If you are homosexual I also have a friend that you would like. A young student. Very nice."

Reese laughed. "No, not for me, thanks. I assure you, I love a woman as much as any man, but I'm here in Cuba for other reasons." Throwing back the liquor, he drained the glass.

The bartender cocked his head to one side. "If not for our women or our men, why are you here?"

Stroking his chin reflectively, Reese leaned back in his stool. "I'm a doctor. I'd heard the hurricane has left people destitute and some medical supplies aren't available. I brought a suitcase-full to distribute and my services as well, if needed."

The bartender nodded. "That is kind of you, doctor. My name is Jorge. "

"Reese."

Jorge refilled Reese's glass. "This one is on me."

"*Gracias, amigo*. Have you heard of any problems?"

Jorge laughed dryly. "Cuba has a shortage—building supplies, food and medicine, especially up in the rural areas.' He lowered his voice. "Even without a hurricane."

"That's unfortunate. It must be rough."

"Yes, but it is what it is."

"And yet you stay."

"I love my Cuba but if I could, I would leave. I have relatives in Miami."

"What about your family?"

"My wife left Havana and took the children to Santiago. I will be lucky to ever see them again."

"I'm sorry."

"The human struggle is endless, amigo." Jorge pointed at the photo on the wall behind him. "See that man?"

A dark-haired handsome man with facial hair wearing a revolutionary cap and khaki outfit stood in a field swinging a golf club. The same man was on posters all over Havana.

"Ché Guevara."

"Who?" Chortling, Jorge smacked his hand on the counter. "Ah-h, Reese, you make me laugh. If you say his name like that people will look at you in wonder. I tell you something. Roll your *r's* to say Guevara. And it is Ché." His lips made a loud distinct *ch* noise.

"I have much to learn when it comes to Spanish, amigo."

"We all have much to learn."

Reese smiled. "A philosopher as well as a bartender. How is this? Ché Guevara." This time Reese rolled his *r's* and said Ché with a *ch*.

"*Bueno*. Not bad for a *touristo.*" Flicking a glance back to the photo, Jorge said, "We admired him. An idealist maybe but a man with integrity. It was a blessing for us to have him come here from his homeland."

"Oh? Where was he from?"

"Argentina." Jorge pursed his lips thoughtfully. "He was a *medico* like you. Poor man."

Reese raised an eyebrow. "Why do you say poor?"

"Died in Bolivia trying to help the people. Shot by the army."

"I thought he was there insurrecting a revolution."

"Bolivia had a government run by the CIA."

"So he thought he could interfere?"

"The people were suffering. No health care or education. He was a good man."

Reese frowned. "I thought he was responsible for many deaths when the revolution ended. Where I come from a doctor saves lives."

"Listen," Jorge whispered, "there were reasons. Honest citizens were imprisoned and tortured by Baptisa's government. Anyone who spoke out disappeared in the dead of night. Those men shot after the fall of Baptista were traitors to Cuba. Ché knew right from wrong. I doubt if he wanted to punish the traitors but someone had to do it."

"And Castro?"

Jorge nodded. "He left it to Ché."

"Convenient. Kept his popularity intact."

"The people felt no anger with Ché. They understood. When Ché spoke the people related. He made them laugh. But most importantly of all, Ché had a dream."

"Which was?"

"To create a society where Latin people do not suffer from poverty and servitude. Where a man and his family could get an education and medical aid."

Reese glanced at his half-empty glass. He had almost finished with this one but the pain was still there.

"What about you?'

"Me?" Reese stared at the bartender.

Jorge dipped a glass in sudsy water and then into some clear water before he picked it up and wiped it. "Do you have dreams?"

"When I sleep."

Jorge guffawed loudly.

The couple in the corner stopped speaking to glance their way.

"It is good to have a goal in life." Jorge picked up another glass and wiped it slowly staring at Reese. "What about a wife?"

"Never been in love."

"That not what I asked. A wife and children." Jorge leaned back, his butt resting on the ledge behind him, and considered the doctor. "You must be a romantic."

This time Reese laughed. "Me?"

"You talk of love. Are you?"

"What?"

The bartender tapped a forefinger on the side of his head. "*Loco* for a woman?"

"As in crazy? I was once but it went wrong. Too old for that business."

"You must have enjoyed the chase?"

"I did my share. Fast cars, women, gambling. But one day when my father threatened to cut me off, I sobered up and decided to go to medical school."

"You're rich?"

Reese nodded. "Very."

"You are fortunate."

Reese looked forlornly at his glass. "Not at all."

"A woman?"

"Yup. A lying scheming woman."

Jorge nodded solemnly. "It happens. He glanced at the gold watch on Reese's wrist. "A Rolex?"

Reese nodded. "A birthday present to myself. It's today—my birthday. I bought it before I left Canada."

"Canada? You're from there, are you? Cold isn't it?"

"Probably snowing as we speak." Reese jerked his chin towards the glasses on the shelf. "Time for me to buy you a drink."

Jorge took a shot glass, set it on the bar and poured the glimmering liquid in both glasses before he set the bottle down. "*Salud! Feliz cumpleaños,*" he said, lifting the glass high.

Reese clicked his glass. "Thanks for the birthday wishes. *Salud to you!* May you see your kids again."

"Health, wealth and love." Jorge chucked down his drink. "Medicine is a fine field and I suppose fulfilling, but a man is only complete with a family. You need a wife."

Reese slugged back the Absinthe and set the glass down. His stomach burned. "A woman, yes, a wife no."

"A wife can be a blessing if she is the right one." The bartender jerked his head towards the man and woman. "See that fellow? That *hombre* comes in here with that lady a couple times a year. Each time with her. I know she is waiting for him to marry her." Jorge sighed. "Very sad."

As if on signal, the big man yelled out, "Amigo! Two more."

Snatching up Bucaneros from the fridge, Jorge uncapped them and trotted over to the table occupied by the couple. The stocky tourist, decked in short-sleeved cotton shirt and tan Dockers, had his arm thrown around the shoulders of a slim brunette in a floral dress. With a beefy hand, he poured a beer into a glass for his date while he drank his straight from the bottle.

Back at the bar, Jorge whispered in a confidential tone, "He's mad for women, that one." Tossing the empties in a bin, he shouted over to the big man, "Gunther. Here's someone from your country."

Lively brown eyes in a freckled baby face brightened. It was the look of an innocent, not a connoisseur of women. His words came out clipped. "Hey, man, you Canadian?"

Reese nodded. "Just south of Toronto."

"*Ja*? That right? London?"

"No, Waterloo."

"Cool."

"I detect an accent."

"Right you are. I'm from Germany. My company transferred me to the Toronto office. I know Waterloo. My aunt lives there."

"He means his girlfriend," Jorge said under his breath. "He's got a woman in every port."

The German tipped back his beer. "You on vacation?"

"Sort of. I needed a break. When I heard about how hard the hurricane hit Cuba, I thought I'd like to come and help. I'm a doctor."

When the man stood up, Reese was reminded of a giant grizzly. Mumbling something to the woman, he sauntered over to Reese. "The name is Gunther. Nice to meet you, doctor," he said, thrusting his hand out.

"Reese."

"Listen, I don't wish to impose but, could you give me some quick medical advice? You don't mind, do you? It's extremely important."

"What's the problem?"

Eyes shot fleetingly down and back to Reese. "I am a man with much appetite, you understand."

Jorge's eyes crinkled at the corners. "And stamina."

"And now you are losing it?"

21

"No, man." Gunther chortled. "A blood vessel broke."

The corners of Reese's mouth curled up. "How do you explain that?"

"The condom was too small."

"Oh-hh."

"So doctor, what would you suggest?"

Reese stroked his chin thoughtfully. "This could be serious…something for a surgeon to see. You don't want permanent problems." He dug in his wallet. "Here is the number of a doctor who could help. Tell him I sent you."

"Surgery?" Gunther frowned. "I would need that?"

"It's possible."

"And then what? No more women?"

Reese shrugged. "I doubt that, but you will have to be more careful in the future. For now, I would suggest you refrain from sex. Rest. Eventually you should be like new."

The German nodded. "Thank you, my friend." He glanced at the dark beauty with the worried expression sitting at his table. "She won't like this," he grumbled, before heading back.

Jorge followed the heavy man's return to his table with serious eyes. "Likes to have a woman several times a day. I think he's not too happy right now."

Reese's mouth twitched. "Interesting. Never had a patient with that sort of problem. Usually it's the opposite…can't get it up."

Jorge laughed. "Gunther is an unusual fellow. Has a girl in Toronto, another in your city and yet one more back in Germany." His eyes shot back to the table. "You believe his story?"

"The blood vessel part, yes…the part about the condom being too small, definitely a lie."

Jorge threw back his head and laughed loudly. "I do know this. He prefers our Cuban women. He thinks they are the best."

He was almost envious of Gunther with his particular obsessive compulsive disorder. "Your women are very attractive," Reese agreed, visualizing Lola's pert breasts in his hands, her body softly compliant.

He had needed that release. But then, the blonde entered his reverie—a woman with a sparkle in her eyes and plenty of curves to make his blood rush. He lowered his gaze to the definite bulge straining his jeans.

22

The bartender leaned forward. "You have the look of a man with a woman on his mind."

A secretive smile formed on Reese's lips. "Not one woman, Jorge, two."

Jorge chortled. "Careful. You don't want to end up like our friend over there."

3

A pain centered in a spot at the back of my head. Voices droned around me like wasps in a hive. From behind wooden counters loaded with goods, vendors shouted out to the tourists.

Tentatively, I explored under my hair. Tender to the touch, I withdrew my hand to see red-stained fingertips.

It brought on a strange reaction. My hands trembled uncontrollably. White haze before my eyes A memory flashed. In my mind I saw a man lying in tall grass. "See anything?"

"It's been quiet. Getting hungry…"

A round of machine gun fire whistled past my ear. Dropping down beside him, I flattened myself into the grass. Bullets scattered closer. Bringing my AK automatic up, I returned fire in the direction of the shots. When nothing further came at us, I breathed out in relief. The noise of combat grew fainter.

"They've gone up river. We're done for today." Tomorrow the battle would be back on. "We should eat. I have bread. It's only a little moldy. Xavier?"

Hearing no reply, I parted the grasses. He was lying still. When I touched his shoulder, Xavier's head rolled to the side. Eyes stared unseeingly. I pulled him up by the shoulders. Where there should have been bone and hair was instead a bloody mess. My stomach churned. Shuddering, I squeezed my eyes shut, trying to erase the vision.

With relief, I saw I was back in Havana. My gaze swept down the row of stalls. Spray paintings, jewelry, t-shirts and souvenirs. As I touched a wood sculpture, the memory faded.

Adjusting my sunglasses, I scanned the area, wondering if it was a premonition or a glimpse from another life. In my mom's last days, I had been told how the sight was inherited. Grandmother was a visual sensitive. She heard angel voices. There would be a story in her art. It was a gap in my life that needed filling.

As I rounded the corner, I heard the melodic strains of a salsa coming from somewhere in the square. On the doorstep outside a simple structure, dusky-skinned women in tight jeans and t-shirts sat chatting. The plaque on the wall of the building indicated it was a revolutionary museum.

A centuries-old cathedral in gray granite towered high just beyond the corner, above the restaurant and museum. With a breeze whirling through the cobble-stoned square, I stopped to look at the huge rectangular doorway framed by swirling ornate curly-cues. Ionic columns bordered the opening on each side.

As my camera zoomed in, the hairs on my neck stood on end. An old place like this had spirits. Things had happened here, some of them not so pleasant. Impatiently, I shook away the energy and walked determinedly to the far end of the square to frame the cathedral in my lens. Not entirely satisfied with the first few shots, I kept at it before dropping the Nikon into my bag.

Across the cobblestone plaza, I passed a small white and brown spotted dog. The terrier gazed up with a hopeful wag of his tail. Just then I spotted an outdoor restaurant directly across the square. I decided to have lunch and save something. "I'll be back," I assured my canine friend before heading over to a wrought-iron table.

While I sat on one of the metal chairs, I checked my wallet. After leaving pesos for the maid, there wasn't that much left. It was time to go to a money exchange but my stomach growled, nagging for a refill.

A waiter strode up. Young enough to still be in high school, he grinned, his eyes dancing flirtatiously. "*Buenos tardes,* Señorita." A menu was handed over with a flourish.

"*Hola.* Do you take MasterCard?"

"So sorry, no."

"Could you recommend something inexpensive to eat? I'm afraid I haven't much money with me."

He pursed his lips reflectively. "Perhaps soup? We have a fine garlic soup. You would like it."

Soup sounded good but was hardly a doggie treat.

"It comes with corn chips."

Pleased, I nodded. "Perfect." The dog could eat the corn chips.

"And to drink?"

When I searched the menu, it surprised me to see water was more than beer. "*Una cerveza, por favor.*"

Smooth strains of a rumba filled the air. At the entrance of the restaurant, a five piece band had started back up. It had to be the same one I'd heard on my way into the square. Pleasing rhythms. The lead singer had a way of crooning a love song that touched the soul. A song about a *corazón*. An aching heart filled with love perhaps. I smiled sourly. Like mine once was.

I settled in the chair and stretched my feet out. The afternoon sun succeeded in easing my state of gloom. I wouldn't think about my heart. Nothing good would come from any thoughts of my ex.

My mother had died of cancer. From her diary, I gathered our Cuban father had abandoned his wife and daughters. I had grown up in foster care knowing nothing about him or my Jewish roots. Somewhere in this city, my grandmother had lived amongst the Havana artists.

The cathedral was impressive. Although Cuba was communist, the people were allowed to worship in church. Even the Jews had synagogues. After lunch I'd have a look at the massive building and if time permitted, search for the synagogue.

Reflectively, I scanned the patrons of the outdoor restaurant. Apart from a table occupied by a group, there was a young couple obviously in love. Two dark heads almost touching, fingers entwined, sitting so close they were almost one.

Not for me. I was alone but not lonely. In fact, it would have been worse if Henry was here. Under his stare, I'd rush to think of topics to discuss, carrying on inanely about anything to drown the uncomfortable silence. Was it even possible that at one time we'd been companions and lovers?

"*Cerveza, señorita.*" The waiter smiled brightly and set a glass and a bottle of beer on the table.

The wail of a trumpet, along with the downbeats from the band's drums, drowned out my thank you. Suddenly aware of how thirsty I was, I poured the beer into the glass and drank. It hadn't been an easy day. Fingertips to the back of my head skimmed a sizeable lump under my hair. I was reminded me of how lucky I'd been to escape a visit to a Cuban hospital.

It would have put a wrench in my plans. I had dreams.

Unrealistic ones, possibly, yet the feeling within me felt so strong, it was as if I was meant to be here.

Balancing a tray on his hand, the waiter swerved in and around the tables, finally reaching mine. "Señorita. Enjoy your soup," he said, setting the soup and chips alongside a napkin and utensils.

"*Gracias.*" I glanced over to the museum steps. The dog was gone. Pensively, I spooned up the soup, deciding to save some corn chips in the paper napkin, just in case.

The soup hit the spot. I'd mistakenly rushed out to the bus thinking I would survive just fine until dinner at the hotel.

A wave to the waiter brought him over. I gave him enough to cover the bill and a tip. It was time to check out the cathedral. The chips wrapped in a napkin, I stuffed them in the side pocket of my bag and, camera in hand, I trekked up a number of steps to the entrance of the cathedral.

The height of the ceiling was impressive. At the front, a stained glass Mary and Child towered above the worshipers. Old ladies in drab dresses, heads covered with black shawls, lit candles in front of altars. Near the entrance, a young man in a tan uniform sat at a desk.

There was a charge for anyone bringing in a camera. After a look around, I discarded that idea. The lighting and the height of the ceiling would make it extremely difficult to capture anything this extraordinary. It was an astounding structure. Rays of filtered light in rose hues and a cool silence inside lent an ethereal air to the cathedral.

Someone brushed by me as lightly as butterfly wings but when I turned to see who it was, I saw no one. A shiver raced down my spine. My imaginings were becoming far too frequent. I was beginning to wonder if I was losing it.

Back outside, I heard a sharp bark. The brown and white dog danced on his hind legs in front of a man in a chef's hat and apron at the restaurant I'd just left. When the man disappeared back into the doorway, the terrier sat back on his haunches waiting.

Was he hoping for more? I dug out the corn chips in my purse and flew down the stairs but by the time I reached the fence around the restaurant, the dog was gone.

A sudden cool breeze signaled rain. Above, dark gray clouds

loomed low in the sky. A muffled bark brought my attention back to the street. I ran over to the door where I'd seen the cook. It was shut.

Just then the dog reappeared. When he saw me, his brown eyes grew sad. From out of the napkin, I placed a few chips on the ground in front of him.

Before chowing down, he gave me his best grin. It was then that the rain started misting my skin lightly. With a final flick of his tongue, the terrier set off down the narrow street. Turning about, he gave me a quick *arf,* trotted ahead and stopped before he eyed me once again.

I stood there, the chips in hand. Undaunted by my hesitation, the tiny dog retraced his steps and let out a sharp bark. Any fool could see he wanted me to follow. I went after him although it would have been a better idea to find shelter.

Halfway down the block, the dark clouds decided to play rough. A thick sheet of tropical rain soaked me in seconds. The dog took cover under an awning. Above his head, a wooden sign read Mojito. The dog sat on a straw mat on the stoop and grinned.

I took his advice and joined him. Others in the street had the same idea and scurried to get out of the storm. I dropped the remaining chips on the cobblestone for the dog. The storm picked up strength, and I moved in closer to the wall. The chill that accompanies a downpour made me long for an armchair in front of a warm fire.

"*Señorita,*" a voice boomed out from behind me, "why not come in out of the rain? You will find it much more pleasant inside."

I had to crane my neck up to see the dark-skinned man's face. An impressive height, he could have been a football linebacker so broad were his shoulders. "I haven't much money with me."

"*No hay problema.* There are men inside," he eyed me speculatively, "who would be more than happy to provide you with food and drinks."

When I frowned, he patted my shoulder reassuringly. "Not bad types. Regular *hombres.*" Grinning, he took my elbow. "And any friend of this *perro* is a friend of mine."

I paused to adjust to the dim lighting inside. "He's your dog?"

"Sometimes. I call him Mojito and this is his residence but he has friends in the square that take care of his food needs as well," the bartender said, heading to the bar.

From the corner, I heard a loud snort. A burly man in casual cotton pants and shirt commented in accented English. "I think he prefers their cooking to yours, Jorge. Who can blame him?"

The big Cuban grinned broadly. "A regular diet of my *frijoles* would get rid of that paunch of yours. Forget your greasy Canadian food. No wonder you have," he swung his arms as if he was embracing Santa Claus, "a big belly."

When I peered over to get a look at my fellow Canadian, a pair of lively brown eyes gazed back. Getting on his feet, he trotted over and extended a big hand. "Jorge is just jealous. Hello, beautiful lady, I'm Gunther. Welcome to the Mojito."

"Anise." I shook his hand. "You're Canadian yet I detect an accent?"

"German. Living in Toronto for now. Come join us." He indicated the petite Latina in a tight green dress sitting with him. "This is my Clara. She speaks only a little English."

Slipping off my damp cardigan and placing it on the back of the chair, I took a seat at the round table. "*Hola,*" I said to the petite brunette.

Clara leaned over, pulled me close and kissed me lightly on each cheek. It was something to get used to.

When soft fur brushed my calf I looked down, half expecting the little dog but it was a golden-eyed black cat with glossy short fur. I scratched the little creature on its head between the ears. My new friend rubbed appreciatively against my leg.

"Negro likes you," commented the German. "He is particular about his associates. This *gato* is a good judge of character." He pursed his lips. "I suppose a cat would have to be."

"Why?"

"Santeria. They sacrifice small animals for their blood. Although birds and goats are the most common."

"That's awful. I have heard of chickens but cats and dogs?"

Gunther shrugged his shoulders. "Who knows? Every Santeria saint needs a different sacrifice. Odd that you don't see many cats, though, isn't it?"

That was true enough. I hadn't thought about it but I hadn't seen one cat in the streets. "It's all very secretive. They claim to be

Catholics but most people belong to Santeria. So, you understand why Negro stays here in the bar. He wouldn't trust just anyone. I think he feels the danger."

I stroked the cat's soft fur. I heard him purr as I scratched him under the chin.

"He thinks you can be trusted."

"What do you know of about this religion, Gunther? Isn't Santeria something like Voodoo?"

"I don't know how they compare, Anise. I can tell you herbs and plants play a role, for sure. There are stores from which to buy the necessary objects for healing. That's right, isn't it, Clara?"

Clara nodded imperceptively. "The priest or priestess helps people," she shook her head, "but I should not speak of it. If you want to be part of Santeria, a *madrina* must teach you."

Gunther pushed his wire-rimmed glasses firmly on his nose. "I can tell you some things. There is a patron saint for each person. They told me mine is Chango." Gunther tipped his beer back. "A saint who has many lovers. Now," he lifted his forefinger and waved it emphatically, "I heard that drug lords pick the god of hunting. How is he called, Clara?"

"Ochosi," Clara murmured, placing a hand on her boyfriend's arm as if to stop the conversation.

But the big man had just warmed up to the topic. "It is quite fascinating. I have seen a little of the songs, dancing and rituals mainly because of Clara."

"Hey, Gunther," Jorge called out from behind the bar. "I think you are being greedy, amigo. You have no need for two women, especially now." He rapped his hand on the bar. "But the doctor here needs to meet a pretty woman. Don't you, my friend?" he said to the man seated on the barstool before him.

"Yes, of course." The German called out to the stranger seated at the bar with his back to us. "Hey, doctor! Foreigners need to stick together." Gunther tossed back the last trickle in his beer bottle. "Bring your bottle over here and be sociable."

4

The stranger swiveled around. Startled, I recognized him. Eyes like a forest at dusk. He wasn't classically handsome but the strong nose, jaw line and eyes made for a magnetic face.

Slick in his black clothing, he was a panther surveying his territory. When he strode over to us, he nodded briskly. "*Hola.* I'm Reese," he said, taking the chair beside me.

"There is no need for you to drink alone. We will help you out." Gunther peered at the bottle of Absinthe Reese set on the table. "Never tried that stuff but always willing to experiment. This is your lucky day, doctor. You met me," he pointed to his chest, "Gunther, and now you will meet," he gestured, "these lovely ladies."

The doctor was some cool customer. Only a few hours ago he had run me down but now it was as if we had never met. He smiled and nodded.

Grinning broadly, the bartender traipsed over and set down four shot glasses.

As Reese poured the green liquid in the short clear glasses, Gunther eyed the doctor. "Shall I introduce you? This fabulous creature is Anise and this sensational lady is my lovely Clara."

"Nice to meet you ladies. *Encantado.*" Reese's look was guarded.

Was he still angry about the accident?

From under heavy-lidded eyes, Clara studied Reese. It was clear she found him attractive. "You are a doctor?"

"*Si.* A pediatrician."

Clara raised an eyebrow.

"*Un doctor para los chicos,*" Gunther explained.

"Ah-hh. *Muy bien.*" Clara smiled and batted her lashes

flirtatiously. "It is a wonderful thing to be a doctor."

"It is." Although Reese spoke to Clara, his enigmatic eyes watched me.

"Where are you from?"

"Canada. Outside of Toronto."

Gunther held his glass up. "Come everyone, a toast, *Salud!*"

I joined the others in clinking glasses before I tipped back the Absinthe. Strange how he lived so close to my home.

Reese touched my hand. "You like it?"

His touch was electric. I withdrew my hand. It was difficult to speak. "Mm-mm," I murmured, drawn to his face more than I wanted to be. "Subtle spices. I'm not sure what. Not mint?"

The corners of his mouth turned up. "It's anise. Absinthe has anise in it."

Gunther laughed. "I think you brought the perfect drink for this lady." He glanced at his empty glass. "Good enough for another," he said, holding his glass for a refill.

With a hint of a smile, Reese poured some more. "Staying here in Havana?"

"Near here."

Gunther squeezed Clara's hand. "We are in Guanoba. What about you, Doc?"

"Outside of the city. A few miles from you—east."

"And Anise," Gunther cocked his head, "where is your place?"

"Same. The Este beach."

Gunther squeezed Clara's shoulder. "It is a great there." He pursed his bow mouth. "Are you here for long, Anise?"

"As long as I need to be."

"Ah-ha, a cryptic answer." Gunther said, leaning back in his chair. "A woman of mystery. Perhaps you can get the goods on this lady, Doctor."

Reese's eyes darkened. I could feel the heat rise to my cheeks.

From behind us I heard the voices of a group of Cubans entering the bar. They sat down at the table closer to the back where Jorge scooted over to bring them a round of beers. Whatever he said brought on titters from the ladies.

Gunther leaned forward. "Tell us more."

"It's twofold. I'm working on a project."

His forehead furrowed as he considered what I'd said. "What is your job?"

"I'm a teacher but I'm on leave to work on a book."

Clara studied me. "My cousin," she pronounced carefully, "teaches in Havana. Where is your school?"

"Kitchener, a city near Toronto."

Clara rubbed the big man's arm. "Ah, yes, I know of it from my *novio*." She sighed. "I hear it is *muy linda*."

I smiled. "No palm trees."

The big man displayed even white teeth as his mouth widened into a smile. "Clara has never left Cuba."

She shrugged her shoulders delicately, a forlorn look on her heart-shaped face.

Cheerfully, Gunther continued. "Still, Clara is lucky. Both she and her sister work in the Hotel Nacional. The one that Frank Sinatra and Ava Gardner stayed in."

Clara nodded. She tilted her head. "You said you have leave. Explain, please."

"I don't get paid but I'm allowed some time off."

Reese leaned in. "You are a writer as well?"

"It is a picture story of Cuba. I'm a photographer."

Suddenly up on her feet, Clara said pointedly, "*Baño,* Anise." She motioned towards the back.

Figuring she wanted me to go to the washroom with her, I stood up. The room whirled before me—the occupants of the table a swirl of color. I gripped my chair to steady myself. Reese rose and flung his arm around my waist. "Are you alright?"

'Yes. I'm good." His arm was charged with energy. Through my thin cotton dress it sparked into my body. I had never felt that from a man.

Reese let go hesitantly when Clara extended her hand. I took it gratefully and was somewhat relieved to get away. The hand-holding was a little strange but what the heck, when in Rome.

"Hurry back, *Liebchen*." Gunther tossed back a glass of Absinthe and said something under his breath to Reese as Clara led me over to the door labeled *Damas*.

The bathroom was tiny with a single sink to the left and two stalls straight ahead. Clara tried the doors and found they were occupied.

In front of the mirror over the stained sink, a trim lady with brilliant yellow hair was straightening her mini-skirt but when she saw me she stopped and checked me out instead. She spoke Spanish while studying my face and hair. Grinning, she made a comment.

Clara struggled to explain but the words failed her and she pointed at my eyes. "She says your eyes are strong."

Did she mean the color? "*Gracias*," I thanked the lady who now placed her hands on the straps of my dress and loosened them an inch or so before tugging the dress down a fraction.

Her large almond-shaped eyes sparkled as she spoke. I wasn't too sure if it was my cleavage she liked or the yellow dress.

Amused, I left everything the way it was. When I reappeared from the stall, Clara presented me with a tissue while my hands hesitantly entered a stream of yellowish water trickling from a rusty tap. With no soap, I shook off the excess and patted my hands dry.

It was then that a small painting caught my eye. Blues and yellows in the expressionistic style. A sad blonde woman looked over the bow of a ship, her clothing reminiscent of the forties with shoulder pads and a huge hat. It was skillfully rendered. At the corner etched in red paint, "A Sommerville". The name startled me. When Clara took my hand, my mind raced. A self-portrait. The lady in the hat had to be my grandmother. She was Ana and I was Anise. Our initials were the same.

In a bit of a daze, I returned with Clara. Jorge had taken a seat back at our table. The men were laughing. Apparently Reese had said something funny. Somehow I hadn't pictured the man as anything but serious. Catching me staring, Reese's face once more became a mask as he lifted the bottle and poured everyone a refill.

"To new friends," he said, eyes meeting mine.

"Am I forgiven then?"

Sensuous lips curled up at the ends. "I think I could be

persuaded."

"Hah! The doctor is a sly fox." Gunther chuckled. "We heard the story while you were in the bathroom. This guy goes around Havana running down attractive women. I suppose that's one way to get them to notice."

Jorge pulled out a cigar from his pocket and clipped off the end. "I think a person needs to watch out around the doctor." Remembering his manners, he offered them around the table but only Gunther pulled one out of the package.

Flicking his lighter, Gunther took a drag before passing it to Jorge. "And I'm beginning to think Reese is not quite the do-gooder he pretends to be."

"Pretends?" Reese downed his Absinthe in one quick swig. "I take my profession seriously."

"Maybe, but you are a danger to a healthy woman," the German said, gazing at me as he spoke.

"Anise is in no danger. She's…"

"Hot? Which makes her in danger." Gunther grinned. "Still, it's a strange meeting you have to admit. Driving into a woman?"

"Not ideal, I agree, but what the hell. I forgave Anise for nearly killing us. My plans would have been shot if I'd ended up in the hospital."

His plans? What about mine? Arrogant man! I shot him an evil glare.

"And your plan is?" Gunther probed.

Reese avoided my look and turned to the big guy. "Biking inland and helping Cubans."

Out of the tourist area—inland. This was something that could work for me. If only he could be persuaded to take me along, but then, did I want to go with him?

"It's rough up there, buddy." Gunther ran his fingers through his curly mane. "Hey, maybe you could stop in to see Clara's brother. He'd put you up. He has a sugar cane farm. I'll draw you a map. We'd go with you but I think I'd better see the surgeon tomorrow. "

"And my cousin Julio has a house overlooking the sea up the coast. It's in the cliffs, mind you, but still very nice." Jorge's chest puffed up like a rooster's. "Julio is a government auditor. He might like a visit."

Accommodation would be perfect. God knows I didn't have the money to pay for another hotel. "I need to see the area outside of Havana for my book project."

All eyes turned to me.

"Cuba was the place my grandmother settled in during the war. She was an artist. I thought if I came here I'd understand more about her. And then I found myself channeling into my creative side. The areas outside of the city would make interesting photographs. Already I have pictures of Havana which show the spirit of the people."

"How did you expect to explore Cuba? You are alone, aren't you?" Reese leaned back in his chair.

I nodded.

"It's not safe."

"I can take care of myself." For a number of years I had been a student of karate. Self-defense was muscle memory for me but I understood his point. Once weapons were involved it was infinitely more dangerous. "This is important. I need to see more of Cuba. The mountains would be perfect. Would you take me with you, Reese? Please. I'll pay my own way—gas, whatever."

"No way, Anise," Gunther patted my hand, a big grin on his face. "You don't want to go there with him. What do they say about doctors? Or is that nurses?"

My cheeks flamed.

"Shut up, you fool," Jorge broke in. "Can't you see you're embarrassing the lady?" He turned to Reese. "Well? She wants to be there as much as you. Are you going to help her out?"

Reese's eyes glowed like embers in a fire. "I'd like to know more about the whatever."

Gunther chortled and slapped Reese on the back. "Funny fellow." His face became suddenly serious. "It's no place for a lady like Anise. She should stay here where it's safe."

I directed my gaze to Reese. "Is that what you think? I should stay in Havana and take photos here?"

Reese leaned back in the chair and let his gaze drop down the length of my body. "Well, you look healthy enough."

Jorge's eyes dropped to my cleavage. "*Muy guapa,* Reese."

"She can't be any healthier," Gunther piped in. "See what I mean?" He glanced around the table. "He wants to play doctor but the patient is a vibrant beautiful woman with no need of his probing."

I rubbed my forehead, aware of the pain that had crept up on me.

"Anise?" Reese took my hand and pulled me towards him. He peered into my eyes. "Are you sure you're alright? Your pupils are very large."

"She's not the only one, doctor. The Absinthe could kill a horse." The German glanced around the table. "Or cure us of all that ails us. In my case, I would hope quickly. Poor Clara hates to be deprived."

Reese stood and picked up the Absinthe. The green liqueur filled a third of the bottle. "Still lots left, Gunther. Save some for me, eh?"

We watched him head for the *baño* at the back. Again I saw him limp.

Gunther slurred out his words. "That man has something wrong with his leg."

I was feeling the effects of that potent green liquor, myself. "He was hurt when he collided into me today. Out near the square. I was trying to take a picture and he didn't see me." I faltered in my story as white flashed before my eyes. A cold current entered my body. I saw an icy road. A car out of control. Shrieks…pain… and then everything turned black." I shivered before the image left.

"Anise?" Jorge shook my shoulder. "You've gone all pale. I think you need to lie down. The Absinthe is strong." He glanced at Clara, whose head slumped down on the edge of the table.

The bartender was right but that didn't account for the visions. There was no use telling them. That would bury me as far as the motorcycle trip was concerned. "I should have eaten something. At the café, I had soup."

"What do you have for us to eat, Jorge?" Reese said from behind.

"Pork, rice and beans. You buying, doctor?" Jorge asked.

Gunther waved his hand in protest. "No. Let this be on me. We will have all the food you have. Four plates, *por favor*."

Nodding, the bartender headed behind the bar where a small doorway led to another room. He disappeared in what I supposed was the kitchen.

My stomach was somersaulting and my head felt heavy.

"I'll ask Jorge if he has a room upstairs you could rest in," Reese said in my ear.

I hardly dared meet his eyes. "No, I'll feel better after I eat, I'm sure." Something strange had happened with that whisper. A rush of energy had coursed through my body.

"*Gut, mädchen*. Stay here with us," Gunther poured another shot for each of us. "We are here to enjoy Cuba, right?"

Clara stirred restlessly, muttering something in Spanish as Jorge appeared carrying a tray piled high with rice, beans and meat.

Jorge grinned. "I see I must join you or one meal will go to waste. The *señorita* will be better after she sleeps it off. Would you like to take a room upstairs?"

"*Ja*, that might be necessary."

Jorge pulled up a chair from the other table and joined us. "Take the lady up to the first bedroom on the right."

"Sure, but first," Gunther picked up a fork, "I must sample the dinner. I can't wait. This poor belly," he patted-the pillowy tummy, "needs a refill."

Though my stomach begged for food, I found it hard to focus. The Absinthe had sent me into a spacey state. It took an effort to stab a slice of pork and bring it up to my lips. A savory morsel, unlike anything I'd ever had. Not spicy but delicious nonetheless.

The men stared as I chewed.

"Well," Jorge said. "What do you say? *Bueno*?"

I swallowed the tender meat. "It's great." The combination of rice and beans hit the spot.

"I will return," Gunther said, lifting Clara in his arms. "The room on the right?"

"*Si*," Jorge said between mouthfuls.

Gunther returned in record time and dug in with the rest of us. For a few minutes, the topic of conversation was forgotten in the enjoyment of the Cuban feast.

"Good job, Jorge," Gunther muttered between bites. "What say you to the dinner, Reese?"

"Mm-mm," was all he got out of the doctor.

At the other table one of the men took up a guitar and started to strum as the blonde from the washroom tapped rhythmically on a small drum. When the group sang a soft melody, Jorge stopped eating and joined in on the chorus.

The song was about a woman. Although the music was pleasant, an alarm sounded in my head.

Suddenly, Reese jumped to his feet, his face flushed. "Come on, Anise. Let's dance." He bowed in a sweeping motion.

"Dance?"

A glint in his eyes told me he meant it. I dropped my fork.

Taking my hand, Reese pulled me up out of my chair. "Yeah. Life is more than pictures."

I hadn't danced for a couple of years but salsa was easy to pick up again. My right hand held high, I was led into a spin. Managing that one with no mishaps, I sashayed back, remembering to swing my hips to the beat. Every step I took gained attention from my partner whose eyes glittered like emeralds from under heavy-lids. His gaze struck my body like a thunderbolt.

Absinthe is a strange brew. Hands thrown up, I wiggled my body to the rhythm of the music.

Shouts and whistles from the next table encouraged us to move even more flamboyantly. How I managed a double spin was beyond me. I was flying. Soon we weren't dancing alone. My *amiga* from the *baño* decided she would take Gunther on the dance floor for an impromptu lesson.

It was all fun until I lost my footing and pressed against Reese for support. "Sorry. I slipped." The glimpse of pain on his face surprised me. "Did I hurt you?"

"No-oo. Of course not," he muttered, before taking me back to the table and dropping into the nearest chair.

Jorge called out. "Anise, I think the doctor is done. Come, we will dance." And catching my hand, the bartender led me into the next melody.

It was a fast salsa and with an expert dancer. I swiveled in the wrong direction but he pulled me back into a left-handed spin. Happily, I flew into the motion until in the corner of my eye I spied Reese gripping his calf.

I stopped dancing. "I think there's something wrong with Reese."

"The man has had his fill. This is to be expected, Anise. Absinthe is a powerful liqueur." Jorge cocked his head and had a look. "But you may be right." He dashed over to Reese with me right behind. "How are you, amigo?"

"Ice?"

"For the Absinthe?"

Reaching in his bag, he pulled out a pill box. "No, I need it for my leg." Reese tossed a white pill down his throat before he followed it with a slug of Absinthe. "A bag of it if you have it."

"Reese, I didn't realize you were in pain. Perhaps we shouldn't have danced."

His green eyes met mine. "It's nothing to do with you, Anise. I wanted to. No worries. The injury is an old one from a..."

"Car accident." I finished his sentence without thinking.

Reese shot me a look. "How did you know?"

I shook my head. "I'm so sorry I stepped on you." I didn't know how I could tell him something so personal.

Jorge interrupted. "Come, I will take you up to one of the rooms. You can ice it there." With a hand under Reese's arm, he helped him up. "This way." He jerked his chin in the direction of the stairs.

"Let me bring the ice." I headed over to the fridge and opened the freezer door.

"I'll take him up. First room to the left," Jorge shouted over his shoulder.

With a plastic bag of ice from the freezer, I picked up my tote and turned to go.

"What's up, Anise?" Gunther's large frame was sprawled in a chair beside the blonde.

"Jorge is giving Reese a room. He's in pain."

"And you are bringing ice? Very nice. Such a lovely nurse for the doctor."

"He needs it, Gunther, and heaven knows it was my fault aggravating an old injury."

"Well, we shall all stay here tonight then." The big man smirked. "See you in the morning, Anise."

What other choice was there? Glancing out the window at the darkness, I regretted my impulsive decision to come to the Mojito. The last shuttle must have left hours ago and I didn't have enough money for a taxi back.

On the way up, I turned right, opening the first door. It was dark and at first I didn't see Clara in bed covered by a blanket. Realizing I had gone the wrong way, I was about to leave when Clara called out, "Anise, *por favor.*"

Her voice was so quiet, I came nearer. When she sat up suddenly, I was taken aback by her drawn face. "What is it, Clara? Are you ill?"

With a wave of her hand to the bed, she indicated I should sit. As I took a seat beside her, a haze of white appeared around her body and then a deep purple bordered the aura. I had seen this particular aura around Christmas.

Slurred words and a frozen expression made me believe she was in a trance when she spoke. "I am afraid for you, Ani. Be careful in your journey. There is evil in the house." And with that, Clara's eyes closed and sleep overcame her.

With the effects of the Absinthe, I was not myself, but I was convinced that Clara was a medium. Others spoke through her. Who was it that was trying to communicate with me? Clara had said Ani, the name my mama had called me.

Aware of the cold sensation in my hand, I gazed down at the ice pack I held, realizing I needed to get it to Reese. I retraced my steps to the first door on the left of the stairs and knocked.

"Good," Jorge said, swinging the door wide, "you are here. Please, you must help me. The doctor has consumed too much Absinthe. I can't take his clothes off by myself. Set the ice on that dresser and come here."

With his head propped up by a pillow, eyes half closed, Reese had stretched out his long jean-clad legs the length of the bed. "Anise?" he croaked.

"Yes. Don't worry. The pain will lessen. I've brought ice."

"I think I need more than ice," he murmured hoarsely.

There was no question about what he needed from the way his eyes slowly consumed my body.

Jorge grinned. "Reese must not be in pain if he's thinking of your womanly charms."

"Don't be silly, Jorge. Where do you want to start? His t-shirt?" I asked hurriedly to change the subject.

Jorge nodded. Reese sat up in the bed and waited expectantly for me to proceed.

Tentatively, I slid my hands down his shirt, feeling hard abs through the cotton. Gripping the edge of the shirt, I tugged upwards. The fresh scent of spice assailed my nostrils. I leaned closer to breathe it in. I was so near I could have kissed his chest but instead pulled away to let Jorge jerk the tee off.

Overwhelmed by the strange stirrings inside me, I could only watch as Jorge undid Reese's belt. It wouldn't be easy to undress him. The doctor, although lean, was also muscular and a big man.

"Come, amiga. Help me. We need to take his pants off."

A giggle caught in my throat. Embarrassment made me laugh but to be honest, I had to be kidding myself if I denied my excitement. What red-blooded woman wouldn't want to unwrap this fine male specimen? "What should I do?"

"Hold him while I pull the jeans off."

I sprawled over his chest to grip him and Jorge grabbed and pulled the jeans down.

After we finished the job, I couldn't help but smile, pleased by what I saw.

"He is still quite the man," Jorge muttered, a hint of wonder in his voice. "I would have thought with so much liquor…" He glanced at me. "You have a powerful effect on the doctor, Anise. Poor man has two swollen parts."

I shook my head, not convinced. "No, Jorge, it has nothing to do with me." I pointed to Reese. "See, I told you. He's asleep."

"But he is aroused because of you." Jorge snickered. "That's what his body tells me. No denying the obvious." Taking the ice off the table, Jorge wrapped it in a towel. "The bruise is on his calf. It'll be better to flip him on his stomach. Hold this."

Jorge turned Reese around. The purplish raised area of Reese's calf had a bloody gash. Taking my hand, he placed it on the bag. "You will need to hold it here for a while. I'm sorry, amiga, but I must go. I leave you to care for him." He paused at the door. "You don't look well yourself. Rest here. Don't worry about the room cost. The doctor will pay. In the morning we will all have breakfast."

The door clicked shut and I was left to press the ice on Reese's bruise. Examining his face in profile, I was fascinated. His features were irregular but somehow the combination of the slightly crooked nose in a narrow face and full lips all melded into sizzling sensuality.

If I took an ice cube and ran it over my body, would I be able to cool down the heat that consumed me?

With a sigh, I kicked off my sandals and, with my hand on the ice pack, lay down on the bed trying not to think about the sizeable bulge in his gitch. Was it really for me? Had Reese found me as attractive as I had him?

Averting my eyes, I rested, drinking in the scent of his skin. My hand against the ice bag, I slid closer to Reese, sure I should leave but pulled in as iron filings are to a magnet.

An arm pulled me in. "You smell so good, Anise," he whispered in my ear. His lips touched the nape of my neck. Tingles leaped to my core. I waited for more but his breathing slowed. The absinthe had lulled him into sleep.

My outstretched hand came to rest on something soft and warm—a black patch of fur, my feline friend from the bar. The deep throaty purring eased my tension. I drifted off until the rumble of thunder from outside awoke me.

A flash of lightning lit the room. I raised myself on my elbows and looked over to the window. The room spun around so rapidly, a green vapor formed. From within the haze an athletic man with wavy dark-hair and whiskey eyes stepped towards me. Casually attired in a white cotton buttoned-down shirt tucked into khaki trousers, his confident smile spoke of warm sultry nights.

He sat down at the foot of the bed and gazed soulfully. "I have searched for you. It is my good fortune that I have finally found you. Please, tell me you are happy to see me."

My jaw dropped. For the life of me I had no idea who he was.

Positioning himself next to me on the edge of the bed, he looked around the room in amusement. "I love you but three in a bed? This is not exactly what I had in mind when I requested to be reunited with my lover. Shall we go and let him sleep it off? You'll come with me, won't you?" He took my hand and pulled me up in a sitting position.

I didn't dare take my eyes off him, this time in case he disappeared as he had last night. "It was you in my room last night."

"Mm-mm. You found me out, *cariño.* He shrugged his wide shoulders and grinned, a glint of mischief in his eyes. "But surely you can't blame me for that? I needed to see you." Taking a strand of my hair, he slowly threaded his fingers through. "Lovely."

Heat flushed my cheeks. "I'm not going anywhere with you."

"And why is that, *mi amor?*"

I shook my head in frustration. "Who are you?"

"If I said I was the man for you, I know you wouldn't believe me, so I'll just say I've been waiting to come back into your life."

"Back? I don't know who you are."

"You are an unusual woman that envisions things others cannot."

"That's true but..." How did he know this?

"Soon the truth will reveal itself. Be patient." Stretching out beside me, my mysterious caller pressed a leg against mine. His heat warmed my skin. A warm rush of energy perked my nipples. "It would be better to speak in private, wouldn't it? For all we know," he jerked his chin in the direction of Reese, "he might wake up."

The man brought my hand to his lips and let them brush against my wrist.

"How beautiful you are," he murmured. "Your eyes are not

like any woman's I've ever known. Blue as the Caribbean and yet other times they have the fascinating ability to change to icy silver. They see into the beyond."

His husky voice sent shivers down my spine. This wasn't for real. It couldn't be. I glanced up at him and met his eyes so illuminated with life. I didn't understand. First the accident that brought Reese into my life and now this charismatic ghost. What was happening?

"Stop thinking, *cariño*. It is what is meant to be. Our time is precious and there is too little of it." With those words, he pulled me close. His mouth caressed mine softly at first before my lips parted to receive the tip of his tongue. A slow sizzle. Then, fire. The bruising kiss left me breathless. "I need you," the spirit whispered hoarsely. "We must try again. We can beat fate. Come back with me." Lightning flashed from outside the window. The green vapor in the room dissipated, leaving a white mist, and then there was darkness. Drained, I fell back on the bed. My visitor was gone and I felt strangely sad.

5

Thunder-thrower, they called him. Axe ready for battle. In ancient days he was known as Thor but here he was Chango. The priestess needed Orisha power.

The white sheer dress was what tradition decreed and she wore it proudly. Around her neck, the red and white beads were the same colors as the clothes on the doll. From the floor, she picked up a drum to beat a steady rhythm as she sang softly to summon Chango.

It wasn't often she would ask for something for herself but the time had come to have the man she wanted. And didn't she deserve a husband like him? Handsome, intelligent, and a good provider? Too many months had been spent pining away for a man who'd betrayed her for another woman. His love had been false or else why would he have gone back to her? The priestess thought all these things as she set the drum aside and took out the shells. As the cowry shells scattered on the table, she fell into a deep trance.

The priestess called on her ancestors. They would help her foresee the future. It was her legacy. Many years of training had fine-tuned her psychic abilities. Love, health and revenge spells were her specialties.

Images appeared in the contours of the shells. Through a fine white mist, she made out the figure of a man. At first it was difficult to see his features but then the vision cleared. He was tall and dark. She sensed highly evolved energy with psychic strength.

Two figures appeared before her. They gravitated to each other. As they embraced, a flame encircled them. Writhing in passion, the blood red fire swirled and enveloped the figures. Would he be hers, she asked the shells? At first they nodded yes but then they shook no. She frowned, not understanding the news. In a haze, a second vision took over. The man's skin glowed in the morning light. He was lean and hard muscled. Desire was in his eyes yet when she slipped off her gown and pressed her breasts against his chest, he was unresponsive. In the distance, a fair-haired woman approached. The air was static with gold energy. No longer charmed by her lovely nude body, the man turned from the priestess.

Fingertips at her temples, the priestess realized her rival was no ordinary female. She had powerful premonitions yet she was not a Santera. *Who was she?*

Rage built inside the priestess. It was not right! This golden woman must not win his love. She must be stopped. But how? If this woman had great psychic ability, she would be warned through her senses. It was clear the priestess would need Chango's help. When the string holding her dress loosened, it dropped off her shoulders and fell to the floor. She stood naked.

Inside the cage, the chicken looked at her curiously with one orange eye, its russet red head bobbing up and down. She gritted her teeth and with determination undid the cage door. Quickly, she snatched up the screeching fowl. The knife flashed in the sunlight as she put an end to the bird's cry.

With the freshly killed victim held high over her head, bright red blood spurted onto her neck and shoulders, dribbling down in rivulets, spreading warmth to her inner thighs.

Back on the ground, the headless rooster ran in circles convulsing as the priestess sat cross-legged pounding the Santeria rhythm, singing Chango's song. In her heart, she knew a blood sacrifice would satisfy her god.

When the fowl stopped its dance of death the priestess felt strong once more, ready to fight for what she knew should be hers. Gold bangles on her wrist slid down as she sprang up hands high, breathing out the ancient words. The priestess stared into a dream. It was time to shape shift.

6

Absinthe hurled Reese into an abyss. An endless black hole. Tumbling in continuous motion much like a circus acrobat flying off a high wire, he flew downwards into an endless tunnel.

Reese wasn't afraid. Wherever he was going was well-deserved. Fate had taken over. No one could stop the inevitable and if punishment meant death, so be it.

Green flashes shot through the steamy air as he neared what he knew must be the final length of the journey. Twisting and turning with the force of the air current, the trip ended in a sudden jolt as he crashed down, the wind knocked out of him. A kaleidoscope of colors swam before his eyes. When his vision cleared, he saw an orange sunset dipped in blood reflecting over the scarlet hues of a natural pool. On the rocky edges, towering Royal palms bordered the water.

The sweet sound of female voices brought his attention to the trees behind him. They must have approached silently because he hadn't heard them, awed as he was by the view.

Three statuesque women with flaming red hair wearing long gauzy black dresses sang a magical melody in a lilting language that could have been Spanish or Portuguese. When they ended their poignant song, one of the damsels stepped out from the others. She was definitely the fairest of the three. With a swaying hip motion she waltzed forward, stopping in a position directly in front of him.

Thin ruby lips turned up ever so slightly at the corners, yet her smile did not quite reach her eyes. "Finally you have come. We have been waiting for you," she purred in a deep voice.

Reese was fascinated. Whatever this place was, it had women. Hot women. If this was a dream it was definitely not a nightmare. "Hey. Let me introduce myself. My name is Reese."

The auburn beauty nodded. "I know. I am called Sangra."

The other two women had spread a fluffy red blanket on the grass.

With a jerk of her chin, Sangra motioned them back and then settled herself on the blanket. "Come sit with me."

Reese obliged, sitting down across from her. He saw no reason not to. Besides, the journey had tired him and it would be pleasant enjoying the sunset with an attractive lady. He smiled, thinking what a sap he was for nature and romance.

Under the scrutiny of the redhead's slanty eyes, he shifted uncomfortably. They were almost hypnotic in their intensity. A more relaxing experience would be with the very charming Anise back in Cuba.

Sangra snapped her fingers at the nymphs standing under the palms. "We are ready. Bring the wine." She whispered coyly, "We must celebrate your arrival, Reese."

One of the women came forward holding a tray. The other one held a huge fanning device and proceeded to wave it in their direction.

In the newly created breeze, Sangra's long tresses fluttered over her face. She brushed away a tendril in annoyance. "That's enough, Lucinda," she said rather sharply. And then her tone softened, her gaze on Reese. "I think it's time for the wine." The auburn beauty waved her hand in a come forth gesture.

After he took the offered glass, Reese thanked the server and held it up to admire the berry hue. "A cabernet?"

"No-oo. It is what you like most. This is one of our finest wines. A vintage shiraz."

Reese laughed. "You know my liking for shiraz, yet I'm a stranger in your land. How is that possible?"

Sangra patted his hand. "Patience, my handsome visitor. Soon all will be revealed. First, a toast to you, Reese." Clicking his glass, she downed most of the wine and set it on the grass before guiding his goblet to his lips. "Drink." Sangra waved her hand to the others. "Leave us."

The two women curtsied and silently made their way to the pool.

A sly smile came to her lips as she watched him tip back the goblet. "What do you think?"

"Excellent."

"And the finish?"

"Nice. Flavors of chocolate."

"How perceptive of you. Do you find it smooth in the mouth?"

"Mouth embracing."

Sangra's eyes smiled. "Good. This one is called Pasión, the finest shiraz in our world. I knew you'd like it, especially with the hint of chocolate."

Reese grinned. "I'm a fool for dark, but don't tell anyone. A man with a chocolate addiction on planet Earth isn't perceived as being too macho." Hands outstretched behind him for balance, he studied the vixen seated directly in front of him. "So why is it you know so much about me?"

"Attractive men interest me." She pointed a finger at the pool. "See that? The water is a natural hot spring. You will swim with us later. It will take away all your stress and you will want to stay here with us always."

"Always? Aren't you presuming a lot?"

"No." She slid her hand down his cheek. "You are lucky to have been chosen but this was not a random decision."

"And you chose me because?"

"You are exceptional."

Reese laughed. "Nothing like flattery to give a man a big head."

Sangra's almond eyes darkened to the color of a rain cloud. "I speak the truth about you and about everything we have here in our world."

"And this world is?"

Without answering, Sangra sprang up and muttered something under her breath. A gust of wind blew through her thick wavy mane and whipped the diaphanous black dress upwards, revealing long shapely legs. Hands thrown up towards the sky, she shouted, "Nuncamorir!" Thunder rumbled and a jagged flash of lightening lit the evening sky.

It was an impressive display of magic. The woman was undoubtedly more than a hot babe.

Sangra raised an eyebrow. "Well?"

Reese got to his feet. "At your service."

Eyes sparkling, Sangra's glance swept the length of his body before it returned to his face. "Since you are already up, why don't we go to the spring?" With her arm looped into his elbow, she propelled him to the pool. "We will entertain you and then later who knows."

Reese lifted an eyebrow.

"We are women of many talents and I am the empress of this land. No one is more gifted than I." Her hand pointed to a tree stump near the edge of the pool. "Sit there, Reese."

The other women must have sensed her intention. They took positions on either side of her, fingertips pointing to the sky. Slowly, synchronizing their movements, they unfastened the straps at their necks, allowing the flimsy dresses to slip to the ground. Three curvaceous females in lacy black under-things.

A strip tease was not what Reese had expected but it had his complete attention. At that point all of them turned their backs to him. Shapely trim bodies with full rounded hips and generous asses. His one thought was whether this was the prelude for a fantasy millions of men dreamed about.

In a throaty voice, Sangra sang a slow seductive song with the red-heads crooning backup. Though his eyes searched the palms, it was impossible to see the musician who played the melody but at this point, he hardly cared. What he saw was more interesting than music of any kind.

His breath caught as slinky lingerie slid to the grass to join the discarded gowns. It was a bit disappointing that the sirens didn't turn to display their attributes. Nevertheless, Reese found the plump cheeks wiggling in time with the music more arousing than any pole dancers he'd ever seen on terra firma.

"Stop listening! It will do you in." A tinkling voice whispered urgently in his ear. "We need to go." A finger flicked the back of his head.

"Ouch! What the…!" Reese turned around. He couldn't believe his eyes. A small female in a silver body suit, long legs encased in sparkly leggings, gripped his arm, dragging him away from the pool. "Quickly, we have no time to lose."

"But why? They're not doing anything wrong. What's a little

strip act going to do?"

"Reality check! Those nymphs have a seduction plan going." The pixie pulled him along. "Any moron can see the nymphs are into black magic and you're their next victim. Think with your brain, Earth man, not with that thing below."

This teenager had him nailed. What man thinks when he's turned on?

The heart-shaped face, framed with auburn hair cut in an edgy jagged style, looked innocent at first glance but there was more to her. Impelling eyes that sparkled emerald green made him question his initial assessment. On reflection, he had to agree with the pixie.

With a glance back at the undulating nude dancers, he remembered how Sangra had said he would stay in her world. When he'd arrived he hadn't cared if he died but once they'd had the shiraz, his mood had lifted. Still, it was not his intent to stay in some strange fantasy land, no matter how enticing.

Sangra was luring him in for her own purposes. He wasn't born yesterday. "Why do they want me to stay?" he finally asked.

"Look, there's no time to explain. Trust me, it's not good. They'll be done any second. Hold on to me?"

Reese nodded.

"Ready?" With a jerk, she shot up into the air with Reese hanging onto the tiny hand.

They soared rapidly in the sky, gaining momentum as they flew higher. The fluffy white mass in front of Reese felt moist as they swooshed through. A cool mist sprinkled over his bare chest and legs. He shivered, not quite understanding what was happening.

"We're going through a cloud, Earth man." The pixie grinned. "What a kick, eh? Nothin' cooler than flyin'."

Inside the cloud, they hovered a moment. The pixie giggled.

Reese looked down at his damp gitch clinging to his body. He wished he'd left his jeans on. Then it dawned on him that he hadn't taken them off. So where were they?

"You don't look so good, Earth man. Don't worry, your *cojones* aren't gone permanently. With a little warmth, they'll come back."

Reese sure hoped they would. A man's balls were very dear to him.

"By the way, did you have anything to eat or drink?"

"Shiraz. That's all."

"Oh!"

"That's bad?"

"Damn right it is. When we get to the golden arch, I'll give you the antidote. Lucky there is one or you'd be totally messed. You lucked out this time." The pixie's eyes blazed feverishly. "The wine is deadly. Now that you've had a taste of it, any other shiraz could set you off. It'll be a burning urge like a drug addiction. Your energy field will want to return to Nuncamorir. If that happens, I'm not sure I'll be able to save you again."

"What can I do?"

She pointed her forefinger up as if to test the air current. "You must find a woman that loves you or she must find you. Loving her will make you forget. When that happens, you can return to Earth."

"I'm not in love with anyone."

The pixie giggled. "So says any sane person. No one can predict the future. There is a woman on Earth that is your soul mate. All that you need to do is open your heart."

What she said was the stuff fairytales were made of. True love and redemption. There was no way he could ever be free of the guilt. Had he been man enough, he would have stopped Lisa from driving. Now and forever he would be responsible for her death. So what did love have to do with it?

"You get it, Earth dude?"

"You're only a kid. What do you know about life?"

The pixie's eyes narrowed. "You think 'cause you're old you have smarts? My life hasn't been bliss and cotton candy either. Now, shut up and concentrate. I don't need to be searching for you."

Reese knew when to stop arguing. After all, she was helping him. Why, he didn't yet know. Over a dark thundercloud, they floated towards a crimson sky that seemed to get redder the higher they flew.

"Why is it all so red?"

"She's made it like this. Sangra put a spell on Nuncamorir. The sun never sets. It's always at the point of setting." Head first into another cloud, the pixie pushed ahead. The palm of her hand slid down and clasped his fingers tightly.

"Don't let go. This cloud could be trouble. It's a sirus. They're the worst. Stubborn things. I've never seen one that has any respect for sky travelers, especially sky sprites." A faint smile formed on her bow-shaped mouth. "I'd hate to have to drag you back up here again."

"And if I fell, would I die?"

"Stop, already. This obsession with death you've got is getting a bit lame. Don't you have a job to do in Cuba or was I crazy hearing about how you wanted to help the hurricane victims?"

"You heard me? Wow, you are amazing, girl!"

They started to whirl in the billowy gray cloud. It was scary but exciting—something like scuba diving in sand clouds instead of the ocean depths.

Feet straight out, Reese concentrated on going through using his hands to shift cloud matter. "What did you say your name is?'

The pixie grinned. "I didn't, but my name is Tora because I was born under the sign Taurus and in the year of the Goat."

"I like it. I'm Reese."

Tora rolled her eyes.

Reese laughed. "Stupid me. Guess you would've known that. Thanks for helping me, Tora. It was irrational mixing a painkiller with Absinthe. It could have done some serious damage."

"Guilt." Tora did a twist and they both tumbled into a white fluffy cave.

"Right. I tried to let it go but I'm responsible for Lisa's death. It never should have happened."

"So now you have to live with it."

Reese frowned. "That's the hard part." He caught onto her hand again as an air current rocked them.

Tora steadied him with her elbow. "Did you drive the car in the ditch?"

"No. I was the passenger. She was upset. Started to cry. The road was icy."

"And she was crying because?"

"She thought I was having an affair. For months she'd been telling me I was in mid-life crisis."

Tora shot him a look. "And were you?"

"No-oo," Reese said slowly. "I wanted to work out and go for runs. Sometimes I went to restaurants alone."

"You did this often?"

"Not intentionally. She wasn't interested in anything I talked about."

Tora steered them away from a black shelf and brought them over a ridge. "So what does that tell you?"

"We grew apart?"

"Were you ever together?"

A throbbing pain centered his forehead. "Still…"

"Let it be. You'll finish yourself off and who will care?"

Reese could feel the truth of her words.

"Almost there." The pixie's hand pointed to a structure in the distance. "Do you see it?"

Reese strained his eyes.

"Get ready." Tora pulled Reese closer. "We are going in for a landing." She positioned her hands in a prayer position. "Hands together like so," she instructed. "Now arch and bend down as if you were diving in water."

Just ahead, Reese saw a brilliantly illuminated golden arch. "Okay, let's go."

With a powerful descent, they shot down but unexpectedly slowed as they neared their destination. They glided onto the summit to perch like hawks on a branch. Living the life of a medical student had not prepared Reese for sky diving experiences but he appreciated the novelty—and what was life without surprises?

From out of her pocket, Tora found the tiny antidote wrapped in gold shiny paper. "Eat this. It will bring you back to your world. Don't expect to remember much. The shiraz was like taking a roofie."

Upon unwrapping the paper Reese examined the dark brown square with a familiar scent. "Chocolate?"

The pixie grinned. "Only the finest Belgium for you, doctor."

"Mm-mm," was the last sound he uttered before he was blown back into oblivion.

***

Reese's fingers running through my hair had been soothing and gentle until his mood shifted. When his hand pulled on a tendril, I rolled away. My eyes opened to the morning sunlight filtering through the woven blinds.

In the corner of the room there was a small sink and mirror. I took my makeup bag from my purse and padded over. After washing my face, I applied eye liner and a couple coats of mascara. The reflection staring back at me wasn't too happy. Red streaks marred the whites of my eyes. Hangover—the after-effects of partying. I looked like I had tied one on and I guess that was true enough. With a glance over to Reese tossing and turning, I thought I might be a little better off than he was.

From the edge of the bed, I studied the doctor. The bruise had turned green and the swelling had lessened. So had the bulge in the gitch. The rest of him was worth a second look. Broad muscular shoulders, a firm chest and abs tapering to a narrow waist. He had the hard arms of an athlete and the long, powerful legs of a runner. The strong feet and hands matched the rest of the six feet frame perfectly.

I sat down and leaned over to tentatively touch his streaked hair. It was as soft and silky as a poodle's fur. The soapy smell of his skin brought me closer. With my nose at his neck, I detected a hint of spice. I closed my eyes and reveled in the scent, breathing it in.

All that ended abruptly when Reese muttered, "Why are you here?" He groaned and turned away. "Just go. I don't want you anymore. We're done. Finished! Understand?"

Taken aback, I was disgusted with myself as much as I was with him. I swung my feet down and stood. What was I thinking staying here with a stranger who obviously treated women like dirt? Just like Henry. How could I have been so taken in by this man? It was just as well. I had enough problems. He could go to hell. Grabbing my tote, I headed out the door.

On the way down to the main floor I started to worry. How would I handle this journey without Reese? But then my confidence returned and I pushed the negative thoughts away. I would figure it out somehow.

"Hey, Anise!" a big voice boomed out from the table by the window. "Remember me?"

I looked over. Was it Gunther from last night?

The big man seemed glad to have surprised me. "Jorge's making *huevos rancheros* and sausages. Please, *mädchen*, Join us. I'm buying."

I inspected the German, bright-eyed and bushy-tailed. Amazing. What resilience! I, on the other hand, quickly concealed the puffiness around my eyes behind a pair of large-framed sunglasses.

The bartender strode in from the kitchen carrying a tray full of food and set it on the table. "*Hola, amiga*! Take advantage. It's not often that Gunther is so generous." He stared pointedly at the sunglasses. "A difficult night?" he asked breezily, without waiting for an answer. He shook his head. "Absinthe…powerful stuff. Where is *el doctor?*"

"Sleeping it off. Jorge, I'll need to eat and run. The shuttle is going back to my hotel soon." Taking a seat next to Gunther, I placed a napkin on my lap.

A sad dog look. "You will return? It's not often I am blessed with such a lady as you." Jorge sat down with Gunther and started to fill his plate with eggs and sausage.

"Me?" I paused, egg on my fork.

"*Si,* a very pretty woman."

"*Ja,* Jorge is used to a much uglier clientele. Especially his girlfriends." Gunther brayed loudly at his joke. He wolfed down a sausage.

Hands on his hips, the bartender glared before he tore into the heavy man.. "It always amazes me how an *hombre gordo,* such as you, could find himself a young woman like Clara. But I think it has more to do with size of the wallet than your looks." Jorge pulled out a chair and sat down.

"Women love me, *compadre*. Get used to it." I am more of a man than many, even with my," Gunther patted his round midriff, "excess tire."

"You need to control that mouth of yours, *amigo* or someone might take offence. Cubans have quick tempers." Jorge nodded wisely. "That is good advice, *hombre*."

"*Ja,* sure," he said, shoveling up some eggs. "I'll give you Clara's brother's address, Anise." Digging in a pocket of his shirt, he came up with a card. He took a pen from Jorge and scribbled something down. "If you go there, soon we may meet up again. Her brother has a birthday and Clara has asked me to drive them up to their house in the mountains to celebrate with the family."

"They wouldn't mind me being there too?"

"Oh, no. They like to have lots of visitors and family. Cubans are very sociable." He dropped some pesos on the table. "Besides any friends of mine are like family," he added.

He stood and shoved his chair back into position. "The good doctor told me I must check on my problem, Jorge. Perhaps you can direct me to the nearest hospital?"

"*Si, no hay problema, amigo.* I have already phoned for a taxi to take you there. It should be here in a few minutes."

The heavy German grabbed another sausage from the serving plate and gazed at me. "It shouldn't be too difficult for the doctor to find this place either. It's the second, I think, or third farm. And if Reese gets lost he need only ask for Luis. He has the biggest place on that road." Gunther handed me the card.

"Thank you, my friend." I tucked the card in my purse.

"Have you made plans with the doctor?"

I clenched my jaw. "No, and I doubt if he'll want to now."

Jorge scratched his chin reflectively. "I don't understand. It was my impression Reese liked you very much. Did something happen during the night?"

"No, nothing," I snapped.

The men grinned.

"Not that I wanted something to happen."

Gunther nodded wisely. "I can see why you are pissed off. Idiot was too drunk to perform."

I shook my head. "No, it wasn't like that. I wasn't thinking about him in that way."

Jorge rolled his eyes.

"He was overly medicated and combined with Absinthe, he slept restlessly," I continued, somewhat flustered. I looked from one to the other. "Listen to me. All I ever wanted was to take pictures of Cuba. My aim is to do this book project and…"

"What?"

"I am curious to find out about my roots. My grandmother was a Jewish artist. This may seem bizarre but I am sure the painting in the bathroom is hers."

Jorge's blue eyes met mine.

"The one in the women's washroom. It's signed *A Sommerville*. That's my grandmother's art."

"Very possible. All the paintings are from Havana artists." Jorge scratched his head. "There is a synagogue here in Havana. They might know of your grandmother." He gestured. "Eat, *chica*. You are too thin."

The sausage was sizeable but cut easily with a knife. "Very good, Jorge." I took a sip of coffee. "I intend to find the place but something tells me I must go into the mountains first."

"Reese will take you there. I was just joking about how you can't trust him," Gunther said earnestly.

"No, he and I are not meant to be. I will plan something else."

"Plans can change." Jorge cut into his eggs.

"Anise needs the doctor for this trip."

Jorge nodded, his mouth full.

"Perhaps we will meet up when I bring Clara and her sister." He grinned ruefully. "We won't be able to do much else, especially if I have that surgery. If the doctor is not for you, go with someone else. There are plenty of fish in the sea. Besides, Luis will put you up regardless."

A horn honked outside.

"Thank you. I appreciate it."

With a wave, Gunther headed out the door.

Jorge shuddered. "He is a brave man submitting himself to the knife that way."

I dug into the sausage. "What surgery is he having?"

"Ah, I forgot you weren't here when Gunther told his story. It's a broken blood vessel."

"Blood vessel? Where?"

"The tender male area, *amiga*." Jorge grinned broadly. "Who knows how it really occurred. He claims his condom was too small."

"Oh-hh," I said, understanding at last. "So that's why he said…"

"Exactly. I will give you the address of my cousin with the house by the sea. It is a beautiful place. You could stop there as well." Taking a business card from the table, he wrote a name and address on the back and, after that, picked up another card and handed it to me. "Write for me your name and hotel, just in case."

"In case of what?"

"If the doctor is as you say he is."

Silently, I set the coffee cup down, avoiding his eyes.

"*Entonces*, I am your friend. Perhaps I can find someone else for you to travel with. Someone trustworthy, but in my opinion, *el doctor* would be the best *hombre*. He will protect you."

I snatched up a coaster from the holder with Mojito embossed on it. and glanced up at his serious face. "Don't look so worried. I won't go with just anyone."

"*Dios mio!* I would hope not. There are bad *hombres* out there." Jorge shook his head in dismay. "It is dangerous for a woman alone."

"Okay. You win." With the pen he handed me, I wrote the name of my hotel and my name.

"*Bueno*." Jorge took the card and pocketed it. "Now, go catch your bus. I will call if I find someone but if you should change your mind…"

I stood. "*Gracias*, Jorge. I won't change my mind."

***

Reese woke with a start. The vivid dream of Lisa lingered. She'd tried to pull him into bed but this time he had resisted. After drifting out of his dream he'd reached out for Anise but felt only a blanket. He opened an eye to discover the lady was gone.

Last night was a haze. Staring at the empty room, his mood spiraled downwards. Had he ever met a blonde goddess by the name of Anise? He rubbed his throbbing temple, swearing softly. Absinthe was lethal. Could Anise be as unreal as Sangra and the pixie?

He flitted his gaze to the clock on the dresser. Eleven twenty.

Lola. He had promised to check on the daughter. Glancing down, he was taken aback. What had happened to his jeans and t-shirt? Swinging off the bed, he scanned the room to find a neat pile of clothes folded on the rattan chair.

Over in the corner attached to the wall was a sink. A few splashes of cold water didn't kill the hangover but it was a start. Damn leg was acting up again. Running fingers through his hair, he reflected that Absinthe had given him more than he'd bargained for.

Another glance around the room confirmed that the hot blonde was indeed gone. Could it have been something he'd said? And then it all came back how he'd accused her of causing the accident. Yet, as the evening progressed, hadn't they put that behind them?

Artsy types tended to be spacey. He should know. Drawing had always been something he enjoyed when he'd had time. But all that had gone by the wayside after he'd entered medical school. From then on, there had been only work.

Tugging on his jeans, a snippet of his dream came back. A world with the most amazing sunset. It was where he had been sent guilt-ridden and depressed, thinking his life was finished. Hence, the strange dream of the otherworld. For a moment, he wondered why he was back but as hard as he tried, he couldn't remember. He shook his head, giving up. It was time to return to reality.

He needed to man up and get on with his mission. Still, he had to wonder if there hadn't been some unconscious desire to be with the redhead. But no, she wasn't the *one*. There was another far more enticing woman. His jeans grew uncomfortably tight imagining slowly kissing her.

Annoyed with himself, Reese pulled on the black t-shirt and tucked it into the jeans before zipping up again. Rearing to go in search of Anise, he grabbed the backpack, shot out the room, raced down the stairs and entered the bar.

"*Buenos dias, amigo.* Why do you hurry? Come sit." Jorge leaned back in his chair. At the round wooden table, covered bowls as well as a carafe of coffee had been randomly placed on an embroidered cloth.

"*Hola*, Jorge." Reese glanced around but there was no sign of the blonde. "I can't stay long. I have a patient to see."

Jorge dished out some eggs and sausage from the bowls. "Freshly made. *Huevos rancheros.*" Shoving a plateful of eggs and sausage over, he added, "The patient can wait. Surely not an emergency."

Reese took the seat opposite the bartender. "No…I think she'll be fine but I promised to check in."

Jorge watched him eat. "Good?"

"Very. Thanks."

"*De nada.* If I become ill, I hope you would come to my rescue as urgently as you were about to set out for this patient. A beautiful woman?"

Reese picked up the coffee carafe and filled the mug. "No, a teenage girl." He laughed. "With attitude."

"Then even more reason not to hurry."

Long black hair and alabaster skin flashed in his mind. Reese grinned. "Her mother is beautiful."

"In that case, I will close the bar and accompany you."

"That should solve my problem."

"Problem?" Jorge raised an eyebrow. "What's wrong with beautiful?"

A sudden vision of Anise swinging her hips in a slow salsa wiped out the memory of Lola.

Jorge grinned. "I know. It is the one that ran off that fills your thoughts."

A wistful smile played on Reese's lips. "It's the way she moves."

"Go after her, *amigo.*"

"Anise left without a word. She doesn't like me." Reese poured milk into his coffee mug. "It's a done deal. A *fait accompli.*"

"I don't know French or your Canadian slang but you must know the woman had eyes for you."

Reese laughed. "Me? If that were true she would have left a phone number." He set down the coffee, fuming. "And wasn't she keen on going up into the mountains? Something must have turned her off."

"It was you in your underpants. I thought you had a good display for her but," he shrugged, "perhaps she has seen better."

That set him off with a loud snort whereupon he slapped the doctor soundly on the back.

"Why was I lying there in my gitch, anyway?"

"Gitch? Strange word." Jorge picked up a sausage. "Listen *amigo*, I had her ice your bruise. She didn't seem to mind taking care of you. I think you have the wrong impression. Anise liked you well enough until this morning. Did you do something to her in your drunken stupor?"

Reese shook his head. "No, nothing that I recall. But, hey, I had a crazy dream."

"Did you hit her in your sleep?"

Reese's eyes widened. "I wonder if that could be it? The Absinthe and the pain killer put me in a strange state. I was half way awake at times."

"The Absinthe put her to sleep, too. But women are different than men, *amigo*." Jorge rocked in his chair, lips pursed. "No matter. There is only one solution."

"And that is?"

Refilling their coffee, Jorge set the carafe down. "Go after her."

"What? Are you crazy? I have no idea where she is."

"You are the one that is *loco*." Jorge jabbed his chest with a forefinger. "I have her name and hotel," he pronounced.

"Really?"

"Yes, but she will be a difficult fish on the line."

"Why?"

Jorge punched him on the bicep. "I think *el doctor* is full of himself today. The lady has secrets."

Reese rubbed his chin reflectively. "True. I know nothing about her."

"But, do not let such a thing stop you. You have the advantage."

"Why?"

"Why, why, why! You are so dense, *amigo*. You have something she needs."

A glint came into Reese's eyes.

The bartender broke out laughing. "No, not your prowess. Absinthe has left you with only half a brain."

"Then what?"

"The motorcycle."

"Of course. What a fool I am. Anise wants to get up into those mountains and can't just go on her own, can she?" he said smiling. "It would suit her purposes to contact me," Reese eyed Jorge speculatively, "through you."

"The lady might go with someone else."

"Who?"

"Any sane man would take her—a woman like that." Jorge swished his fingers in the form of an hourglass and whistled.

"Then there is only one course of action."

"*Bueno.* Now your brain is functioning. Go see your patient and come back here. Then I will give you directions to find Anise."

Pushing the plate away, Reese took out his wallet and stuck a few pesos in Jorge's hand. Enough?"

"Most generous, *amigo.*"

"*Gracias*, Jorge. I appreciate your help.

***

A brilliant smile on her lovely face, Lola waved him in wearing a thigh-high clingy black dress. "*Hola*, Reese. Your arrival is timely. My daughter is awake." She led the way down the hall, clicking ahead in high-heeled stilettos.

In the bedroom, Lola directed her daughter to sit up. After checking ears, eyes and throat, Reese listened to the girl breathe. "She is much better and," he pronounced, with a glance at the thermometer, "the fever has passed." But the look she gave him was as sullen as ever.

"Ah-hh. That is a comfort." In rapid Spanish Lola instructed the girl before she took Reese into the lounge and gestured to the couch. "I have made coffee for us."

Disappearing a moment, she entered again with delicate cups and saucers and placed them on the table. She poured coffee into each cup, and handed one to Reese. She sat next to him on the couch.

"This is very kind of you but I can't stay long. I have another appointment."

Lola nodded. "Your mother is friends with my Aunt Delores?"

"Yes, Mom lives in Miami now. That's where I met Delores. I gather you have more family in Miami?"

"Aunts, uncles and cousins." Lola sipped her coffee before continuing. "Mama had planned to send for us but she died." She crossed her leg; the dress fell back revealing a pale thigh. "Apparently my aunt is wealthy. Is that true?"

Reese thought back to the last conversation he'd had with his mother. "She has a house on Biscayne Bay. Yes. It's a beautiful place, according to Mom." He paused. "But she suffers," he added, patting Lola's hand.

"Suffers?" Lola scoffed. "She took everything from Mama to set herself up and then married the rich *Americano*."

"She can't have any children."

"And that is the cross she must bear." Lola sniffed. "Let's not talk of her. It makes me angry." She gazed into Reese's hazel eyes. "How long are you intending to stay?"

"Long enough to feel like I've accomplished something."

"As a specialist you can help. Will you leave the city and go inland?"

"I hear that's where they need supplies most."

Lola's full mouth parted. The tip of her pink tongue flicked over her lower lip. A smoldering gaze shot in his direction. "Hopefully, you will visit again?"

"Cuba?"

"Yes." Straightening up, she held her head high, giving Reese a direct gaze. "The Red Cross has provided supplies as have several countries but still, after a hurricane it's hard for everyone. You are welcome here."

Reese glanced at Lola. "I want to be honest with you. I am not looking to get involved."

"Friends then?"

Reese smiled. "That's good for me."

Setting down the cup, Lola leaned over, pulling Reese's head in to press her lips to his. The kiss was returned with the intention of making it short and friendly but Lola's insistent tongue invaded. His barriers dropped and he began to enjoy the heat of the woman. Fingertips scraped his neck and his body responded.

A flash of gold. Anise's slim form appeared, swaying enticingly. Through the center of her body, an orange flame leaped out like a fire. Her eyes sparkled turquoise. Reese pulled away from Lola's demanding kiss.

"What is it? Are you ill?"

Reese shook his head. "No. I must go."

"But..."

Grabbing the bag, Reese stood and headed to the door. "Thank you for the coffee. See you."

"Soon," Lola whispered, as he shut the door behind him.

7

On the shuttle back to the Caribe, I stared blankly out the window. How was I to do this? My photos needed to be unique.

With Cuba's cratered roads, renting a scooter would be ludicrous. And then there was the safety factor. A woman traveling alone had to be cautious.

Tours seemed to be the only option yet when I pictured a shuttle full of vacationers, it seemed all wrong. As the bus pulled into the circular driveway, I was one of the first to jump off. Sunshine would help my mood.

I changed into a bikini and wrapped a pareo over the bikini bottom and slipped into a pair of sandals. Tossing a paperback into my bag, I headed out down the tile walkway past the restaurant to the sign that read *piscina*.

Outside it had cleared. Sun filtered through puffy white clouds. A forceful breeze tossed my hair wildly about. A row of yellow lounge chairs occupied with sun worshipers were lined up by the pool. I passed behind them and made my way through the gate to the beach.

A wide expanse of sandy beach, more tan than white, was broken up with lounge chairs occupied by hotel guests. Weaving in and out, I spotted a chair close to the sea. After spreading my towel over the chair, I climbed on, closed my eyes and drifted off to the sound of the waves crashing on the shore.

Voices from the neighboring lounger woke me. Two mulatto women slaved over a tanned middle-aged man, coating him with oils. One kinky-haired charmer took on his bottom half, while her slender café-au-lait sister slid her hands over his chest, smoothing on the liquid in a circular motion. He smiled lazily, making a soft remark that brought on titters of laughter. Catching my stare, he gave me a slight, almost imperceptible wink, much like an iguana blinking in the sun.

When a wiry fellow approached, dripping wet from a swim, the sheikh made a quick remark in Italian.

His friend laughed and cast a look in my direction. "*Hola. Parli Italiano?*"

"No, sorry. English."

"Ah-hh." He studied me with slate-gray eyes. "Too bad. I speak only a little English."

I turned away, thinking about another man that did speak my language. The sun on my flushed face grew uncomfortably hot. A vision of those unusual eyes appeared and then a flashback of the two of us dancing. The warmth of his fingers had ignited a flame. Our movements had magically synchronized.

My Hormone voice agreed. "There was some big time chemistry going on."

"He had his chance and he blew it," Logical snapped.

Hormone sighed. "He was hot."

True enough but men were trouble. It only stressed me out thinking about them. Glancing at the waves breaking on the pristine beach, my black mood lightened. A swim would relax me.

I threw my beach bag on the towel and ran to the water's edge. Near the catamarans, a red flag flapped in the wind. There was current but I would be careful. Up to my knees should be safe enough. I ventured in slowly. A wave crashed hard on my thigh. The surf sent my pulse racing. It was wonderful. Sun, surf, and a sandy beach—everything I needed to feel alive.

Another powerful wallop from the ocean set off warning bells. Any fool could see the ocean meant business. I began to regret my decision to live on the edge. As the sea hurled me further, I switched direction, turning back, but the force pushed me out.

I was almost out of the current's pull when everything went wrong. With a giant's strength, the ocean grabbed my ankles and pulled me down. My face hit the bottom. Powdery particles whirled around as I held my breath. Finally, it let go and I jerked away and surfaced. Mere seconds passed before the fight began all over again.

The sea wanted to take me down but I wouldn't let it. Shooting up to the top, I sprung forward. Then, with all the energy I could summon, I flew through the air, arms out, readied for a landing, but instead of hitting the sand, I head-butted the man standing at the edge of the shore, flattening him with my weight.

I lay on top of him, exhausted. A familiar pair of jungle-green eyes met my stare.

"What are *you* doing here?"

"Coming to your rescue," Reese drawled with a wide grin.

"I didn't need rescuing."

"Like shit you didn't. I dragged you out." He waved his hand at the surf. "You think you did it all by yourself?"

"What bull. I swam out."

"Want proof?" Reese jerked his hand high, dangling my bikini top from his fingertips.

I snatched up the flimsy material.

Reese's lips twitched. "Need help?"

Covering myself with one arm, I sat up and turned away before bringing the bikini top to my breasts. "Tie it," I hissed.

"Are you sure? Topless is fine on Cuban beaches."

"Interesting. Where I come from it's legal too, but most women wear the bikini top. Now, tie it!"

"If you insist."

Reese worked slowly. Maybe doing up a string bikini with his rather large hands wasn't so easy. I waited impatiently for him to finish and then swung around to confront him. "Explain why you're here."

Leaning back into the sand on his elbows, Reese took me in. "You look cute when you're mad."

I glared at him. "That's nervy of you after what you said this morning."

"What do you mean?" he asked, his brow furrowed.

"You ordered me to leave, remember?"

Reese's eyes widened. "I said that? I must have been dreaming, Anise. I don't remember any of it."

"Sure…some excuse. And I think you still hold a grudge for the accident."

Sitting up, he brought his hands to my hips. "Me? No, not at all. You're just a little spacey. You can't help that."

"Why? Because I'm a blonde?"

"Yup."

"Well, my hair is ash. Those are highlights."

Reese smirked. "So you're a dirty blonde I'd say. A stealth blonde. But, no, I didn't mean it was a blonde moment. I was thinking because you're a creative type." He squinted at my hair. "By the way, you've got great hair when it's not wet."

"You think I look a mess?" With one finger, I slid it down his sand-streaked face. "That's like the pot calling the kettle black." His messed up hair caught my attention. "You're almost a blond yourself."

"Just a few sun streaks in my case." Shaking his wet wavy locks away from his eyes, Reese smiled. "You're damn lucky I sacrificed my GQ appearance. Don't you wonder why?"

"Yes, good question. Why was that?" I stared at him defiantly. "I was aware of the current before I went in, and," I pointed my finger in the air significantly, "I made it out no problem. After all, I was barely in the water. I doubt if that qualified me as shark bait. But thanks for caring. That's a switch from this morning."

"Anise, believe me, I really wasn't talking to you. It was all part of this dream. A nightmare." Reese frowned. "And yet, it seemed so real."

I recalled the spirit man's kiss, so softly sensuous." The thought of his lips made me tingle. The memory had been so real. Yet that was just a vision. I stared at Reese. "Too much Absinthe."

"That's true, but if I tell you about the dream maybe you'll understand. Will you at least listen?"

My wandering eyes spanned the sand-caked t-shirt and jeans, and I decided to give him a break. "Alright. Let's sit on those lounge chairs. I think you need to dry off."

Reese pulled himself up. Either his leg was better or he was a master at hiding pain. We headed over to the lounge chair where I'd left my bag and towel.

Sitting down on the chair I'd occupied earlier, I watched him tug off the soggy black t-shirt. After tossing it on the chaise lounge beside mine, he unzipped his jeans and let them drop. "European-style swim suit." He spread his clothes on an empty chair alongside the t-shirt. "What do you think?" Reese posed for me and when he saw me grin said, "Oh," and rubbed his chin thoughtfully, "I forgot. You've already seen me in my gitch."

I fumbled in my bag until I found a pair of sunglasses. "Not because I wanted to. It was Jorge's idea to take off your clothes." I tried not to focus on his strong lean body.

His eyes glimmered in the sunlight. "But you helped."

"I had to. The Absinthe did you in."

Reese shot me a look of admiration. "You did alright with the stuff for a tiny woman." He sat down on the chair beside me.

"Tiny? I'm small and powerful, buddy." My hand closed in a fist and I lightly punched him in the chest. "German heritage. I was raised on Schnapps shooters and beer."

Reese laughed, leaning back in the lounge chair. "This is nuts but you kind of remind me of the pixie in my dream."

"Pixie? That must have been some dream."

"You don't know the half of it."

"I'm listening."

Eyes half closed, Reese spoke quietly. "I was in this land with palm trees. There were these three beautiful redheads."

"It doesn't sound like anything upsetting. So you snarked at me because I woke you up?"

"There's more to this, Anise. Listen," he continued, his voice softly melodic. "The sun was setting and the sky was brilliantly red. These women greeted me and gave me wine before they started to dance. They were evil. The main nymph, Sangra, well, I'm not sure what she wanted."

"It sounds like a sexual fantasy to me. I think you have a thing for redheads."

"No-oo. It wasn't like that, although," Reese gazed out at the sea, "I have to admit I was blown away by the women. But I was suspicious. When I came back to Earth, Sangra, or was it Lisa, the two women merged into one. She called out for me to return and I told *her* to go away, not you."

I straightened my bikini strap. "And why was there a pixie?" As I questioned Reese, a hazy form appeared before my eyes. A lithe girl clad in a silver body-suit. Her face came into my line of vision and zoomed in closer. Auburn hair and slanty green eyes. She mouthed something I couldn't understand.

"Anise? Are you okay?"

I turned to Reese. "The pixie wore a silver outfit."

"How did you know?" Reese said slowly, staring at me.

I closed my eyes. The pixie reappeared shooting up into the clouds. "She flies."

"This is bizarre." Reese got up and sat down at the edge of my chair. He took my hand and regarded me earnestly. "How do you know all this, Anise? It was a dream—*my* dream."

"I see things," I said quietly, meeting his eyes.

"You're psychic?"

I nodded reluctantly. He would think I'm crazy but I had to be truthful. "It comes and goes but yes, I think so."

"Then you know I'm telling you the truth."

I studied him. "Yes, I think you are."

"If you still want to go, I'll take you into the mountains."

"You're not put off by my abilities?"

Reese shook his head. He placed his hand over mine. "You're not the only one."

"What do you mean?"

"I see auras."

"Really? You're not pulling my leg?"

With a grin, his eyes swept down my body. "Touching it would be more my style."

I rolled my eyes. "How is your leg?" I asked, glancing down at it.

"It's much better after icing. Thank you for staying last night." His eyes glittered. "You didn't need to but you did. Why?"

"I felt responsible, I guess." Feeling self-conscious, I looked away to the foamy surf pounding the shore. "If I hadn't walked into the street, you wouldn't have hurt yourself."

"Don't feel guilty. If I hadn't had a weakness in that leg, nothing would have happened. I'm a skilled motorcyclist. I've raced."

"So the injury is not from the car accident?" Even as I said those words, an image of a cold winter storm and a road covered with black ice appeared before my eyes. I trembled. The scenery blurred with the speed and a cry of a woman echoed in my ears. Pain tore through my body.

"Anise!" Reese gripped my shoulders. "What is it? Why are you shaking?"

"A woman died."

Dropping his hands, Reese flashed me a look. "What?"

"She was in the car with you."

Our eyes locked. What I saw in his scared me. "She drove."

"You saw her?"

"No. I only felt her pain."

"She wasn't supposed to be there. I was angry and didn't want to talk. I wanted to drive but she jumped in. It was all my fault."

I shook my head. "No, it was the ice."

"I should have stopped her." Reese stroked my hand gently. "Please. Let's not talk about the past, Anise. I'd rather forget." He attempted a smile. "Why don't you go to your room and pack a bag. We'll meet up in the lobby in twenty minutes. Does that give you enough time?"

He was so sure of himself. "Make it forty. I need a shower."

***

What does a woman take on a trip to the mountains? A party for Clara's brother called for a dress and heels. Other than that, shorts, a couple of tops, jacket, and sandals were good enough. And a bikini if we made it to the beach. Was I done? Hm-mm…not quite. I smirked, thinking of the glimmer in Reese's eyes. I picked up a few pieces of lacy underwear and tossed them in too.

Before I left, I found the directions and stuck them into the pocket of my jeans. Bag in hand, I trekked down the stairs to the lobby.

Reese leaned against the wall just inside of the entrance, watching the arrival of a tour bus. Dark sunglasses and the slightly hooked nose made him appear both rugged and dangerous. The form fitting t-shirt on his broad shoulders and the jeans on those slim hips rooted me to the spot. My pulse fluttered erratically.

Yet there was reason for concern. Here I was going away with a man I barely knew. Life with Henry had been so boring I was throwing caution to the wind.

"Anise!" Reese called out. He approached confidently. "Give me your bag." Lifting the fabric suitcase, he suddenly let his hand drop and let out a low moan. "Oh-no! The rock collection." Although I couldn't see the expression in his eyes, a smile played on his lips.

I pulled down the sunglasses perched on the top of my head. "My Nikon."

"Ah-hah. I guess there's no point in suggesting you leave that behind." Bringing a hand to the small of my back, he guided me out to the curb where his motorcycle was parked. The hotel doorman stood there waiting.

"Wait," I said. "What is your last name?"

"Lyon. What's yours?"

"Sommerville. Nice to meet you."

After passing a bill to the attendant, Reese loaded my bag into the carrier at the back, grinning. "The pleasure is mine." He shot me a look. "Smart."

"What?"

"You put on jeans and a jacket."

"I'm a stealth blonde, remember?" Climbing on behind him, I looked out at the sea. "It seems a shame doesn't it, leaving a beautiful beach behind to drive inland?"

Revving the motor, Reese spoke over his shoulder. "It's great up in the mountains. You'll love it, but I agree there's nothing like the beach."

Holding on tightly to Reese's waist, I brought myself close to his back. "Where are we going?"

"I thought we'd head over to Clara's brother's house first. Jorge said you had the directions. You did remember to bring them?"

"I have them and the directions to Jorge's cousin's beach house." I tapped the paper I'd tucked in my pocket.

He threw me a wicked look. "I repeat—smart blonde."

I smiled. This might be a great trip, after all.

The breeze and the traffic made further conversation difficult. It wasn't easy either. I clung on for dear life as we swerved out of a truck's path.

"*Cabron!*" Reese yelled out at the smirking driver.

"What is *cabron*?" I asked, as we came to stop at a light.

Reese grinned over his shoulder. "Goat."

"Goat?"

"It has a little stronger connation in Spanish."

"You've got to ignore the idiots on the road, Reese. They're crazy around here. They could arrest you. We're in Cuba, you know."

"Yeah, but they're Cuban. One thing these guys respect is attitude."

"Men," I muttered, as we shot back into traffic.

Reese was a thrill junkie when it came to driving. Aggressively, he edged out of a tight traffic jam and brought us into the open road again. Before long we reached an intersection. Slowing, we veered off to the left. This was the way towards the mountains.

The narrow dirt road was an obstacle course of pot holes and scattered rocks. Thankfully, Reese slowed down. The last thing we needed was a flat tire or worse.

With the heat of the day and the dust flying into my face, I was beginning to think this trip might be more than I'd bargained for. Every bump jolted my back and this was just the beginning.

Here and there a house broke up the monotony of farms. My guess was sugar cane. With the heat and the jolting, I was ready for break. When a roadside stand appeared ahead, I yelled, "Let's stop there, Reese!"

He swerved onto an expanse of gravel and stopped in front of a little white house. First, I would check out the fruit. The plantains were a gamut of colors and sizes in pink, red and yellow. Cubans don't think of these as fruit. They mash them like potatoes.

I recognized oranges, guava and pomegranate but the others were clearly a mystery. The lady behind the counter produced a knife and cut open a purplish fruit with a bumpy exterior. The inside was yellow holding tiny black seeds. I took the sample from her. Sweetly tart and juicy. "What is this?"

The old lady grinned, a tooth missing. She spoke quickly in Spanish. I shot a look at Reese.

Reese grinned. "She said it's an aphrodisiac."

I poked him in the ribs.

"It's true. That's what she said." Reese gave the woman some pesos for the fruit which she wrapped in brown paper. When he headed back to the motorcycle, I wandered over to the house.

Two teenage girls sat behind a stand on the deck. From the similarity of their appearance I guessed they were sisters. Corn crafts and bead jewelry were for sale. The small, slim brown-eyed girl met my eyes. I felt her dig into my energy. "Your saint is Yemaya, *señorita*."

"Hm-mm?"

"Mother of the waters." She produced a narrow necklace of

blue and white beads and pulled it over my neck. "Yemaya beads. One peso."

I knew nothing of what she spoke. "Why do you think she is my saint?"

"Sorry, my English is not good."

Glancing down at the corn cob animals, I saw a doll with a white and blue dress.

"*Si.* Yemaya." She smiled. "Five pesos."

With the house so broken down, I felt I had to buy something. "Just a minute." I went back to the bike, unzipped the saddle bag and grabbed up my Nikon pouch. I found the money and exchanged the coins for the doll. The tiny corn doll squeezed into the lens pocket. Then I asked for the *baño*. Not only would a pit stop be great but I was very curious as to the interior of the house.

The young girl motioned for me to follow and we entered a tiny dark room with a small couch, a stuffed chair and a wooden rocking chair. We stopped near the end of a dark corridor. Ahead, I caught a glimpse of a kitchen. To the right, a wooden door leaned against a plain white wall. Just beyond that was a seatless toilet and a basic pedestal sink. A draped area hid the bathtub. Puzzled, I looked at the unattached door. She gestured for me to step in and picked up the door, setting it into the frame. No hinges. After washing my hands, I lifted the door from the frame and returned it to the spot against the wall.

On my way out, I paused to peek into the living room. The rich colors of an oil painting caught my attention. There was a dark sky with a lone ship tossing in a turbulent sea. The people were back lit with yellow. Massive waves pushed the boat on a precarious angle. The artist had skill. When I stepped closer I saw the signature. My jaw dropped. *A Sommerville.* Tentatively, I touched the signature. Sparks flew to my fingertips.

"Anise!" Reese called out from outside. "Come on. We need to get going!"

With one last puzzled look I made my way outside. "*Gracias,*" I said to the girl, and climbed on behind Reese when I remembered. "Wait! I just need to take a couple of photos." Before Reese could object, I climbed off and ran out to the grassy ridge by the highway. The Nikon zoomed into the green valley between the purple mountains in the distance.

Satisfied, I ran back to the motorcycle and climbed on behind Reese.

He sighed theatrically. "Was there some reason I agreed to take you?"

"You were overcome by my devastating beauty?"

He revved up the motorcycle and swung out onto the highway in reply. A dilapidated pick-up carrying farm workers and produce rumbled past us with a chorus of shouts and whistles. Feeling carefree, I waved and got more hoots.

When we slowed for a fallen log, Reese called over his shoulder. "Anise, you want to cool it down? Those boys aren't ready for blondes. You don't want to get them all worked up. Remember these are Latino guys. You know, fire in their veins."

"Really?" I shouted. "Are you sure you're not jealous?"

"What's to be jealous of? You're with me." Reese grinned. "And I have you for the rest of this trip."

***

Like an over-ripe peach, the sun hung mid-way in the sky. The humidity was so intense it rose from the ground in hazy steamy waves. Hot, and tired, I longed for a tall, cool glass of water.

When we entered a narrow road surrounded on either side by acres of sugar cane, Reese made a stop. I looked over the directions and told him to keep on going.

With only a light breeze, my skin was filmed with a coat of sweat. I wasn't the only one. Reese's spicy scent mingled with soap. Breathing in his flavors, I sighed with pleasure.

Reese swiveled around when we came to a stop. "Is this the turnoff?"

Again, I pulled out the paper that Jorge had given me and checked. "I'm not sure," I said, shaking my head. "It should be the second or third farm. It's hard to read. He said if we had trouble to ask someone."

Reese stopped. He grinned ruefully looking up the road. "Easy for him to say." Glancing out at the fields of towering sugar cane, he frowned. "I can't see anyone. Can you?" He snatched up the card without waiting for an answer. "My guess is that's a three. Gunther should be a doctor with this handwriting."

I shivered. A flash of white.

"You okay, Anise?" He ran his hand down my cheek. "It must be the heat. We've got to get you somewhere out of the sun fast."

It was hot but I knew it was something else—nothing to do with the heat. I was standing waist deep in cool, sparkling water. Beside me, a man laughed. On the far side of the river, lush green vegetation bordered the bank. The hairs on the back of my neck stood up.

"Anise?"

The sun was strong on my face. I waited for more but nothing came. "I'm okay, Reese. Don't worry."

He stared at me. "Are you having some sort of vision?"

I nodded. "I was in water, a river. Somewhere tropical. There was a man beside me."

"You shivered. Did something happen?"

When I closed my eyes once again, I tried to bring it back but my mind denied me. "No, nothing, but it was almost as if something terrible was about to happen."

"We've got to find Luis and have you rest. I understand you are psychic and that could leave you confused but I'm a little worried. You fell hard on that road. It could be that the concussion is responsible for this."

He had a point but I thought that it must be something else. These premonitions seemed to be getting stronger and each one was leaving me with less energy. Somehow I had to regain my strength.

Revving up the motor, Reese drove on and entered a narrow road. Half way down, a girl and a boy were playing with toy cars. He slowed down within a few feet of them. "*Hola, muchachos!*" he yelled.

They looked up curiously.

"How's your Spanish?" Reese whispered, helping me off the bike.

"*¿Donde esta Luis, por favor?*" I called out to the kids.

Two pairs of large dark eyes gazed up, followed by giggles.

"Hey, how about this?" From out of his backpack, Reese dug up a bag. "Chocolate?" he said, offering one to me.

"Oh-hh…thank you." I unwrapped a milk chocolate square.

"The good stuff. I always keep some."

"Mm-mm." I took the bag from him and waved it in the directions of the children. "*Chocolate, niños?*"

They hesitated a split second before they crept up, hand in hand. When I filled their open palms with tiny treasures, their faces lit up. The chocolate was a definite ice-breaker. I don't know which one of us looked happier, all of us savoring the sweet feast.

After she swallowed, the little girl enthusiastically said, "*Muchos gracias,*" nudging her brother.

"*Gracias, señorita.*" His big brown eyes regarded me hopefully. I gave them both another one and then, finding I needed more, took another for myself.

Reese's lips twitched. "Hey, how come they like you? It's my private stash."

"I'm the blonde. They love blondes in Cuba. What's better than a blonde offering chocolate?"

"True. I'm just a doctor."

"*Un doctor?*" piped up the little girl.

"*Si,* where do I find Luis?" Reese tried again.

The little girl shook her head and looked at me.

"*¿Que es tu nombre?*" I pointed at my chest. "Anise."

"*Hola, señorita* Anise. I speak English." She drew out the *e* when she spoke. She patted her brother on the head. "This boy is Guillermo and my name is Luisa." Then, forgetting her English, she chattered away in Spanish.

I nodded encouragingly, hoping I'd understand something. Suddenly giving up or just plain impatient, Luisa gestured towards the bend in the road ahead of us. When I stood there staring in confusion, the dark-eyed munchkin decided to take the lead, grabbed my hand and started to pull me along.

Guillermo snatched up my other hand, following his sister's lead. "*Vamanos!*" he urged, and laughed.

"They want me to go with them, Reese."

"I have a feeling we're at Luis's farm and these kids are his. Go with them, Anise. I'll drive. Can't leave my baby here. See you up at the house in a bit."

With the children pulling me, I headed down the road. Reese zoomed by a moment later. When we rounded the bend, I saw what Luisa wanted to show me. It was a long white bungalow with a red tile roof and wooden window frames. Not fancy but attractive.

Broad-leafed plants with red blooms edged the porch. On the front deck, a gray-hair old woman occupied a blue couch. A motorcycle was parked off to the side but there was no sign of Reese or the bags.

"*Hola, señora.*" I pointed to my chest. "Anise."

"*Buenos dias, señorita,*" she said, with a toothy grin. "*Doña Esmeralda.*"

The rest was lost to me. "*¿El doctor?*" I asked.

Before *doña* Esmeralda could reply, Luisa grabbed my hand, and pulled me up the steps of the porch past the old lady. Her little brother thought it was a fun game pushing me from behind. With the children giggling at their new game, we came to a door.

From the entrance, I saw it was a kitchen. A slender woman leaned over a gas stove, slowly stirring something with a heavenly aroma. Pitch black hair was braided and pinned in a tight bun, revealing an oval face with symmetrical features. A green tank top tucked into flared blue jeans belied her somewhat old-fashioned coiffure. Gold sandals encrusted with sparkling rhinestones were modern enough.

Swiveling about, a large spoon in hand, her face lit up in a smile. "So sorry, my English is not good," she said softly. "Please, *Señorita,* come in," she urged, waving the utensil.

"*Gracias.* Call me Anise, and your English is just fine.*"*

She smiled. "My name is Linda.*"*

"Nice to meet you.*"* I was beginning to wonder if everything was alright.

Linda must have read my concern. "You must not worry. *El doctor* is with my *esposo.*"

Her eyes were the same as those of the children—the color of chestnuts, large and doe-like, fringed with thick black lashes. Imagine the money these women saved on mascara! Linda means pretty and she definitely was. No wonder the tourist men sought out Cuban women.

The kitchen was small. A narrow refrigerator, half the size of the one I had at home, was situated close to a gas-powered stove. It amazed me how Linda managed to make a family dinner with such limited counter space.

"Mama, can I bring *señorita* Anise to Papa?" Luisa begged.

"*Si, hija.*" Linda paused, looking from Luisa to me, "Anise, you and *el doctor* will stay with us. Luisa, take the *señorita* to the men. Tell them dinner will soon be ready, please?"

Luisa nodded, and once more took my hand. With Guillermo scampering behind we headed to the far end of the kitchen. A door opened to the balcony.

Outside, a tall fair-skinned Cuban man, his head shaved clean, leaned over the railing and pointed with his cigar to the trees. Beside him, Reese's eyes followed the motion. The cries of birds came from the underbrush.

The doctor was slightly taller than the other man but both were powerful in build. My pulse fluttered. An unexplainable rush of energy entered my center. A brilliant emerald haze surrounded Reese, yet in the center of his body, I saw a wild red flame.

Reese stopped talking and waved his cigar. "Hey, Anise! Come here and meet Luis." Turning to the man, he explained. "Anise is a photographer. She wants to take pictures of Cuba for a book."

Sparkling gray eyes swept down and back up to my face. "*Bueno! Hola,* Anise. It is a delight to meet you. Cuba has much to photograph. Do you like it?" He waved a hand expansively in the air.

My eyes shot down to the cliff in front of me. A wooden railing was the only safety feature protecting us from a sheer drop. Palms majestically dominated the smaller trees laden heavy with green fruit.

"Cuba is a magnificent. Your English is very good, Luis."

"I'm not your average farmer. My father sent me to university. I decided to study languages. You can imagine how my father took that news. After two years, he insisted I return and learn about sugar cane."

"That's too bad."

Luis nodded in agreement. "I think I could have found a government job but," he shrugged, "what was I to do? I had only sisters. Someone had to run the farm. As it was, papa lived only half a year after I returned. Luckily, I learned quickly."

"I'm sorry to hear that. Is *doña* Esmeralda your mother then?"

"Oh, no, she is my aunt. My mama died in Miami just weeks after she arrived. Her heart was weak. The trip was too much for her. *Doña* Esmeralda was her older sister. Unless Linda allows her the rare treat of cooking she prefers to spend her time on the porch." He turned to Reese. "I think my wife guards her territory. Do your women fight over the kitchen?"

Glancing in my direction, Reese's lips twitched. "Some love the kitchen and others spend so much time at work they know nothing about cooking."

I couldn't keep my mouth shut with that comment. "Canadian women are so busy with their jobs, they let the men do the cooking."

Luis looked from me to Reese. "I think you two are, how do you say, pulling my leg?"

"I was teasing Anise." Reese smiled. "Let me explain. In Canada, women cook and have jobs outside of the home but there are also men who understand the fine art of gourmet cuisine."

"You see, Luis," I tapped his arm, "when a man cooks, he is a gourmet chef but a woman is only doing what she ought to be doing and even if she is fantastic, she is still a cook."

Thoughtfully, Reese puffed on his cigar before he spoke. "Words, Luis. In Canada, women have equality. They've been able to vote since 1919 and be part of the government."

"Really? Women were given the right to vote here too but it took much longer for them to be part of the government." Luis studied his cigar. "The revolution had many Cuban women involved. That led to other things."

"Like what, Luis?" I was beginning to think there was more I should know.

"Women started to form groups."

Reese flicked ash over the railing. "Equal rights groups?"

Low in the pale blue sky, a dark form swooped down towards the trees and then up again. I blanked out the men and became the hawk. My destination was a plain white building. Inside, the chatter of women was loud, full of enthusiasm.

With a clap of her hands, a trim blonde brought the group to silence. Motioning the ladies to sit, she spoke to the Cubanas. The lady was more than pretty. A bright orange energy surrounded her. A glow lit her face. She captured their attention with the intonations of her voice lilting musically. Although I couldn't understand the Spanish, I sensed she was telling them about women's rights. In this meeting room, an overwhelming feeling consumed me. I felt sweaty and the pit of my stomach churned. It was impossible yet I realized I was her.

Reese slid his hand along my cheek and gazed into my eyes with concern. "Anise, you okay?" To Luis, he said, "We've had long road trip and Anise was recently injured in an accident."

"A Cuban dinner will make our lovely guest feel much better." Luis smiled. "Linda is a good cook, or should I say chef?"

"Papa." Luisa picked up the ashtray from the patio table. "Mama said to come in. She is almost ready with dinner." She wagged her finger. "Don't forget to put out your cigar." Her eyes flicked over to Reese. "You, too, *doctor.*"

"See how bossy the little girls are? Imagine what it is like to have a Cuban woman conducting your life?"

With a grin, Reese butted out his cigar and motioned for the children to proceed. He placed his hand on the small of my back and guided me back into the house.

The kitchen was cleaned up and Linda was nowhere in sight.

"Come, *amigos.*" Luis directed us to a room to the right.

Doña Esmeralda waited with Linda behind the chairs at the end of a heavy oak dining room table. "Your place is here, *doctor,* and Anise will sit next to you. Is that good? We will sit where we always sit. I think Isabel may decide not to come."

Luis pulled out a chair for me. "Why is that, *mi amor?*"

"She is…" running out of words, Linda rapidly explained in Spanish.

"Go get your sister," Luis instructed Guillermo with a frown. Watching the youngster leave, he said tightly, "Teenagers! Isabel is upset about her appearance." He pointed to his eye. "She was out with her friends and now her eye is not good." He waved at the table. "Please sit everyone. We must not let Linda's excellent dinner get cold."

Reese sat at the head of the table. "Was her eye injured?" he asked.

Linda shook her head. "She thinks not but it is red today. Since yesterday she refused to leave her room."

Guillermo skipped back into the room, tugged on his father's arm and whispered. Luis pointed at the chair beside him and the boy took his seat. "Isabel is being stubborn. Please excuse her."

"If you will permit it," Reese said, placing the napkin on his lap. "I could check in on your daughter later."

"Certainly, *gracias*. After dinner." Luis picked up his wine glass and held it high. *"Salud!"*

8

It felt good to be amongst a happy family, something I'd never had. Tomorrow I would take photos. Life was good. Henry was out and Reese was in.

Luis interrupted my thoughts. "I am worried about Isabel. You did say you wouldn't mind checking in on her, *amigo*?"

"Of course," Reese said. "Maybe Anise could come with me?"

"Good idea. I'm sure Isabel will be more comfortable with the presence of a woman."

Pushing out my chair, Reese waited for me to stand before grabbing the medical bag where he'd left it.

Luis spoke over his shoulder as we followed him down the hallway. "The children have bedrooms here but you and Anise will be staying in the addition just past the kitchen. By tomorrow, our house will be full. It will be a happy time with my family visiting. Perhaps we can celebrate a betrothal as well as a birthday."

I was hardly convinced of that. For Clara's sake, I hoped I was wrong.

Then I remembered her warning. When she'd called me Ani, those were my mama's words. Clara was a medium receiving messages for me. Angels guide us. We don't see them but they are everywhere. Usually they are people we knew or who knew us. I was more certain than ever these angels were taking me on this journey. One of them was my mother.

Luis tapped lightly on the middle door. "Isabel, I have brought you visitors. Reese is a doctor. Will you permit him to check your eye?"

When the door opened, I was startled to see a slender fair-haired girl of about sixteen sitting on the bed. With two dark-haired parents, she was most unusual.

"*Hola,* Isabel," Reese said quietly. "I am sorry but I speak very little Spanish."

"Please, come in. I speak English."

"I will leave," Luis said in an undertone. "She may prefer that."

Reese nodded. "This is my friend, Anise."

Isabel grinned mischievously. "Ah-ha. You mean girlfriend. I can tell by the way you look at her. Am I right?"

If I didn't know better I would have sworn Reese blushed. It was endearing to see a sweet side of him.

He avoided Isabel's question. "Anise is in Cuba to take photographs for a book."

Isabel's hand shot up to cover her eye. "Not of me!"

I nodded. "Don't worry. I wouldn't take it now. Perhaps when your eye is better?"

Isabel grinned. "Only if I can wear jeans." Suddenly animated, she asked, "Would you take a photo with my *novio*?

"Sure."

Reese sat down in the arm chair, bag in hand. "Were you hurt?"

"No, but it's very red."

I settled on the edge of the bed and watched Reese shine a light into Isabel's eyes.

"Looks like pink eye, *chica*. Don't worry, it will be gone in a day or so. In the meantime I'll give you eye drops. It's contagious so make sure you wash your hands with soap." Reese slipped on a thin pair of latex gloves. "Look up," he instructed, as he dripped eye drops out of a bottle.

"*Muchos gracias, doctor.*"

"Glad to help." With a hand on my elbow, he steered me out of the bedroom.

I was really pleased he had included me. Seeing him do his work was great but I sensed something I didn't like. I glanced up. "What is it?"

Reese frowned and shook his head. "Teenagers. They keep popping up."

"The dream?"

"Yes, and another patient I saw in Havana."

From the lounge, the sounds of drum beats and guitar invaded the hallway. Reese jerked his chin in the direction of the living room. "Let's see what's going on." He stepped back for me to go ahead, walking a pace behind.

In the lounge, Linda was singing softly as the children played. Luisa strummed the guitar while Guillermo beat on a tiny drum.

Luis waved them in. "Come, *amigos*! It's time for some fun." He thrust out two glasses filled with a pale green liquid. "Try. There's nothing better than these."

Reese tilted his head to eye the green sprig decorating a pale drink. What's in it?"

"Mint leaves, lime and rum. You will like it. I make one which rivals the Bodeguita de Medio."

Reese perked up. "The Hemingway's hangout?"

"*Sí*! Their mojito is the specialty of the restaurant." Luis beamed. "And you, Anise? Have you ever tried one?"

"Years ago in Santiago." I wasn't at all sure why I said that. This was my first trip to Cuba.

"Ah-hh, our oldest city." Luis nodded approvingly. "What did you think of it?"

"I remember an old fort."

"Well, you saw the best of Santiago. The city is not as interesting as Havana." He turned to Reese. "You are a lucky guy. Anise is *guapa*, like my Linda."

"When is Isabel coming?" Luisa piped up. "She could sing. Mama needs to have a mojito too."

"She is wise already." Luis handed Linda a glass with his special mixture and then, seeing both his guests had finished, he passed us another. "Can either of you sing?"

I shook my head. "Not me. Maybe Reese."

"Not in Spanish. I used to play in a band. Old eighties music. Sometimes we did classics." He peered at the children. "Play any Elvis?"

Guillermo laughed but Luisa nodded and whispered hurriedly to her brother. "Do you play, *señorita* Anise? We have an extra guitar." From behind the table, the girl picked up a guitar and handed it to me. "You can do the back up."

Slowly, I took up the guitar and placed it on my lap. My

fingers seemed to move on their own accord.

Luisa nodded approvingly. "She does it well, doesn't she, papa?"

"Our guest has talent. I think I recognize the piece."

It was as if I was possessed. A force propelled my hand like magic over the strings, a task that should have been impossible. I had never learned to play an instrument. As my fingers slid over the strings, I tried to recall the words.

White flashed before my eyes. I was no longer in Luis's home but in a small room, seated on a rattan couch with two young women sitting before me. From outside, the noises of cars and the honk of a horn shattered my words as I explained how to play a chord on the guitar.

As I flicked the final note, the room fell silent before appreciative applause broke forth.

"Excellent! Thank you!" Luis turned to Reese. "Now I call upon you, *doctor*, to sing for us. *Niños*, you must play that famous song, *Love Me Tender*, for him." He nodded at Reese. "You know that one? Luisa will give you the lyrics. Right, *hija*?"

"*Si*, Papa." Luisa shuffled the sheets on the table and triumphantly dug up a slightly crumpled sheet. "Here they are."

Linda laughed. "Now you must sing. I am looking forward to this. Luis is far too shy to sing in front of people." Turning to her husband, she kissed him on the cheek.

When the intro finished, Reese sang in a deep baritone, his voice suiting the Elvis song perfectly. "*Love me tender, love me sweet…*" Each word was sung meaningfully. I was moved, never having seen this part of Reese.

A smile formed on Reese's lips as his gaze swept the room, finally resting on me. It surprised me how well he sang, his voice raspy and low, full of emotion. I felt a stirring in my core. Warmth filled me. I could feel the depth of his love. His eyes closed with the line, "*Take me to your heart—for it's there that I belong.*"

Who had Reese been thinking of? What woman had touched him so profoundly? I cautioned myself. That song hadn't been for me. I tried to see her but nothing came. I knew it was something I couldn't call on at will. These premonitions came and went, sometimes leaving me confused.

I felt a tinge of jealousy. Why had no one ever loved me like that? My fate was to be a wanderer on planet Earth, always alone.

The enthusiastic applause in the room knocked me back to reality. Linda wiped a tear from her eye.

Luis nudged me. "Put the guitar down, Anise. Finish this drink. I will prepare more," he said, disappearing out of sight into the kitchen.

"*Salud!*" Reese clicked his glass against mine and then Linda's. "*Muchos amores.*"

"*Bueno, doctor*. But I think you need only one. A good one."

"You misunderstand, Linda. Reese and I are only friends."

Reese squeezed my shoulders. "Don't be *so* serious, Anise. Linda, do you play, too?"

She nodded.

I set down the empty glass. "Did you teach the kids?"

"I did, but you must understand, in Cuba, music," she said, fingertips at her heart, "it is in the *corazón*."

I agreed. It was hard to teach someone who couldn't feel the music. I knew this, but how?

"I enjoyed the melody you played, Anise. What was it?" Reese asked.

"A folk song." Another enchanting melody surfaced in my mind and I caught up the guitar once more.

Surprisingly, Linda hummed along with the tune. "I can't remember the words but I've heard it before," Linda said, reflectively. "It's from South America, isn't it?"

The words which came from my lips were from another level. "Argentina. Mercedes Sosa was beloved by us all. *La Voz de la Zafra*." Then, realizing how absurd that sounded, I fell silent.

Reese's forehead furrowed. "Mercedes Sosa? You know her music?"

I shook my head. "Reese, I really don't know why I said that."

"Were you in Argentina?"

A vision of brilliant green fields passed before my eyes. Tall grasses dispersed with bright sunflowers. A small blonde girl flitted through the grass, long hair ruffled with the breeze, floating out behind her. The white hazy film surrounding the lithe figure lent her the appearance of an angel on Earth.

Snatching up a sunflower, the child twirled around until, swaying dangerously, she let herself slump back onto a bed of grass. Her turquoise eyes stared up into the cloudless blue sky seeing something incomprehensible. She seemed unhurt yet her expression frightened me. What was it she was seeing? A chill shook my core.

"Anise?" Reese bent down beside me and took hold of my hand. "You look so pale. Are you feeling okay?"

Linda glanced from me to Reese. Her eyes shot over to the door where Luis stood holding a tray full of mojitos. "Luis, no more for Anise. She is not well."

Her husband set the drinks down and arched his eyebrow.

"I'm good. It was nothing." I picked up my mojito and tapped his glass lightly. "*Salud*, Luis."

Clinking his glass with Linda, he held it up. "*Bueno*. I am just so happy to have visitors. It gets lonely out here on the farm. I am grateful that you both are here. What more can a man ask than laughter and song? Let the children entertain us."

Luisa looked up at us. "Did you know Vera Matson wrote that Elvis song? I thought he wrote it. Why do people disappoint us?"

I bit my lip thoughtfully. "Believe in yourself. People can be deceptive."

"Yes, *señorita*. You are right about that. Especially friends, right?"

I shouldn't have said what I did to Luisa but it was true and there was no point in living in a fantasy world.

"Papa sing," Luisa commanded.

When Luis started to sing, the words blurred. It was a lovely tune about a woman yet I had that same dark feeling I'd had in the bar in Havana. An ominous feeling of loss.

It cheered me when they switched to another piece of music. I felt Reese take the mojito from my hand and place it on the table next to the guitar.

"It has been a long journey."

"Of course," Linda said, "I will show you to your room. The children have already brought your bags there. I hope you will be comfortable." She motioned for us to follow her.

"Goodnight. Thank you, everyone, for the wonderful evening." And then, remembering my rather difficult situation, I couldn't help but frown.

Sensing my discomfort, Luisa squeezed my hand. "I will show

señorita Anise the bedroom, Mama. You can stay here with Papa."

"Alright, *hija*, you may, but I am coming, too."

Pulling me along past Linda, we traipsed down the hall. "The *baño* is next to your bedroom. Lucky you. There is a giant bathtub and the bedroom is cozy, *señorita*. Very private."

That was exactly what worried me—a room with Reese. A few paces behind, speaking in undertones, Linda and Reese followed. The narrow hallway ended with two bedrooms. A partially opened door revealed a spacious room with terra cotta walls. A delightful old-fashioned porcelain tub majestically stood on ornate claw feet off to one side.

Luisa pointed to the room beside the bathroom. "That one is yours. The other one is empty tonight. Tomorrow, my aunts will arrive and stay there." She giggled. "Unless of course, *Tia* Clara comes with her *novio*. They will need two bedrooms then. *Tia* Clara," she placed her hand over her heart and rolled her eyes up dramatically, "is in love!"

I laughed at her dramatic gesture. "With Gunther?"

"*Si. Tia* Clara wants to marry him. He is rich." Smiling impishly, she probed, "And you, *señorita* Anise, are you?"

"Rich?"

"No-oo! In love," Luisa whispered. "*El doctor es muy guapo.* He would make any woman crazy. My sister Isabel was quite overcome with passion.

I grinned. "She said that?"

"*Si*! When I went to get her to come down for supper she refused. Wouldn't want *el doctor* to think she was ugly." She shrugged her shoulders. "Such a silly one. With so many boys her own age crazy about her, she thinks about an old man." She gave me a look. "What do you think, *señorita* Anise?"

"Reese is attractive."

"Yes, but *señorita,* isn't it more than that? There is romance in his song."

My pulse skipped a beat. "He has a wonderful voice. And you played well, too, Luisa."

"*Gracias*, but I think, not everyone has your skill with the guitar."

We stood at the door of the bedroom waiting for Reese and Linda. They had stopped a few feet back. I retraced my steps to join them and found them discussing the merits of a painting.

It was of a mother with her child. My jaw dropped.

It was signed *A Sommerville*—Ana Sommerville, my grandmother.

I grasped Linda's arm. "How did you get this painting?"

Linda pulled back. "Are you alright?"

"Yes. What do you know of the art?"

"My father-in-law bought it in Havana from an old Jewish woman. She sold them in the market. Why?"

"The artist is my grandmother. I wonder if she could still be alive?"

Linda shook her head. "This was years ago."

I rubbed my temple.

"What a coincidence," Reese said. "You wanted to find out about her and there is a painting right in the house."

"I saw three paintings of hers. One was in the Mojito Bar, and another in the house where we stopped and now here."

In the dim hallway light, a white film backlit Reese. "It is a strange coincidence, Anise." He swung around to Linda and Luisa. "Good night, ladies."

Luisa giggled until Linda silenced her with a look. "*El doctor* and his lady need some rest." Linda drew me in and kissed my cheeks. "Sleep well."

I embraced her in return. "Thank you for your hospitality."

Sherry-brown eyes sparkled. "*De nada. Mi casa es tu casa.*"

By the time I came into the room, Reese was sprawled out on the double bed, long jean-clad legs stretching to the ornate pewter footboard. The bed stood in the middle of large room. The terra cotta walls glowed warmly from the light of the lamp on the night table.

"No use delaying the inevitable, Anise."

"The inevitable?"

"Us—sharing the bed."

"Reese, our relationship is strictly platonic."

Emerald eyes gleamed in the dim light. "A man can fantasize."

"We just met."

Leaning back on his elbows, Reese grinned. "Don't tell me you haven't had thoughts in that direction."

"If I did, I would hardly tell you. Your ego is big enough."

"Other parts of me are quite sizable."

"Braggart."

"All true. But I know a woman needs more than that. Don't worry, babe, I can be enticed to give you everything you want. In fact, it would be my pleasure."

I picked up my bag. "I'm sure, however, I have something better in mind besides enticing you."

"What could possibly be more exciting than the two of us making love?"

I zipped open my bag and shuffled through the clothes.

"What's up, princess? You look put out."

"I didn't take anything to sleep in."

"You mean you sleep in pajamas?"

"No-oh. Actually I don't but I wasn't prepared to be sharing a bed with you. I know I should have packed for this, but somehow it escaped my mind."

"That's because you were in shock, honey. You nearly drowned, remember?"

"I was not in danger. That's only your perception of it." I waved my hand impatiently. "Reese, I need something to wear. Help me out here. Is there something of yours I could borrow?"

"I have an extra pair of boxer briefs—black. You'd look cute in those."

I tossed my bag on the armchair near the door and glared at him. "I'm thinking something a bit larger, like a t-shirt?"

Reese's eyes shot to the ceiling. "There's a fan in here but you must have noticed the temperature is only slightly cooler tonight than it was during the day. A t-shirt wouldn't be my choice. I'd suggest you go with the gitch and a bra."

"No thanks."

He laughed. "No bra, then. Live a little. Go topless."

I hissed through my teeth. "Reese!"

"Alright, if you insist on covering up, a gitch and one of your tight little tops."

"The problem with the heat can easily be solved." I strode over the far side of the room and unlatched the shutters. Standing there a moment, I was disappointed to find there was absolutely no breeze. With the night air only slightly cooler than the room temperature, we were in for an uncomfortable sleep.

"Good thought, but Anise, you can see my point."

I could. "Alright, Reese. I'll borrow the boxers."

"You sure? They'll be a bit warm, don't you think? Why don't you just leave your panties on? I'm sure they'd be much sexier." His lips twitched. "I'd guess lacy or am I wrong about you, Anise? Do you wear those plain cotton undies?"

"Lacy low rise bikini," I snarled, snatching up his bag and pulling out a pair of black boxer-briefs. "But I'd prefer these." From my own tote, I located a top and toiletry bag. With both articles in my hand, I headed to the bathroom.

The cream shade of the lamp cast a golden glow to the terra cotta walls. I could almost picture myself submerged in the old-fashioned bathtub. I peeked into the mirror. A streak of dust ran from the corner of my eye to my chin. As I cast my eyes downward, I noticed dirty smudges on my arms.

I should have asked if any one else would be using the tub tonight but the heat and my dusty state made me selfish. Placing my clothes on a bench, I turned on the taps.

On the shelf above, I found some bubble bath. I was sure Linda wouldn't mind if I used it just this once. A couple of drops of the creamy liquid frothed powerfully in the rapidly filling tub. With the pink foamy bubbles threatening to spill over the top, I shut the water off.

I shed my clothes, filled the nearby sink and tossed my top, shorts and underwear in for a rinse. Perhaps, I'd even wash my hair, I thought as I squeezed out the excess water from my clothes and hung them on an empty railing. A quick tap on the door startled me. "Yes?"

"I've brought towels," Reese said. "Linda came by and said we were to use the facilities tonight as the family takes turns in the morning. May I come in?"

"Hand me a towel," I said through a crack in the door, "and wait there."

A fluffy white towel was pushed into the gap and I caught it up. Quickly, I wrapped it around and tucked it in above my breasts before I opened the door.

Reese came in wearing only his jeans.

It took a little self-control not to stare at his buff body but my eyes made their way back to his face. I didn't know if that was a good idea either. Those mysterious eyes made me quiver. Even worse, the upward curl of those shapely lips struck me dumb.

"I see you were about to go ahead without me. Luckily for you I brought towels." He scratched his head. "No, Reese—not so smart. You would have been standing lovely as Eve had I forgotten the towels."

"Funny."

Reese walked over to the bath tub and cocked his head contemplatively.

I stepped up beside him. "If you think you're sharing a bath with me you're sadly mistaken."

"Well, since we're both dirty and sweaty."

"Speak for yourself."

With his index finger, Reese stroked my cheek thoughtfully. "Apologies. Since you're dirty and I'm sweaty, I think we both need to get cleaned up, don't you?"

I rolled my eyes at his implication. "I won't be long. Come back in half an hour."

"As much as I'd like to oblige I was also told if we want showers we'd have to hurry," he glanced at his watch, "and be out in forty minutes for the kids to take baths."

"Why didn't you say so?" I pushed him towards the door. "I was here first. You'll have to wait. Should be about twenty minutes or let's say thirty minutes. I'll need to dry my hair, too." I smiled happily at my plan.

Reese didn't move.

"You need to go."

Silently, he unzipped his jeans. I shot him a look. Gazing back at me, he pushed his pants over his hips. My jaw must have dropped because he laughed. "No need for me to go, babe. I'll use the shower."

"What? I was here first." I pointed over to the bathtub. "See—it's ready."

"We could share and save water."

"I think not."

"I'd wash your back, although I would prefer other parts."

The man frustrated me. I wanted him yet it was too soon. After Henry I couldn't jump into sex with a stranger.

"Okay, you win, Anise. Use the bath. I'll take the shower. How's that?" Reese chucked me under the chin. "I won't look. Promise." Turning to the small shower enclosure, he reached in and activated the spray. "Now if you'll excuse me, I have a shower to take."

He started to pull down his boxers-briefs, and I froze momentarily. Before heading over to my bath, I had to admit I had caught a spectacular view of a well-rounded ass. I didn't feel bad about it, either. After all, the man had intruded on my time, which reminded me that I needed to get into that tub ASAP. Gathering up shampoo and conditioner, I placed them on the tiny table at the end of the bath tub.

Cautiously, I stuck a toe in and finding it perfectly wonderful, dropped my towel on the tiles and slid into the bubbles. Once I'd adjusted to the temperature, I picked up a wash cloth and cleaned my face. It was only one day into this motorcycle journey and already I felt it. The muscles in my body needed the warmth of the water. Lifting my leg out of the suds, I gently scrubbed off the dirt.

The next task to deal with was my hair. I ran fingers through the layers and wasn't surprised to note it had lost its clean silky feel. A quick dip into the water and it was ready for a dab of shampoo. I would have preferred a shower for this but I had no regrets about choosing the tub. Let Reese do his thing in the shower.

Over at the other end of the room, I heard the rush of the water and I breathed easier. I should be finished before he got out but I'd be damned if I let that man take away precious bath time from me. Working the conditioner through to the tips of my hair, I pushed it from my face and sat waiting for it to work. I closed my eyes and leaned back, totally relaxed.

"Keep your eyes closed and hold your breath, babe."

"What!" I sputtered as lukewarm water poured over my head.

"No need to thank me, Anise. I saw the pitcher and figured you wouldn't want the suds left in your hair. You want a towel?"

With my fingertips, I swiped the water from my eyes and squinted at my tormentor. Reese stood above me, looking Greek god-like, a towel draped low on his narrow hips. A wet sheen covered the muscular body where the towel had missed doing its job.

"This is not a free show," I said dryly.

Reese peered at the bubbles clinging to my breasts. "Don't worry. Unfortunately, the twins are covered." He stood back. "Nothing like a sexy woman in a tub except maybe a generous woman who wouldn't mind sharing the experience," he said admiringly.

I smirked. "Hope runs eternal."

"So you're hoping I'll join you? I'm clean but what the hell." Reese placed his hand on the knotted towel.

"Go!" I hissed, pointing at the door.

"So soon? Okay, if you insist. See you in the room, sweetheart." Reese tossed my towel on the wicker chair by the door before clicking the door shut behind him.

Sighing with relief, I got out of the tub and dripped my way over to the towel he had so inconsiderately thrown as far away as possible. After drying off, I took out my mini dryer and a brush and worked some magic. Finally, in a tank top and Reese's boxers, I emptied the tub and cleaned it before I headed back to the bedroom.

The light was on but the room was cloaked in shadow. From above the fan clicked rhythmically. Outside the night was silent. This somewhat reassured me. Insects and bats would not be my bedmates of choice.

After all, I already had one. I might have rebuffed Reese but I was a passionate woman with needs. It's not easy to be cool around an exciting man like him and not sample what's offered. On the other hand, good things are worth waiting for.

It wasn't about a puritanical desire to stay chaste. I was ready to rid myself of Henry, but was I up for a man like Reese? I needed sex with love. That wouldn't be possible because I hardly knew this man. And I couldn't ignore my instincts either. Reese wasn't ready for me.

"Anise?"

"Yes?"

"I took this side. If you'd rather have the other, tell me."

"No, that's good for me, too." I placed my things on the dresser and got into bed. "Luis and Linda think we're partners, don't they?"

"I suppose. If we weren't it would be awkward tomorrow with

the family arriving. I'm not sure what they'd do with us. They don't have enough rooms."

I fluffed up my pillow and lay down. "You don't snore, do you?"

Reese laughed. "I don't think so, at least not usually. How about you?"

I jabbed him in the ribs. "Did anyone ever tell you what an irritating man you are?"

"Persistent, persuasive and passionate, but no, not irritating."

I sighed. "I guess I'm stuck with you."

His face was inches away. "Lucky woman," he said, his voice husky before gently kissing me. Soft warm lips that promised more. A kiss that burned to my core.

He brought his hand to my face and stroked my cheek. "Goodnight, Anise."

"Night," I whispered, rolling over on my side to face the window. I lay there waiting for my pulse to slow down.

"Has anyone ever told you have the most amazing ass?"

"Not for a while."

"Well, you do," Reese murmured, his voice muffled from the pillow.

When I heard his breathing deepen, I figured he'd drifted off. I was a little envious. It always took me a while to fall asleep but the bed was just right and the man in my bed had a comfortable body temperature—not that unpleasant heat that Henry generated, only a satisfying warmth.

A subtle scent filled the air. I flipped around. I breathed in soap and spice. Tingles of arousal shot down my body. In the dim light I examined his cheekbones, slightly crooked nose and full lips. The man was as delicious as rich creamy chocolate.

I turned away, my eyes shifting to the window. At first I didn't see him. The silhouette of a tall man was backlit by the moon.

"Soon you'll be back in my arms," a soothing voice whispered.

"Why are you here?"

"It's been almost forty years. I need you, *cariño*. You must leave with me."

"You're mistaken. I don't know you."

"Oh, but you do. Our lives are entwined forever."

I sat up in bed to protest but my visitor had vanished, leaving a white mist where he had positioned himself in the chair by the window.

The air was oppressively heavy. A flash of lightning charged the sky and from somewhere in the hills, thunder rumbled.

The rain poured heavily as I fell into a restless sleep.

9

The grass rustled. It could have been anything. I wasn't curious enough to pursue it. The last thing I wanted to see was a hungry creature with sharp teeth eager for a taste of my leg. With the late afternoon sun glowing with hues of gold, I took advantage of the perfect lighting on the cliff and snapped a few photos before heading back up.

From a distance a pile of rocks was just that—brown with an interesting pattern. I stopped dead. The zigzag design was a boa. Looped several times around the rocks, I estimated nine feet of snake. At this point my hands trembled as much from excitement as from fear. I knew something of these snakes. Boas are carnivorous, suffocating their prey before they ate, yet otherwise calm.

I ensured a safe distance between us. The lens zoomed in. Pleased with the shot, I was ready to leave. I threw my camera back in the bag, and climbed the remaining distance to the path leading to the house. Earlier, Luis had gone off with Reese to a nearby village and I'd made the most of the location taking shots of the landscape. The morning light had given the hills a different flavor with mystical blues and emeralds cloaking the hills.

By the time I returned to top of the cliff, it was like a set change. The foliage was vibrant with ochre while the hills blushed pink with the caress of the sun. If ever there was a place described as breathtaking it was here, east of Havana. Nature was alive with the music of birds and insects. This was Eden.

Henry had scoffed when I'd told him about Cuba and my project. It wasn't always like that. At one time he had been kind and supportive. But what I saw then was a camouflage. Underneath the friendly mask was a depressed angry man. It took time to be revealed. I should never have ignored the feeling I had when we moved in together. Had I listened to my voices, my life would be different now.

Music and voices from the balcony told me the relatives had arrived. A jeep was parked in front of the house.

In the kitchen, Luis's aunt was at the stove cooking up a storm. She cheerfully called out an *hola* as I made my way to the balcony.

"There she is! Anise, you take some good pictures?" a guttural voice boomed out from the door.

"Hi, Gunther!" In Bermuda shorts, golf shirt and sandals, the German was the picture of a European on vacation. "Yes, it's great down there."

Pulling me into a bear hug, he whispered cryptically, "Watch out."

He needn't have said anything. Already the hairs on the back of my neck stood up in warning. I followed his gaze to a pale, shapely lady beside Reese, a hand casually resting on his arm.

Behind Gunther, a soft voice called out, "*Amiga!*" Stepping to me, Clara brought me close and planted a kiss on each cheek.

"*Hola*, Clara," I said, returning the embrace.

"Come, *amiga*." Taking my hand, Clara led me over to Reese's lovely companion. "You must meet someone."

"Hi, babe!" Reese was animated. "You were gone a long time. Get some good pics, I hope? Anise, let me introduce you to Lola. It was quite a surprise that we'd already met."

The raven-haired beauty's lips curled into a smile that didn't quite reach her eyes. When she kissed my cheeks, I returned her greeting. The scent of gardenias was overwhelmingly powerful.

Around Lola's body I saw a red haze that filled the balcony. Anger. Or was it all a sexual energy? I saw the way her eyes fixed on Reese, ready to devour him.

I forced myself to keep my voice steady. "How did you meet?"

"Remember how I said I wanted to help Cubans? Lola's daughter was my first patient."

"Oh?"

"My mom retired in Miami. One of her friends is Lola's aunt. My mom thought since I was going to Cuba anyway, I should look up Delores's niece. The letter Lola wrote worried her."

"Does your aunt know Luis's family?" I couldn't take my eyes off Lola and the brilliant fire of her aura.

Reese tapped the cigar on the ash tray. "Delores got out during the revolution. She's never been back. I went to see Lola the day I ran into you with my motorcycle. Remember I said I had to go somewhere?"

I recalled that meeting all too well.

Clara sat down on one of the rattan chairs. "You were at our apartment?"

"Yes, but I had no idea you were related. What a coincidence! It's a surprise that I would meet up with Luis's family and stay here."

Luis took a mojito from the table and handed it to me before taking one for himself. "*Salud* everyone!"

Gunther grinned. "Now, for our wonderful host. A toast to Luis. Happy birthday!"

"And many more," Reese added.

"Thank you," Luis signaled to the children. "Bring out the food, *hijos*. We will eat out here on the balcony tonight."

Seeing Isabel's pout, Linda suggested, "I think the children would prefer to eat inside in the kitchen."

"*Bueno*. They can do that after they serve the food. Doña Esmeralda will stay with them." Luis chortled. "A man needs to celebrate his day with adults."

Gunther tossed back the mojito. "While we celebrate the beauty of his siblings, right, Reese?"

Reese took a cigar from Luis. "I will smoke a cohiba and as I breathe in the fine flavors of chocolate, I'll think about the lovely women here in Cuba."

Luis looked at me speculatively. "You are not in need of our women, my friend. Although Anise is not Cuban, no one would dispute her beauty."

I'd swear Lola pinched his backside from the agonized expression on his face. But Luis, made of sterner stuff, kept a smile pasted on his handsome visage.

Giggling, Clara tipped back her glass. "Lola likes to cause pain, but you must allow it, *hermano*. It helps you grow. Isn't that what they say about a pinch?"

"Grow old," Gunther grunted, "and grow fat."

"Not me, *amigo*." Luis lit his cigar and puffed. "Weren't you the super size model for Nike?"

I lost what they said as I tuned an ear to hear Lola purr, "I came to see you, Reese, as much as Luis. They won't miss us if we pop out for a bit. There is something I'd like to show you."

"What?"

"We have natural hot springs in the field near the trees." She pointed to a clump of palms in the distance. "I will bring you there. Go put on your bathing suit and I will change into mine. The water is wonderful. Have you ever been to a hot spring?"

"What are you plotting, Lola?" Luis swung around to peer into his sister's face as if to read her thoughts.

Smiling serenely, Lola stood on her tiptoes and pecked his cheek. "We will be back in no time. I must show Reese my favorite spot."

Luis shook his head impatiently. "Our friends are visiting here together."

"I want to show him our hot springs, Luis. It won't take long. Surely, that's allowed."

"Reese came with his *novia*," Luis said sternly.

Lola curled her lip and was about to say something when I interrupted,

"It's alright, go ahead if you want." I stared challengingly at Lola. "Reese can do what he wants."

Placing his cigar in the ashtray, Reese brought his forefinger to my cheek and let it trail down. His touch sparked a flame. I was drawn into his mysterious eyes flecked with amber lights.

"And what I want is to take you. Why don't you get into your bikini and we'll let Lola show it to us?"

"What a sly devil," boomed Gunther. "He is not satisfied with one woman, he must have two. Stay here with me, *Liebchen*." He threw his arm around my shoulders. "The doctor is not man enough. I, on the other hand," he pointed at his chest, "have been known to keep a woman happy for hours."

Clara poked his stomach and hissed something in Spanish that I couldn't make out but from the way her eyes narrowed, I sensed her anger.

With his hand up, Luis signaled stop. "Of course, Lola must show our guests the hot springs. We eat late tonight anyway. No hurry. Enjoy the waters."

Reese took my hand. "Let's get changed." Leading me to the door, he looked back at Lola. "We'll meet at the front, alright?"

Lola pursed her lips and nodded.

In the hallway on the way, I said, "Thanks for including me."

"You know," Reese turned, pulling me closer, his eyes glittering, "it would feel even better without…"

"Without?"

"Clothes."

***

A burst of light. I was swimming—the river waters refreshing on my bare skin. Sunshine overhead sprinkled the tropical broad-leaved plants on the bank with that vibrant emerald hue found only in the tropics.

A dark-haired man popped out of the water, wide shoulders and powerful arms thrust forward in a butterfly stroke. Movie star handsome with an even-white smile that would have charmed a snake, he yelled out, "Feels good, doesn't it?"

With my chin on the surface as I swam, I could see the bright gleam of intelligence in those changeable eyes. The man was a rarity.

"Happy?"

"Yes, but I'm exhausted."

"No wonder. You have done as much as any of those men. It is admirable how you marched for days without ever tiring—a slender woman such as you."

"Thanks, but you know I need to pull my weight. I can't be treated differently." On my back, I sank into a float. "This was a great idea. The water is glorious."

"We'll have a little time alone before they return. Let's go in. I need to kiss you."

With my body tingling in anticipation, I swam swiftly towards the shore. I wanted to be with this very special man. "You're sure this is private? I don't want any of them to know," I said, when we made it to knee high water.

Pulling me along to the trees, he smiled. "If they have any power of observation, they know already. Every time I look at you, I'm happy. I feel so lucky to have met you, *cariño*. It must be apparent to any idiot."

"I don't want them to think of me as your paramour. I've worked hard to be a soldier, doing my share."

"And they know it. The men have respect for you, as I do." Gently, he ran his fingers down my cheek. "You are beautiful both outside and in. We have the same beliefs. You understand what is important not only to me but to all of us."

With my hand in his larger one, we walked to a secluded area behind the trees where our clothes hung on the branches, freshly washed.

"Let's sit." He lowered himself down and held out his hand. "I need to see you in all your beauty."

For a moment he said nothing but his eyes wandered the length of my body. "You are a goddess. No other woman is as alluring as you."

Stretching out my legs towards him, I admired his muscular body, trim from all the walking, the limited rations and the stress. There was no sign of the asthma that tortured him. "I'm glad I still look good to you."

"Always. You are in my heart." Taking up my foot, he kissed my toe and, that not being enough, proceeded to caress the other toes before his kisses trailed to my ankle.

I shuddered with the heat that torched my body. No lover had ever been like this.

"Your skin is so smooth. I love to touch it." His hands slid up my leg while he licked the inside of my ankle.

I dropped down to the blanket, reveling in the sun and the man that adored me. Licks and tender kisses traveled further up to my thigh. I quivered with arousal. I needed to touch him to feel his essence. Lightly, my fingers brushed his shoulders and neck before threading through his thick locks.

"Come up here," I whispered hoarsely Pulling himself up, his face above mine, I saw the passion in his eyes. While wondrous kisses torched my mouth, a hand stroked my shoulder before wandering to my breasts. The soft touch on my nipples stiffened them into peaks. I wanted his attention but I needed his lips even more. My mouth was drawn to his while my hands gripped strong muscular arms. Butterfly kisses ignited an ember lodged in my core. Withdrawing his lips, he nuzzled my neck until I shuddered with every nibble and lick.

It had been so long. I ached for more. Just as I drew his head to my breast, I was startled by the rapid rifle fire in the trees from across the river bank.

***

If ever there was a paradise, it was this. A steamy mist rising from the bubbling pool and shadows from the palms swaying in the breeze while moonlight flickered through the fronds.

Lola had brought towels and had placed them near the stairs. "*Mi amor*, come here." She stretched out her hand to pull Reese closer but he stayed next to me. "How do you like it?" Lola slinked to Reese, forcing him to lift his arm to drape it around her shoulders.

"It's great," he said, pulling me closer, letting Lola slip out from his arm. "Are you alright? You were so far away."

"Mm-mm. I had—" I whispered, "a vision."

"It has upset you. I can tell." He brought his head to my ear. "We can speak privately later?"

I nodded.

Lola squeezed his hand. "Let's get in, darling." She stood and slowly slipped off her bikini. Her body was voluptuous enough to entice any man. "Skinny dipping is the best way." She stared a challenge in my direction.

Reese took my cheek and lightly kissed my lips. Electricity charged my core. "I will, if you do," he said softly. I was up to any challenge that woman could throw out.

For a few minutes everything was forgotten as we swam together. But when Lola popped up next to Reese and kissed him, I was angry.

In the dim light it was impossible to see his expression. All that mattered was that he had allowed it. With an energy I didn't know I had I swam back, climbed out and took up a towel, wrapping it tightly. If he wanted her, let him. I didn't need to chase after any man.

Reese swam to the opposite side of the pool, away from Lola. Eying a colorful plant near the edge, he hoisted himself up and plucked off two brilliant scarlet flowers. With the stems firmly held in his teeth, he swam towards me, Lola several lengths behind.

"For my beautiful companion," he said, presenting the first hibiscus flower to me. Reese handed the second flower to Lola. "And to my thoughtful friend." Had he been watching, he would have seen daggers shoot in his direction.

I handed him a towel which he wrapped and tucked in at his waist. He sat beside me. "Hibiscus. It means delicate beauty," he said. Then Reese whispered in my ear, "Perfect for you."

I met his eyes. "Thank you."

"I don't know either of you ladies well but I know you are both treasures to mankind."

Lola laughed shrilly. "You flatter like a Latino."

"I suppose I am. French and Irish on my mother's side."

The Celts were known for their sixth sense and the French for their romantic souls. An interesting combination.

Lola's eyes narrowed. "Are you married, Reese?"

He frowned. "No."

With his discomfort obvious, I pointed to the gap in the foliage where blood-red streaks marred the darkening sky. "Look at that sunset! Isn't it fantastic?"

"Hey!" A voice boomed out. "We need you people for dinner. The food is being laid out. Clara said I was to order you back no matter what you're up to. Doctor, you are blessed. His eyes roamed from one female wrapped in a towel to the other. "Lucky bugger."

"I think you are the lucky man and don't know it." Reese thrust his hand out to help me up. "Clara cares for you."

"I agree. She is serious about you, Gunther," Lola added enthusiastically, "and she is loyal."

Gunther took hold of Lola's hand and assisted her up. "Clara is lovely. But, ach, tonight there are so many sexy women. Skinny dipping with two ladies, eh," he said, snatching up the pile of bathing suits. "Just like Christmas! Not an ugly one tonight anywhere."

Lola jabbed a finger into his chest. "You need to consider Clara. She could make a good wife for you. It's time to start thinking of children with a loving woman."

Reese pushed back a wet strand of hair that had fallen into my eyes.

Gunther sat down on a rock and stared thoughtfully. "What do you say, doctor?"

"Love is fleeting, my friend. Once you've lost it, the love is gone forever."

"So you're a philosopher now or is that your experience speaking? What brought this on? Some cruel woman broke your spirit?"

"Shit, no!" Reese said lightly, but a shadow darkened his eyes. "Come on, ladies. Dinner awaits."

***

Platters of pork, chicken, black beans, rice and vegetables steamed enticingly on the large wooden table. In adjacent wicker chairs, Linda and Clara sat chatting, plates perched on their knees.

Gunther loaded up his plate and took the chair between them.

A melodic rhythm filled the air. On a wooden stool in the corner, Luis strummed his guitar, singing about something to do with the *corazón*. Was it about love gone wrong or was it about the joy of fulfillment?

I felt my fingers ache to play the song on my own guitar. That was totally absurd yet who could deny last night? I had a talent I knew nothing about.

The flashback had been pleasant. Where was the place I had lived and taught music? Judging from the heat, it was somewhere tropical. I wished I knew more. Sometimes I wondered whether this gift was really a curse. The other memory with the handsome dark-haired man, as much as it had been sensuous, frightened me.

Before I could find some food for myself, Reese thoughtfully brought over a plateful of tasty morsels. "You are lovely in that dress, Anise." His face lit up. "The blue makes your eyes indescribably brilliant. Turquoise instead of silver." When I heard those words I could swear my heart sang right along with the music.

Undaunted by the cavalier act, Lola cozied up to the doctor. "I must thank you again. My girl is so much better now since you cared for her. Our doctor was puzzled by the fever. I can't tell you how grateful I am that you helped her."

"It was my pleasure." From a large silver bowl, Reese spooned up pork in a dark sauce. "I'm so happy that she's recovered. Where is she, by the way?"

"I allowed her to stay at a friend's house. I didn't want her to miss any more school while I was away."

"It's a nice break for you, too, isn't it?"

Lola nodded with a significant glance in my direction. "It's a chance to focus on other things." With her back to us she filled our wine glasses to the brim. "This bottle is nearly empty. Perhaps you could find another bottle for us," she said to Reese.

"Of course." Reese headed to the kitchen.

Lola swiveled around and handed me a glass. "Are you a wine drinker, Anise?"

"I like reds."

"This one is a shiraz. Sip it slowly. It is strong." Lola's bright red lips pinched into a narrow line as she watched me test the wine. "What do you think?"

"Smooth." I closed my eyes to savor it. Already I was feeling mellow. "Blackberries and there's a hint of chocolate." To me there was nothing like chocolate—rich Belgium. With every nibble, endorphins were released within and with that, the pleasure principle.

Some women like chocolate more than sex but not me. The combination of a shiraz and chocolate aroused me like nothing else except a very sexy man with a sensuous touch.

This trip had awakened me. My eyes lit on the object of my lust who seemed somewhat endearing in his confusion. Reese disappeared into the dining room, apparently on a quest of sorts.

Lola sipped her wine. "I think he would make a fantastic brother-in-law, don't you agree?" she whispered conspiratorially.

"Gunther?"

"Yes, admittedly he is a bit of an oaf, but he has a well-paying job and is most generous."

"He brought the wine?"

"Yes, a case full but it's more than that. He has visited us here in Cuba many times. Gunther always brings gifts for the whole family." Tilting the glass back, Lola peered at me from over the rim. "We are not known for our wines, Anise. Cuba has rum, sugar cane, and tobacco but nothing I would consider worthy to be called a wine. The embargo prohibits a great deal." She sighed heavily. "I do so love a California wine or the smooth Australian shiraz he brought tonight. Life is not easy here." Her eyes glittered in the lamp light. "But a Canadian bringing in gifts can make it so much more pleasant."

"Gunther is thoughtful. Is that why Cuban women are interested in the tourist men?"

Lola smiled slightly. "Life can improve with a foreign husband."

I finished my glass and set it on the table as Reese appeared with a fresh bottle.

"So sorry, ladies. I found a corkscrew—finally." With a flourish, Reese poured the sparkling berry liquid into each goblet.

Feeling suddenly disoriented, I rubbed my temples.

Reese glanced at me. "Anise?"

"Excuse me," I muttered, escaping into the hallway. The corridor was dark. Shadows loomed on the white stucco walls. I hesitated, forgetting where the washroom was.

Standing confused for a second, I realized the bathroom was at the end of the hall across from our bedroom. I crept with rubbery legs, a hand on the wall. It seemed an endless journey. Once inside the room, I tottered over to the mirror. The face that stared back was pale as death with pupils unnaturally dilated. Tiny beads of perspiration dotted my brow.

There was a rap on the door. Lola entered. "I thought you might need some help. I suggest you lie down and rest a bit."

Sleep? It might be what I needed. My limbs felt heavy and my stomach was queasy.

"Come, I will help you." Taking me by the elbow, she led me to the room beside the bathroom.

It was good she held on because I lacked the energy. My legs were becoming weaker and I faltered, stopping at the door frame. Lola pulled a switch. A bedside light cast a yellow glow to the room.

The dimly lit chamber was strangely unfamiliar. Our bags weren't here nor were any of our clothes. "This room isn't mine," I whispered.

"Never mind. You will be just fine here," she purred soothingly. "Look how comfortable the bed is?" Lola patted the bed invitingly and smiled. "Reese thought you should stay here."

When the room swam before my eyes, she led me to the bed

and forced me down. Gripping each foot in turn, she tugged off my shoes. "Now help me with your dress. I have undone your zipper. Lift up a little and I will pull it off." Lola smiled. "There. That's better." She took out a gold medallion and held it before me. "Watch the Virgin. See how she is happy?"

"Yes," I said, my voice distant to my ears.

"You will welcome a visitor."

"Who?"

Lola brought her finger to her lips. "Hush, you will soon find out. He is a friend but I can tell he wants it to be much more. Be kind to the man. Let him be your lover."

"But I don't want a lover."

"Yes, you do. I sense it. You have been deprived for too long. You will enjoy it and ask for more. Now, relax. Look at my medallion." Lola swung the locket before my eyes. "See how she watches you?"

The sparkle of the Virgin's face made my eyes heavy.

"But for now you will sleep. He should arrive shortly."

The room was a white cloud. Lola's face was hazy and out of focus. My eyes had trouble staying open. The urge to drift away overwhelmed me.

"Relax, Anise." There was an edge to the Latina's soft voice.

My eyes closed but my gut feeling told me I had to get up. Something was not right here. No matter how much I welcomed sleep, I needed to find Reese. I could feel he was in trouble. I tried to stand but lightheaded, fell back on the bed.

The door clicked shut. It was the last thing I heard.

***

Awakening to the sound of laughter, I became aware of a scent that spicy smell that I knew so well. On the back of his bike, I'd taken in his fresh body scent. I looked about. Reese wasn't there. Was it my lover from the other life?

What had happened to send me into this strange state where I was neither awake nor asleep? Odd. I had eaten and that should have kept me sober.

Feeling cool, I glanced down and found I was wearing only a bra and panties. *When had I undressed and why?*

The skin on my belly felt itchy. Lightly, I skimmed over the curve of my abdomen. Bringing my hand up, I saw a trace of gray powder on my fingertips.

Music and singing came in from the open window. A salsa. The beat of the drums echoed in my brain. I vaguely remembered there was a party in the house. I shook my head. Was I really this wasted? How could one glass of wine be so powerful?

Lilting laughter from the hallway set the hairs on my head on end. Reese was in trouble—I sensed it.

Gathering my strength, I stood up. The room swam before my eyes, but I breathed in. With the air entering my lungs, I collected my strength and lurched to the door. I swung the door open and smacked right into a solid mass of flesh. My eyes shot up. It was Gunther.

"*Liebchen*, why are you leaving?" Squinting to adjust to the low light, his eyes ate me up. "I see you really did want to see me. The lacy stuff is very sexy, Anise." Taking my arm by the elbow he led me back to the bed.

I didn't want to go but resistance was difficult. Memories of green eyes and shapely lips filled me with joy. And then there was the music. Soft hair brushed my cheek as he held me in his arms. I glanced at Gunther. He was my visitor. I liked him yet the memory was not of him. "Why are you here?" I could hardly get these words out. It was too difficult to speak.

"I was so surprised to find your note, but I had to see if you were really serious." He glanced down at my black bra. "Now I see you are."

"Serious?" The room was a kaleidoscope of colors, every corner filled with lights. I had no idea what he was talking about or why he was there.

Gunther didn't wait for me to finish. He kissed me hard on the lips and with his hands on my shoulders forced his tongue in my mouth.

I hated the kiss. The harsh smell of cigarettes and the sweaty odor was wrong, yet I knew I needed to treat my visitor kindly. The Virgin had said so.

"Delightful," he mumbled, pulling me close. The strong scent of garlic on his breath turned my stomach. Sloppy kisses to my neck made their way to my shoulder. "How lucky I am to have you summon me like this."

Why would Gunther think I wanted him? Yet I felt immobilized by an outside force that kept me from telling him. Nor could I refuse him. I shivered not from excitement but from fear. I was a puppet on a string, manipulated by someone else's energy.

"Ach, let me see your treasures, Anise." He shoved my bra straps down and fingered the flesh exposed by the lace. "Nice. I will give them attention. Oh lovely lady, you will not regret asking for me."

With a swoop he picked me up and placed me on the bed. Frozen in a state of inertia, I could only lie there and watch as if this was happening to someone else. The lust in his eyes was apparent. "*He will be your love*r," a faraway voice instructed. I heard it and shuddered.

"I will get rid of these things quickly, my sweet, and you will have every part of me." Undoing the buttons of his shirt, he shrugged off the garment.

When his belt unclasped, I began to feel my world closing in on me. "No!" It came out like an echo in a tunnel.

In the midst of lowering his pants, he stopped and chuckled. "You'd rather I kept my clothes on? Funny lady, hm-mm. Very kinky. I like that. I would never have guessed you were like that but what do I know? I'm just an old guy with a liking for beautiful women." His pants dropped to the floor and he stepped out of them. "I'll keep the boxers on, if you prefer it that way. You will be glad you chose me, Anise. The doctor is otherwise occupied. I know that for a fact. That little minx, Lola, has captured your doctor and put him under her spell. Lucky turn of events, isn't it?"

Everything he said was coming out jumbled. It was as if I was encased in a glass cabinet trying to open a locked door. Yet I resisted. It didn't matter what the voice said. I was interested in Reese not Gunther. I studied his flushed face and knew that somehow I had to tell him.

I tried to get up off the bed but my legs were like jelly and I fell back, my hand smacking Gunther's thigh.

He grunted. "Not so rough, *Liebchen*. We have time." From behind, he reached around to undo my bra. Unfastened, he pushed the lacy straps down and tugged to release my breasts.

He sat back on his haunches to admire what he saw. "Lovely.

Large but not too big—so nicely formed." He scratched his chin reflectively. "I have to admit I'm puzzled by all this. I thought you liked the doctor. Who would have guessed you have needs for a fellow like me." He paused, staring out the window. "I'm a good lover. They tell me so. Maybe that's why you prefer me, a burly guy, to the handsome doctor?"

I could only stare in answer, the words sticking in my throat.

"Whatever the reason, I seem to be particularly horny tonight. Clara is already asleep. We have no concerns in that direction. We will have plenty of time."

From the hallway, loud voices made him pause.

There was a thud on the door, followed by another bang with Reese bursting into the room followed by Lola. He wore nothing but his boxer-briefs. When he saw us, he glared angrily, his green eyes dragon fierce.

I gazed at him in wonder. Why was he here?

"What are you doing, Anise?" His words came out in a slur.

From under his arm, Lola stepped forward clad in a flimsy black nightie. She tried to stop him from entering the bedroom. "Let's go back, Reese! Can't you see they are busy? Anise wants Gunther. Forget about the whore. Come back to bed with me. She doesn't want you. See how she flaunts herself? It's Gunther she desires, not you." Tugging on his arm, she tried to pull him back into the hallway but Reese shrugged her off.

"Are you alright, Anise?" His voice was distant.

I looked on in confusion as Reese wildly lunged at Gunther. Taking him by the shoulders, Reese shook him violently. "Go back to Clara, you idiot. Leave Anise alone. She isn't thinking straight. Can't you see that?" He picked up the lacy black bra and tossed it on my lap. "Put it on, Anise."

Strangely, I wasn't in the least bit concerned about my topless state. Somehow the whole thing was somewhat amusing and since handling the bra and its hooks was beyond my capabilities, I decided instead to concentrate on the drama unfolding.

"Wait." Gunther stooped down and picked up his trousers. From his pants pocket he located a paper and waved it in front of Reese's face. "She wanted me, doctor. Look at this. Proof!" he shouted.

Grabbing the big man by the shoulders, Reese steered him to

the door. "I don't care what it says. Go!"

Gunther smirked. "I think she disagrees with that."

"You heard me," Reese growled, knocking the note from Gunther's hand. "Anise is not your woman."

"Nor yours, either. Last I heard you were with Clara. Now go to her." He picked up Gunther's shirt and pants and tossed them into the hall. "Get out before I throw you out!"

"Alright my friend, but don't blame me for coming here to make love with Anise. Any man would want to be with a woman like that." With a last glance, he added, "You made the mistake of choosing the wrong woman, not me."

Edging herself past the men, Lola dived down to the floor to snatch up the note.

I giggled. Somehow the whole thing seemed hilarious.

"Anise!" Reese looked concerned.

Trying to stop the laughter, I held my hand in front of my mouth.

"Forget about this whore, Reese." Lola held up the paper. "Look here. It proves she's trying to steal Clara's fiancé from her. *Meet me in your room. I want your love. Signed Anise.*"

It was as if she hadn't spoken. Reese sat down beside me and placed his hand on my forehead. "You are feverish, Anise. Please go, Lola. You can see Anise is not herself. I want to talk to her privately."

"You want me to go? We were making love and now you want her, too?" She strode over to Reese and smacked his face. "You are vile. How dare you treat me like this!"

Reese's eyes narrowed. "Please go."

As Lola held her hand up to strike him again, Reese blocked her and seized her wrist. "I don't want you."

"You will regret this." Her eyes pierced. "I shall get dressed and return to the party. I would advise you to do the same." With that she sashayed out the door, slamming it behind her.

Reese glared at Gunther. "I've lost a lot of respect for you, man. Jorge warned me about your Don Juan behavior but I believed you were serious about Clara. It would be advisable to go to her before she dumps you. I wouldn't blame her if she did."

"Alright my friend, I will go but listen to yourself. Your action was no different than mine. I doubt Anise can forgive you. She probably knew you were with Lola before she wrote that note. I wonder that you could blame me for coming here. Any man would want to be with Anise."

None of this was making sense to me. First Gunther…and then there was Reese with Lola. The voice kept ringing in my head. *Be kind to the visitor.*

At last alone with Reese I was confused. I should have been angry but I was overcome by his scent. Such a heady combination of spice and soap. It aroused my hidden desire. I wanted to forget everything and bury my face in his chest to take in as much of him as I could.

"Anise, I'm so sorry. I don't know why I was with her." Reese frowned. "It was all so odd. She was in this white cloud and I knew I had to have her. I don't understand it." He nudged my chin up. "Forgive me, please. This is all my doing. I should never have left you alone." His voice was unusually gentle—the same tone he had used with Isabel and the children. "It's my fault Gunther came here." He shook his head as if to clear it. "I'm not myself, somehow. I wish I knew why I was with Lola." With his forefinger, he stroked my cheek. "Anise, tell me you didn't really want Gunther."

I gazed up at him. "I need help with the bra."

"Of course. Hold out your arms."

With Reese's help pushing the bra over my breasts, I managed to hook it up. I was so sleepy. "Can we go to bed?"

"Sure."

When I got up, my legs buckled. Reese sprang over and caught me around the waist before I fell.

"What's this?" Reese held up his hand. "It looks like a powder."

"What?"

"When I grabbed you, it came off on my hand." He scrutinized my belly where gray particles coated my skin. "It's there, too." He held up his hand to his nose. "An odd odor. What could this be?"

"I don't know and don't care." Although I was tired, I felt this strange arousal, even more so now that he was so near.

"Something strange is going on."

The warmth of his body and his changeable green eyes made me oblivious to his words. I wanted to be with him in the comfort of a bed. *I wanted to be kind to my visitor.*

Reese gazed earnestly at me. "I need to explain or at least tell you what I think happened."

"I already know. You were making love."

"We were together, that's true, but I swear it didn't get past a few kisses. Believe me," he muttered.

"Never mind. It doesn't matter now."

"It does. I didn't really want to be with her but it was as if I had lost my will power. And Anise, while I was with her I had your scent."

"What?"

"I know it all sounds like a wild story. I don't expect you to believe me."

I looked him straight in the eyes. He seemed so earnest yet his story was bizarre. All my life I'd felt like a freak of nature for the visions I'd had. I had to listen to his story and try to understand. "What do you mean about having my scent? Were you drunk?"

"No-oo, I don't think so but now I'm not so sure. I seriously don't know what was going on. She said she wanted to show me something. The next thing we were in the bedroom and we were together on the bed. It was like a dream, Anise. All hazy. One minute I was kissing her and then something happened."

"You had sex?"

Reese shook his head as if to clear his head.

"What are you telling me?"

"I had this overwhelming sensation. Your scent entered the room. It made me feel weak. I couldn't think straight."

"You could smell me? How strange."

"Listen to me, Anise. I was confused. I hardly knew why Lola was with me."

Of course he knew why. He wanted her. Did he think I was naïve? *Why was he telling me this?* If he wanted to be with Lola there was no need to make up some story. I could take the truth.

My interest in Reese was only some adolescent fantasy. Reese was a player. I'd have to be stupid to believe another word.

"Anise," Reese took my hands and held them tightly, "there was this knot in the pit of my stomach. I kept thinking of you. I started to sweat. The room blurred. Somehow I made it to the washroom. I vomited. It was as if I knew something horrible was happening to you. Lola tried to lead me back to the bedroom but I had to go look for you."

I looked at him in disbelief. "And you knew where to find me. How?"

"I felt it."

The room started to swim before my eyes. "You saw us together," I said, slowly turning to him. "Why did you care?"

"I thought you were in danger."

"From Gunther?"

"I don't know why or what. It was this feeling I had. A strong premonition of—"

"Of what?"

"Something evil."

"You were with Lola when you had this premonition?"

"Yeah. Believe me." Reese gripped my arm. "I didn't want anything to happen with her and I didn't allow anything."

"You don't owe me an explanation. It's your choice."

"But it didn't seem to be. Something drove me to her but I resisted."

"You mean you wanted to have sex with Lola?"

"It was like my body had been possessed. I kissed her and fought the impulse to do more." He gazed at me uncertainly. "And Gunther? I don't have a right to ask but, Anise, did you?"

"I know it looked like it." I frowned. "The note—I don't know anything about that."

"Don't worry about that now. We'll figure it out later. Can you stand on your own?"

I nodded.

He bent down and scooped up the pile of clothes on the floor. "Where are your shoes?" he asked, glancing around the room.

I sighed. "Haven't got a clue. Don't remember taking them off."

From under the bed he came up with a pair of high-heeled metallic sandals. "Yours?"

Reese blurred before my eyes. A spacey sensation over came me.

"Anise?"

It took everything I had to focus. The whirling in my head was so strong at this point, the best I could do was nod in reply.

"Lean on me." Something caught his attention. "Wait." Reese propped me up against the wall and examined the shoe. "What the heck?" Reese eyed the silver lining. Curiously, he checked out the glittery item. "There's powder in these as well." With a sniff of the substance, Reese sneezed. "Damn, that's nasty stuff!"

My legs felt like jelly. "Please, Reese, I think I need to lie down. Could you take me to bed?"

"That's a good idea. Take my arm, Anise." He laughed. "No, never mind. I'll carry you."

"Reese!" I protested. "You shouldn't. It's only a wave of dizziness. I'm sure I can walk."

Ignoring me, Reese hoisted me up into his arms. "Shit! This whole thing is insane," he muttered, as he wobbled in the hallway. "No worries. You're as light as a feather."

After he placed me on the bed, he dropped down beside me. Everything was odd yet it felt good to be with him.

"Didn't think you'd be able to carry me. Are you sure you're okay?"

Reese smiled. "Yeah, it's crazy. Like some weird drug trip." He rested his head on the pillows, his arm dropping over the side. Suddenly aware of his backpack on the floor, he asked, "You like chocolate, don't you?" and broke out a bar.

I grinned. "Anytime. There's nothing better," I said, taking a chunk from his hand.

"It's guaranteed to make us both feel better." Throwing another one in his mouth, he savored the sweet, eyes closed, before swallowing. "Nice. I have to confess, I'm a bit addicted."

"Mm-mm. Me too. Chocolate makes everyone feel great. Did you know it releases endorphins in the brain?"

Reese grinned. "Um-mm, pleasure. Yeah, nothing like it." Reaching into his bag, he pulled out something he hid in his hand. "I have something really special."

"And that would be—"

"Close your eyes and open wide."

He didn't have to tell me twice. I couldn't wait. Eagerly, I parted my lips. But instead of using his fingers, sensuous lips held the sinfully delicious chocolate and pressed it on my tongue. My eyes opened wide. I was about to protest but thought better of it. The chocolate was so good.

"Spicy chilies in the chocolate," Reese whispered.

The heat of my mouth melted the chocolate and tingles rushed down to my core.

"Chilies are an aphrodisiac."

My tongue exploded with the flavor. "Oh," I sighed, suddenly breathless. "I thought it was the chocolate."

"That, too."

The chemical reaction in my brain was explosive. One look at the sizzling man in front of me was all I needed to bring a fiery rush to every nerve ending.

When he pulled me close, I didn't resist. The strong arms around me and the scent of spice and soap overpowered me with torturous longing. Although I felt drowsy, sleep was the last thing on my mind.

I was lured in deeper, caught in his net. Shapely lips attracted me like a magnet. Up went my finger to touch each fascinating curve. His mouth gripped my finger and the touch of his tongue sparked a fire. Verdant green eyes flecked with passion hooked me in. I needed to feel the heat from those lips. With my hand at the back of his head, I pulled him closer. The kiss sent liquid fire to my core. His mouth pressed lightly, igniting flames in my body. Nothing had ever felt like this.

"Anise?"

"Yes?" I murmured.

"Is this real?'

I gazed into the depths of those impelling eyes and a shiver ran through me. "I want to make love."

His hand stroked my cheek. "Me too. You are amazing."

"But?"

"There's so much you don't know about me. Things you may not like. I don't want any secrets between us." Reese pushed a tendril away from my ear before he continued. "I have never wanted a woman like I want you. Lola was a mistake. Believe me, Anise, I did not want to be with her. This is special."

When I looked at him I couldn't believe how aroused I was. My brain failed to function let alone get out the words. I wanted him to stop talking and touch me.

"You are special." He sighed. "If only I could stop floating."

I nodded. "It's a strange sort of feeling. Reese do you believe me about Gunther? I would never have asked him to come to me."

For a moment he was serious. "I think there was something in that wine, Anise, but," the corners of his eyes crinkled, "as much as I want to discuss wine and life I would rather forget about it." He kissed me softly on the lips. "I want to make you feel fantastic."

"And kisses will?"

"There are other ways—"

The tip of my tongue, charged with electric energy slid into his mouth. I heard him groan. My fingers threaded through the waves at the back of his head as I kissed him. Fingers explored curves, and our bodies melded tightly against each other, while his tongue tantalized.

His hand skimmed my arm. "Your skin is so soft," he whispered. Butterfly kisses trailed down and teased the valley between the mounds encased in a lacy bra. Sometimes I thought this area was more sensitive than the breasts themselves but I changed my mind as Reese pulled the straps down and journeyed further. I lifted my back to help him. He reached around and quickly unclasped the garment before tossing it aside.

I dropped my head down on the pillow, arching my throat. Warm lips tenderly caressed the hollow of my neck. With each lingering kiss, my juices stirred. I sighed. Butterfly kisses trailed down and teased the valley between the garment before tossing it aside.

Delightful shivers ripped down the length of my body with each light stroke. My sensitive peaks perked, wanting more. By the time he cupped my breasts, the heat radiated from my center.

"You are so lovely," he said, as he caressed my nipple with the tip of his tongue.

A moan escaped my lips.

"Beautiful Anise." His mouth tightened and sucked.

"Ah-h," I murmured. "That's so good." I needed to touch him too. Slowly I reached down, stroking his flat abs before gliding my fingertips to the boxer-briefs. He felt hard and firm.

"Wait!" Reese pulled himself up to fling off his boxers. When he lay back down, I was ready to explore. Playfully, I circled the area and stroked his rod until slippery juices coated my hands. I watched his eyes misty and faraway. With my fingers sliding up and down, he let out a groan.

He laughed. "Any more and I'm done. Lie back, beauty. I want you to feel pleasure." His mouth was back to my shoulder, kissing lightly down over my breasts to the flat plane of my stomach. His tongue feathered my skin sending shivers of delight to every nerve ending. Liquid heat surged to my core. I moaned. With each lick I coasted away.

"Anise?"

Tingles of ecstasy radiated my body. Tiny tremors vibrated in my center, energy like volcanic lava on the point of eruption. "So-oo good," I breathed, wanting him never to stop.

But his tongue teased. I jerked away. The pleasure mingled with pain. But he didn't let up. The intensity of the sensation was driving me wild. My body was shaking uncontrollably, convulsing in waves as I gripped his arm, fingers embedded in his skin.

A scream tore from me as I shuddered in orgasm. I fell back drained and satisfied, a smile on my lips.

"Babe?"

"That was wonderful," I mumbled.

He laughed into the curve of my neck. "Tired? Don't worry, I'm feeling it too." Reese wrapped his arms around me.

In a hazy state of consciousness, his scent filled my senses and I drifted. Just as I floated into a dream, a husky voice urged, *"Sonia, wake up."*

10

Strong hands, slippery with oil, kneaded his shoulders. The fragrance of ripe berries and chocolate filled the air. Curiously, Reese turned his head to take a peek at his mysterious masseuse.

Long red tresses obscured her face as she bent forward to work her magic into his muscles. He wanted to see more of this woman. Whoever she was, he was grateful. His tired body was getting the royal treatment, more than he could have wished for. If he was dead he must be in heaven.

In front of him, luxurious tasseled pillows were scattered randomly on the matrimonial-sized bed. The silken sheets under him felt smooth on his skin. As his eyes skimmed the room, he was taken aback. Everything from the sheer curtains covering the palatial windows, to the walls and floor, was red. This set off a warning bell.

From over his shoulder, Reese saw she was beautiful but his instincts signaled danger. On his back straddling him, she stared back intensely as if she had a secret. A temptress in a black gauzy bra and transparent pantaloons.

"Do I know you?" Reese had a feeling he knew the answer to this but his brain was muddled.

The woman's eyes narrowed before she riveted around and brought the palm of her hand down smartly on his butt.

Reese flinched. "What the hell!"

"That was deserved. How dare you make promises and then run off. If ever I find out who helped you escape, she will regret it."

A flashback of three dancing nymphs and an amazing sunset cleared the fog in Reese's brain. "Sangra?"

This time she pinched his ass.

"Stop that!"

The nymph leaned down and breathed in his ear. "A little pain will make you appreciate the pleasure. My juices flow for you."

Reese could feel himself harden. "What are you saying?"

"You're not an idiot, doctor. Women have needs, just like men. I think it was clear I was ready to give myself for our mutual pleasure but you callously deserted me."

"But I can't do anything with you. It would be wrong." Reese shook his head slowly. "I'm having feelings for Anise. Sorry, Sangra. I'm not available."

Sangra reared up like a snake. "That's ludicrous! Have you forgotten you were in another woman's bed? I don't think you were considering your precious Anise then."

"Believe me, I wish I knew why I was with Lola. The whole thing was insane."

"You don't know why?" Sangra threw her head back and laughed. "Perhaps your Anise is naïve but not I. You were having sex because you wanted Lola. You let your penis think for you."

"Yes, alright. I led her on but it was a mistake. Anise is the woman I want."

"And I believe in fairytales," Sangra snickered, "only because I create them. I can foretell the future. I am better than all your mortal women put together. Did you forget who I am?" She pointed a finger to her chest. "I am Sangra, the Empress of Nuncamorir! You will be mine, Reese. The rest of those tarts be damned. You will do as I wish." With a quick motion, she leaped off the bed.

If the harem outfit wasn't enough, a thick gold chain hung low over her belly button, emphasizing her exceptionally narrow waist. Reese couldn't take his eyes off her.

"It's time for the games to begin."

Two quick claps brought a statuesque redhead to the door. Falling to the floor, the nymph waited, her head lowered.

"Bring the handcuffs." Sangra stroked her lip reflectively. "The silken ones and the whip."

"What! Have you lost your marbles?" Reese stared at the empress. "I'm not interested in your games."

Sangra shrugged her shoulders and smiled seductively. "So be it. You will have your way for now but," she paused, and smiled slyly, "you will come to like my suggestions." To the attendant, Sangra jerked her chin dismissively.

From the entrance at the far end of the room, another nymph appeared with a tray on which were set two glasses of red wine and a bottle.

"Perfect. Just what we need." Sangra smiled. "This will help put you at your ease and we will become reacquainted, *si*?"

At this point Reese was no longer relaxed. In fact, he could feel knots of tension building up in his neck and shoulders. It was all coming back to him. The dream he'd had after the night of absinthe. The guilt he lived with and how he'd wanted to end his miserable life. He still carried that burden. Although Lisa hadn't been right for him, she didn't deserve to die.

"You liked this wine, didn't you?"

"Yes-ss," Reese admitted reluctantly, his thoughts still on the car accident. Lisa had insisted on arguing as she drove on the icy road. She had been so sure that he had another woman. According to her, he was a cheater. And then, afterwards, the whole family had blamed him. They hadn't seen the other side of Lisa. The controlling woman who played the helpless role, always demanding more until he felt he'd lost the ability to breathe.

Reese glanced at Sangra. If only he could remember. But though he recalled meeting her, the events were a blur.

Sangra held out a glass of wine. "Try it," she coaxed. "A delightful finish. You shall see."

Reese took the glass, marveling at the shimmer of the berry liquid. The jingle of the beaded curtain in the arched doorway brought his attention to a very familiar looking girl in a silver body suit and sparkly leggings. She bowed before she spoke. "Empress Sangra, I regret the interruption but I have come with urgent news you will wish to hear."

Sangra's jaw tightened. "Who let you in?" Sweeping over to a gong positioned on the wall, she struck it smartly. In a flash, two nymphs in red tops and tights rushed into the room. "You all know the protocol. Appointments are required!" She scoffed. "And you call yourselves guards." Sangra's eyes narrowed. "If this ever happens again, I will see to it that you are demoted to kitchen cleanup. Is that understood?"

"Yes, Empress Sangra," the guards voiced in unison.

"Take her."

The guards eyed the pixie. With her hands on her hips, the pixie glared right back.

"What are you waiting for?"

With a good six feet in height and an advantage of fifty pounds, the nymphs easily lifted the struggling sprite.

"It's about Crema!" the pixie yelled on the way out.

Sangra sat up. "Stop! Bring her back."

This little drama jogged Reese's memory. It was Tora.

Thoughtfully, Sangra sat down on the bed beside Reese as the nymphs set the pixie on the chair beside the bed. "What is your news, Tora?"

When the pixie stared silently, bright spots of pink splotched the nymph's cheeks. "You have something to say?"

"Mm-mm," murmured the pixie, a twinkle in her eye.

"Well?" Sangra commanded, losing her calm.

The pixie smirked. "I'm not sure I want to tell you."

Sangra's eyes narrowed but she changed her tactic, her voice soft this time. "I spoke sharply. Forgive me, but you know," she patted Reese's arm, "our guest is important."

"Oh?"

Sangra's jaw clenched but she spoke calmly. "As you can see," she gestured to Reese, "I didn't need any unnecessary interruptions. But this is a priority. Tora, please, tell me about Crema."

The pixie surveyed Reese in his blue gitch. Her laughter made a tinkling sound. "Easy to see where your head's at."

"You go too far, Tora. I am always very much aware of my responsibilities as Empress of Nuncamorir." She gestured to the table. "Perhaps you would like something to drink before you tell me your tale."

"No thanks, Sangra. In fact you might want to get on this Crema thing right away."

"Why do you speak of Crema? The sirens have been annihilated. Those that survived the War of Fires now live in the land of Miel."

"Crema is approaching and I don't think she's here for a peace summit."

Sangra gritted her teeth. "Explain!"

"The vixens have banded together with Crema and the remaining sirens."

"Those blonde bitches are here in Nuncamorir?"

Tora nodded, her expression serious. "My spies tell me they have entered the northern border with an army of more than a thousand as we speak. They are already camped on the leeward side of the mountains."

"Your spies are reliable?"

Tora shrugged. "Jeckles. They could be making it up but do you want to chance it?"

Across the marble floor Sangra's heels clicked as she paced back and forth, muttering to herself. Head bent to the marble tiles as if searching the floor for answers, she would periodically clasp and unclasp her hands nervously.

The vixens must be more powerful than the nymphs. Reese had never seen the empress so distraught. This whole dream was a joke. This couldn't be real yet from the expression on Sangra's face, this was serious business.

After a rep of ten, the Empress came to a stop and tossed her head back as an errant lock escaped from her ruby-encrusted head band. "Find all members of the war council and have them meet me in the red room," she barked out.

This was bizarre. Not only was this room red but from what Reese could see of the hallways, they were also the same color. *What wasn't red around here?* The redhead might be hot but he was beginning to have doubts about her sanity. *Blondes might be spacey but this redhead was a few pickles short of a jar.*

A quick glance at the pixie threw him off. Did she have something in her eye or had she just winked? Was it possible she was hitting on him? He stared. Sure, with that auburn hair and cute face she was pretty but Reese had no interest in teenagers.

A spicy scent filled the air. He swiveled around expecting to see Anise, but no one was there. His disappointment was deep. What kind of man would abandon a woman as intelligent and beautiful woman as her? The bad feeling that she was involved in something dangerous prickled inside him. There was no doubt in his mind he had to return to help her. But how? Sangra had him trapped in the palace and he hadn't a clue as to how to get out.

"Stay here with him," Sangra ordered the Amazon attendant.

"Don't let him out of your sight." Then, turning to Reese, Sangra said soothingly, "I shall come back as soon as I can, *mi amor.* Drink and relax. There is no reason for you to be concerned with all of this. When I return we will discuss how you can ease your guilt."

"Guilt? How did you know?" Reese was beginning to think Sangra was not only crazy but had some powerful ESP.

Sangra's chin jerked up triumphantly. "It is not anyone who warrants the title of Empress of Nuncamorir." With a toss of her flaming red mane, she strode out of the room followed by one of the nymphs.

The guard left behind had a mean look in her pitch black eyes. "Take a hike, squirt."

Tora's eyes shot daggers. "Not before I've had a sip of that yummy shiraz." With a twitch of her dainty shoulders, she flew over to the tray set on the edge of the bed.

"Get away from that!"

"I want it and I'm taking it." Tora lunged at the tray and captured a glass of wine. Teasingly, she brought it to her lips and sipped.

This infuriated the muscular nymph. Attempting to retrieve the article wasn't easy. The pixie thrust a hand out, unbalancing the nymph who in turn stumbled into the table. Quick as a wink, the nymph righted herself and went for the glass. The two of them struggled and the delicate glass was knocked out of Tora's hand, shattering into tiny pieces on the marble floor, the red wine blending into the crimson tiles.

"Look what you've done!" Her jaw tight, the nymph stalked after Tora. "I want you to leave!"

Flying to the bed, the pixie hid behind Reese. "Punch her!" Tora hissed into his ear.

Reese had been raised to never strike a woman and a nymph was the same as far as he was concerned. But he didn't want to see the pixie hurt either. Poor thing was so tiny.

The big woman stomped around the bed. When she jumped at the pixie, Reese grabbed the back of her sequined tube top and held on.

Not to be stopped, the nymph's long arms reached out for Tora causing one round breast to slip out. Temporarily forgetting the pixie, all her anger turned on Reese.

"How dare you make advances!" She glared at Reese, pulling her top back up. "If Empress Sangra knew she would have you mutilated for such an affront. A swipe of a machete and you would no longer be able to call yourself a man. Ungrateful swine. Do you not know you were meant to impregnate her holy vessel? Yours is a special mission. You were chosen to…"

That lecture was cut short when a bottle of shiraz crashed down on her head. It was quite a wallop. Reese winced as the nymph's legs crumbled beneath her.

Tora's tinkling laughter filled the air. "Good distraction, Reese. Thanks!"

In doctor mode, Reese sprang down to the floor beside the nymph. Bright red blood streamed down from the wound onto her forehead. "Why the hell did you do that? She's unconscious," he said accusingly.

Tora's lip curled. "Good! Now we can get you out of here."

"What's wrong with you? That's no way to deal with a situation. You could have killed her. That bottle is heavy." Reese stared at the pixie. "You used magic to do that, didn't you?"

"I am more than I seem." Tora flew up to his face, slanting eyes sparkling maliciously. "Don't waste your time pitying that slug. She and I go way back. Sangra should have put her to work in the kitchen long ago. Besides, you want to escape, don't you?"

"Yes, I do." Reese frowned. "But not like this. Violence is wrong. I'll find a way out on my own."

The pixie shook her head sadly. "That's being stupid," she muttered. "You haven't got a chance. Okay, I admit it. Maybe I jumped the gun a bit." She patted his arm consolingly. "Don't you worry, Reese. That bozo will be just fine. Nymphs have hard heads. They're not like humans, you know."

From the floor, they heard a loud groan. Reese kneeled, leaned in and swept the nymph's head with his fingertips.

Tora landed on the bed and looked on, rocking forward and back on her heels. "See-ee? That didn't kill her."

"She's covered with blood and there's a huge bump. Thank God she's regaining consciousness." Gently, Reese removed a sliver of glass embedded in her skin. "That piece almost hit her eye. She could have lost her vision."

"Oh?" Tora flew in to take a look. As Reese gave her some space, she curled her fingers into a fist and brought it down on the nymph's other eye. "Too bad, so sad." When the guard moaned, Tora giggled, and punched the nymph's nose. Blood poured out on the attendant's red top.

"Are you nuts? Stop!"

"Yeah, you're right." Tora jerked her chin in the direction of the window. "It's time to hit the road. You want to get to the land of the humans, don't you? We've got some flyin' to do."

Reese was confused. Tora had been so sweet but now he wondered if she was unbalanced.

"Forget about that cow. She'll recover, but if you stay, you'll die."

Before he could decide if he should trust Tora, she grabbed his hand and forced him upwards until his feet left the safety of the ground. Her hand was a powerful instrument which transferred energy, enabling him to defy gravity. Her magic shot them out the open skylight window into the air.

Over the palace wall and up towards the towering royal palms, they flew hand in hand. In seconds, Tora took them higher than fifty feet over a green meadow. As they neared fluttering palm fronds, Reese shielded his face from the pointy ends. As it was before, the sky was crimson and orange with the hues of sunset.

How was this possible? A man flying? Although it was dependent on the Tora's energy, not his, it was an experience that boggled the mind.

As they soared through the air, a thick canopy of red tree-tops below made him aware of how much higher they now were. A few minutes later they leveled off and increased their speed as they zipped closer to a red-capped mountain. The air here was cool and hazy with a silver mist. The cold chilled to the bone. Reese hoped this was not their destination. By that time his arms had grown numb, but eventually their direction changed and they flew down into a valley.

Blue grass with a scattering of smoky-red broad-leafed trees covered the area. It was a dense forest that seemed to continue for miles. Reese grew a little apprehensive. *Where was the pixie taking him?* Did she know where she was going? He gritted his teeth but as they went on it was obvious she was familiar with the area.

Minutes later, they were at the edge of the woods twenty feet up from the ground. Reese prepared himself for a landing.

But apparently, this was not the plan. Just beyond the forest was a sparkle of crimson water. The closer they came, the more brilliant the sea. Waves reared up and crashed in the rocky shore, spewing up a foamy froth.

The rumble of thunder sounded in the distance. A storm was nearing. Tora came to a stop. Her pointed ears perked up. She hovered like a hummingbird, steadying Reese at her side.

Specks of white and red appeared in the distance. As they watched, the specks grew larger.

"What is it?"

The lines around her eyes tightened and her bow-shaped lips became one thin straight line as she listened. "Drums. They're here."

"Sangra?'

Tora nodded. "Her army. She must have found out that Crema and the vixens are not invading Nuncamorir or she decided she would send a unit after us. She'll be in a bitchy mood. She doesn't like anyone ruining her plans."

"And I did?"

Tora's slanted brows rose. "We both are responsible for that. The army is here to take you back, I suppose. You like a slow death? They're known for it."

"Why would she want to kill me?"

"For running away. Your purpose was to provide her with a child. It already angers her that you became involved with other women. She wants to be the only one who carries your child. No one else must have your seed. It would compromise the regency if you impregnated another woman. You have to stay pure and true to Sangra."

"I only want to go back to Earth. There is a woman there that I am very drawn to, perhaps even in love with. Tora, please, help me. Can you bring me back?"

Tora smiled surreptitiously. With a powerful tug, she pulled him down to the surface of the crimson waves.

This alarmed Reese quite a bit. *Surely she didn't think they could hide in the sea?*

Red water enveloped them. The ocean was a pleasant

temperature but that didn't make Reese feel any better. He was in a panic. Tora was taking him deeper. They would die if they kept going.

Dying wasn't the answer for him anymore. He had too much to live for. Funny how much he had wanted to die before, but now Reese knew he wanted to live more than ever. Was it because of Anise? The connection with her was much stronger than he'd had with any other woman.

There was no way he was about to let Tora drown him. Ready to fight for his freedom, he struggled just as she signaled a stop.

From the pocket of her silver body suit, the pixie produced a clip resembling a clothes pin. She brought it up and plugged it in her nose. When she took a similar object out of her other pocket for Reese, he followed her example. To his surprise, he found the device was some sort of regulator. Air filled his lungs. Amazingly enough, the water didn't sting his eyes. The sea was soothing like a milk bath.

Relieved, and finally at ease, Reese was able to take note of his surroundings. The underwater world before him captivated with its dazzling colors. Brilliant bronze orbs darted between the stag-horn coral that grew randomly dispersed with fan and sphere-like brain coral. He had never gone diving but had always had an interest in the ocean and its creatures. As he peered at the fish, he realized why they were everywhere around the coral. It was lunch and the coral was the entrée.

He felt relief at that realization. The smaller fish had taken nips at him on the way down. Rather fond of his body parts, Reese was worried that a hungry six foot grouper might follow their example and take a chunk out of him.

Yet the experience, although strange and possibly dangerous, was also fascinating. No matter what type of coral he saw, it was always red or a shade of red—cherry, burgundy, pink or orange. Even the fish, striped, spotted or needle-like, were variations of red. They blended in so much with the coral, he almost missed the barracuda.

From behind the brain coral a massive head appeared, a round glassy eye fixed directly on him. Five feet of red-hot danger. Reese knew barracuda weren't aggressive but when he saw the powerful jaw with a mouth full of razor-sharp teeth, he shrank back. Warily, he watched it lunge for a small grunt that miraculously escaped into the coral. Reese almost heaved a sigh but remembered he was in the deep and didn't dare breathe out. Luckily, Tora surged in another direction towards a tremendous coral overhang.

Why were they there? As far as he was concerned, the jury was still out on the pixie. She had seemed so sweet on first encounter but today, it was as if something was off. His guess was a personality disorder. Bi-polar? In his practice he had encountered those who went from a hyperactive stage to one of extreme depression. Who was to say it didn't happen with pixies? Tora could be as psychotic as Sangra.

And there was another thing that bothered him. His life appeared to be an open book to everyone in this bizarre place. Sangra needed a man to use for her own purposes and it was obvious the empress knew everything about him as did the pixie.

From out of a rocky crevice, the enormous head of a ruby-spotted eel appeared. A dead-pan eye stared menacingly. It was like one of those monstrous images sci-fi technicians come up with, however in this case it was terribly real.

A gravelly voice grated ominously, "Go back, Children of the Land. You are not wanted here."

Tora bowed her head ever so slightly to the creature. "We are here to make a request of the Almighty Tortuga."

The eel gazed scornfully. "If you have requests, go to your own kind."

"The Almighty Tortuga will want to hear the latest news. It concerns Sangra."

The large crimson eye froze. "You dare to speak her name?"

"I am not afraid, nor should you be. I am here for the safety of all the sea animals."

"Proceed," the eel said grudgingly before he slipped away under the coral overhang.

Reese was mystified. There was a great deal more to the Sangra story. At this point the truth wasn't clear, but he had a feeling he'd know soon enough. When they hit the bottom, there was no need to speculate further as a barely discernible door in the crystal white sand opened before them.

11

A gentle hand stroked my cheek.

"How are you feeling, *cariño*?"

Intense eyes the color of dark chocolate. It was the sexy ghost man. "You're back?"

Even white teeth flashed with his laugh. "No, you are. I'm so glad you're better. I was afraid the fever would never break."

"What do you mean?"

"You've been ill. I was afraid you wouldn't pull through."

Truly I felt as if I had been dragged through the wringer but seeing him was unsettling.

My Hormone Voice grew excited. "Omigod! The stranger is real and movie star handsome. Girl, you have lucked out!"

"I wished I'd had something to lower the fever," the man said seriously.

Hormone snickered. "A cold shower might settle those endorphins."

His shapely lips turned down at the corners. "As the man who loves you more than life itself, it's been a frustrating experience."

Logical was skeptical. "This man is a dark spirit. He already clouds your mind. Tell him to go to the light."

"You're telling me you love me?"

"Yes, I do. Very much, Sonia. My heart beats only for you."

"Why did you call me that? My name is not Sonia."

The phantom man looked puzzled. "No? Who are you then?"

I didn't know what to say having no idea what my name was.

"Perhaps your illness did this?" He pondered for a moment.

"A few days of jungle fever can leave a person with a bad case of memory loss."

I rubbed my forehead, trying to remember.

"Don't worry. It will all come back to you. Don't rush it. You are a strong woman. All our members hold you in high esteem."

"Don't listen to him. You've been drugged," Logical warned.

"They know you are more than just a beautiful face."

"I am?"

"Beautiful is an understatement, *mi amor*. Yes, you are physically exceptionally attractive but much more. You have placed your life at risk on numerous occasions."

"I did?"

"Yes, with high officials in the Bolivian government. And you helped us with your broadcasts. For our cause you sacrificed so much." He ran his fingers through a strand of my hair and chuckled. "What a shock it was to see you as a brunette." He laughed. *"Dios mio.* I'm so glad it has washed out. I love your golden hair. You have the sunny disposition that goes with the hair."

"I'm blonde?"

The man smiled.

"Why did I dye my hair?'

"You've forgotten that, too? Brunettes blend in with the Bolivians. Many of them are aboriginals."

"And I'm not a native Bolivian?"

"No, you are Argentine."

"Ah-hh." I digested this knowledge as I looked around. It was green everywhere. Trees, bushes, grass and in the distance, a glint of water.

The handsome stranger followed my glance. "It's the river we will eventually cross." Pulling me close, he searched my face. "Surely you recall how we made love on the embankment?"

I felt heat rise to my cheeks. *Had I been intimate with this man?* "I'm sorry."

Falling silent, he stared towards the flash of blue though the underbrush. When he spoke again, his voice was soft and distant. "It was at least thirty kilometers north of here. All of us were together but we managed to escape our troop to be alone. We swam and then we rested at the shore. Loving you has turned me into mush. Disgusting, aren't I?"

"Why?"

"It was wrong of me to lead you on but," he sighed, "I couldn't resist you."

"And you wanted to have sex because?"

His eyes shot back to me. "You are so lovely."

"Surely, I was part of that decision?"

Intense chocolate eyes studied me. "I have a responsibility to others. Not only was I the commander of this mission, it was my concept."

"You mean it was an issue of sexual harassment? A person in authority intimidates a woman in the ranks? I take it we are in some sort of army?"

"Yes, we are comrades in arms, but no, it wasn't because I was intimidating you. Still, I should have been more protective. But believe me, *mi amor*, I didn't want to fall in love. I tried to fight it. I will try to explain. Come, let's sit."

I let him pull me down beside him. The tall grass made a comfortable resting place.

"We met in Germany. I was there representing Cuba. There was a party held by the Russians. We danced." His eyes drifted to the river. "You were breathtaking."

Music flowed through me. I visualized myself in a long white dress in the arms of a strong man, swaying and spinning.

"A black tie affair." He smiled. "I'd rather wear my cap and khakis any day but something told me that night would be special. I had a premonition I would meet someone special and I did. You mesmerized me."

Drawn to his strong profile, I took that opportunity to examine each feature—the masculine nose, sensuous full lips and riveting eyes. "Why?"

My companion turned to me and smiled. "Such modesty. Of course, you were the loveliest woman there. You were an angel. Hm-mm. But it was your passion that drew me in. Freedom and equality for every class of people. We both believed it was our mission. You were a woman with heart."

A white flash and I was there in the whirl of dancers. The music was South American. I could hear the strain of violins and a rhythm that left me breathless.

It was as if he had read my mind. "A dance for lovers—the tango." The stranger met my gaze. "I miss Argentina."

"You are not Cuban?"

"In a way. I was given honorary citizenship by my comrade and friend." He frowned. "Which I had to eventually renounce when I left the country. Yet in my heart, Cuba is my second home."

"This friend who gave you citizenship must have been powerful. I thought it wasn't allowed for foreigners."

"We fought together. Through all the struggles to liberate Cuba we became very close."

"I still don't know your name."

"I will give you something to refresh your memory." He bent his head to place a kiss on my waiting lips. There was no awkwardness. Soft lips tenderly meeting mine. The full lips awakened my senses and a torch ignited my body.

Angling yet another way, those lips were sweet as wine. Each kiss brought me into a magical space and the world around me disappeared as those strong arms held me close.

"You fit like a glove."

I nodded, still too stunned to speak.

Sumptuous lips rode mine once more and warmth entered my mouth before sweeping down like a tide to my core. *Had my fever returned or was this man capable of magic?*

"You must feel it too. No matter if you recall my name or not. Admit it, Sonia."

I pushed him away. "No, I'm not Sonia! I don't know you nor do I know—" I threw a glance at the grove of vibrant broad-leafed trees, "this place."

Pain shadowed his eyes. I regretted my hasty outburst. Whoever he was, I was wrong to think he was conning me in any way. My instincts told me he was someone I could trust.

The dark embers of his eyes searched my face. "*Cariño,* look at me." He tilted my chin up. "That party at the socialist conference where we danced in Leipzig for the first time, surely you remember?"

Dazzling ladies in silky gowns dancing with dashing black tuxedoed men flashed through my brain. My handsome partner laughed at something I said and we exchanged remarks, this time on a serious note. Our words were in Spanish yet the intonations of German and Russian surrounded us. The lilt of his Spanish was like being home again.

"Those days we spent together; walking through the gardens, telling each other what we wanted to accomplish. I know how I was attracted to you on so many levels."

I saw myself walking with a man in a park, deep in conversation, through sculpted olive trees. He was mine even then. It was destiny. I turned to him knowing this was the same man.

"I speak Spanish."

He nodded solemnly. "Another thing we have in common. We're both from Argentina. You were born in Buenos Aires and I was almost."

"Why do you say almost?"

"My parents were out of town when I was born prematurely. They had quite the time of it. I had asthma. We ended up moving to the country on the doctor's advice."

"It must have been bad."

He rubbed his chin thoughtfully. "At times, but my papa was determined that I should grow up to be a strong man. I swam and played soccer. Anything to overcome this weakness. My parents were exceptional."

"Mine too," I replied without thinking.

He nodded and gazed at me seriously. "They raised you to believe in equal opportunity."

"And yours?"

"Mama had me reading Sartre at five. French lessons, too. She was a huge supporter of the avant-garde, as was papa. They let me have my little rebellions." He laughed loudly. "Can you believe showing up in shabby clothes for a birthday party? I was an embarrassment to my classmate's parents. What made it even funnier was when my father decided to appear in his scruffiest trousers to lend his support. I think we were both told to leave after that." His bourbon eyes twinkled merrily before he continued solemnly. "My parents gave up a lot for their first born, their sickly son. Things would have been different had we remained in Buenos Aires. My father's business suffered and so did our finances." His eyes drifted to the river. "Money or the lack of it broke up their marriage."

"So now Bolivia. I don't understand. Why?"

"I saw the truth. But, enough about me. I have to tell you something, Sonia, while we have this opportunity."

I gazed at him curiously. He seemed so bold and self assured.

"I need to tell you how honored I was to meet a woman of your vision. I think you are the bravest woman I have ever met."

I lifted an eyebrow.

"Yes, really." He took up my hand and stroked it. "You followed your dreams. The hardships of this mission never once stopped you—the heat, fatigue and lack of food. Many of our best men gave up and returned to their homes but not you. You are my Wonder Woman. No matter what, you kept on. Your belief in righting the world was so strong. Even though this is not your country, you understood. You care so deeply. I admire you, Sonia."

A picture flashed before me—the thin faces of a starving peasant family standing fearfully outside their hut. I was part of a motley crew of guerrillas. "The government told them we were dangerous. That we'd steal their food and kill them. It wasn't true, was it?"

Sorrow etched itself on his face. "I tried to teach our boys the importance of our cause, the necessity to protect the innocent." The corner of his lips turned downward. "There were those who found our hardships impossible."

"And they?"

"Deserted. I'm ashamed that they proved to be everything they thought. Please, Sonia, understand. Nothing is ever black and white. There are shades of gray in everything. I tried to teach them that we were here for Bolivia, nothing else. Those that caved in to their bestial natures were without education. In my opinion that can change an individual. It is crucial. I spent a bit of every day teaching our men. Through knowledge they can find wisdom. So many needed guidance to be better human beings."

"And the peasants were sacrificed for their betterment?"

Dark eyes widened. "No. Not at all. Everywhere I went I made it clear to them. I wanted them to know we were there to help them. They were always shown respect. We paid for their animals and food. It was important that they knew we were fighting for them and that we were not the derelicts the government said we were."

A memory crowded my mind. I saw him holding a physician's black bag crouched in front of a little boy. The youngster sat smiling with a bandaged eye.

"Are you alright? Are you remembering something, *mi amor*?"

I had to confirm the image that had appeared. "Are you by any chance a doctor?"

"I studied medicine in Buenos Aires."

"What made you want to become a doctor?"

His eyes crinkled at the corners as he smiled. "The asthma. It's been difficult but I didn't let it defeat me. Instead," his face became animated, "I let it inspire me to learn."

"And you had a practice there?"

"No, I never finished. I was a few courses short when I caved in to my craving for adventure." He laughed. "It happens to the young. The urge to see the world. In my case I had to see the rest of South America. My friend, a bio-chemist, decided to come with me. We were such young idealists, but who isn't at that age? Not much money, on motorcycles with a lot of macho bullshit to keep us happy."

"Wine, women and song?"

"My friend liked a good party but for me it was to learn about the world. I'm not a drinker. I was there to experience life."

"And so you went on this adventure. Did you see everything you wanted?"

"Argentina, Chile and Peru before we parted. For the first time I was out of my comfort zone. I saw things that were wrong in Latin America. Systems that worked against the common man. It should be everyone's right to have a doctor's care, Sonia."

His words brought me to a different place. A memory of the two of us sitting on a park bench in Germany. Not a cloud in the sky. The day cool and crisp. Autumn leaves. My hand was in his just as it was now. This same man had been serious as he told me about the plight of the miners in Chile and about his stay at the leprosy hospital. "That trip was upsetting for you."

"It was, extremely so, but through the journey my destiny became apparent. The colonial system was archaic yet so many countries depended on a class system. It was my dream that the poor should have free medical assistance. No one's children should die of a disease or from lack of medicine."

A soldier and yet at the same time, a doctor? "What's your name?"

He brushed a strand of hair back behind my ear and smiled slowly. "I'm afraid it's not too exciting."

"It will help."

"For you to remember?" His smile was charismatic. "Of course. It's Francisco."

"I like it."

"I'm glad."

"But I'm not happy with being called Sonia. It doesn't seem right somehow." I rubbed my temple, willing myself to remember the right name. And this tropical place was so unfamiliar. Beyond the tall grasses, a glimpse of sparkling azure. The river we had crossed earlier and had played in. That memory visited me as an insect landed on my arm. I swatted it in annoyance."It's so hot here. Nothing about this is familiar except maybe the river."

"We were in the river together."

I felt myself blush, not sure why.

"Yes, Bolivia is extremely tropical unlike Argentina, or," he tilted his head, "your Germany."

A vision of a large city with tall white buildings appeared in my mind. "It's odd but I miss Argentina more than Germany."

"Oh? You remember? Good. See," Francisco held his finger in the air, "it will all come back. Perhaps, calling you by your adopted name, Sonia, is wrong. It was the name you took for this mission. You'd rather go back to Sylvie. I understand. It's was your name in Germany and how they called you back in school, isn't it? All of us are different here. They don't call me Francisco, either. I have a nickname. As he gazed at me he took his finger and swirled it around until it finally landed on my nose.

I pushed his hand away protesting. "Hey, no kid's games."

"Not for little Sylvie." He grinned. "I can just imagine what a cute little girl you were. Petticoats, frills and a bow in your beautiful hair. Your mama wouldn't have dressed you in khakis and denim."

"You're right. Mama was traditional." I recalled a gauzy white dress with crinolines. "Funny how I loved to dress up for parties." I smiled, the memory so vivid. "I just saw the dress in my mind!" Was my memory coming back? Hopefully this was only temporary amnesia. I closed my eyes and imagined a young girl of eight in a lovely frilly dress. "But, Francisco," I said, with a glance at my denim blouse and baggy pants. "I'm in some sort of combat outfit." I shook my head in frustration. "I wish I could recall more."

Francisco dropped back on the grass and pulled me down with him. "Let it happen. You can't force it. But I do have something that might help."

On my back, I rolled onto my side and searched his face. "What?"

From underneath lowered lids, the bourbon eyes flickered with a fiery passion. "It's called muscle memory," he whispered.

The kiss struck me like lightning. Electricity coursed through me. It was as if his energy entered my body, channeling through my lips. Before I could withdraw, he assaulted my mouth once more, a hand at the nape of my neck threading my hair. I was caught up in something enticing. All I wanted was another taste.

And I wasn't disappointed. Those sexy lips molded against mine and then retreated before they returned to fire my world. I closed my eyes to feel the sweetness of his kiss. But then I was tempted to see the man who was doing this to me. The passion in those brandy eyes was unmistakable. *Had any man ever looked at me like this?*

When his hand stroked my breast every nerve under my skin sparked with awareness. I needed him to cup the soft mound and never let go.

But that thought rescinded when he began to undo the buttons on the rather utilitarian blouse I wore. Squirming on my back, I arched my neck as licks descended over the curve of my breast. I couldn't help a sharp intake of breath as fire lit my center.

Tender lips sought mine and any inhibition I might have had was no more. I fingered his shirt to free him of it. He tore it off and tossed it into the grass. Pulling my hand to his trousers, Francisco held it to the hardness and whispered, "You do this to me, Sylvie." He sighed. "My lovely Sylvie."

12

The turtle was massive. High on a golden throne of brain coral, the loggerhead, as immense as a Volkswagen Beetle, stared down at his visitors. He was incredible with a lipstick-red segmented shell, dark shadowy eyes and a mouth big enough to swallow the pixie whole. On their approach, the turtle's flippers tapped impatiently on the conch in front of him.

They found themselves in an immense coral cave that glowed with the same hue as a summer sunset. Since the water was barely to his knees, Reese removed his breathing device and gripped Tora's arm tightly, whispering in her ear, "You're sure about this?"

Her bow-shaped lips narrowed into a thin red line. "Most definitely. We have no choice."

Closer to the throne, the depth of the water was a mere puddle, trickling over a crystal-pink beach. The beauty of the place was diminished by the presence of the barracuda resting at the foot of the throne.

The turtle watched them. From out of his cavernous mouth a rather surprisingly soft voice intoned, "Greetings, Son of Earth and Daughter of Sky."

"Kneel," Tora hissed under her breath.

Taking her cue, Reese flung himself rather hastily on the sand that covered a jagged bit of coral. His knee bled from the sharp edge "Shit!" he muttered.

"What say you?"

"Nothing of importance, your Highness."

The turtle's jaw clenched. "You are to address me as, Almighty Tortuga, Earth man."

"Pardon me, Almighty Tortuga. I am only a man, ignorant of

your ways. Please forgive my rudeness."

The enormous turtle head nodded in agreement. He looked from one to the other. "You may stand."

Reese extended a hand to Tora but she fluttered up on her own.

"What is the purpose of your visit?"

Tora took the lead and piped up. "It is a matter of urgency. We need sanctuary."

"And why is this, sky sprite?"

"You know of Sangra?"

"Hush! We do not speak her name here."

Pursing her Betty-Boop lips, the pixie stood silently.

"Hence forward you shall call her S," the humongous reptile informed them solemnly.

Color rose to her cheeks. For a second, Reese thought she would explode but finally, she nodded in agreement.

"Tell your story, sky sprite."

"S is angry. I foiled her plan when I helped the Earth man escape."

"Escape? What do you mean? This man was her prisoner? Why?" Tortuga said sternly. "I believe there is much more to this. Details you are hiding."

Tora's eyes shot daggers at the turtle.

"You will tell me the whole story. Leave no parts unsaid."

"Of course, Almighty Tortuga, there is more but I'm sure you don't want to hear it all."

"I want you to start from the beginning. Everything about S concerns me." Tortuga studied the pixie. "Surely you know why the Children of the Sea have suffered?"

"Yes, it was because of S. Her magic transformed the sea and all who lived in it."

"It was not merely the outward hue of their scales or shells. All of them have altered internally. The cycle of the sea is broken. No creature functions as they should. We have lost our emotions." Tortuga shook his head. "Her sorrow caused this."

"How?" Reese asked.

"She came to me for guidance. I was unsympathetic." The Tortuga bowed his head. "I should have listened to her story and been more supportive but I was too self-righteous." He stared at

Reese. "Turtles are highly moral. It stems from our complete dedication to our religious beliefs. But that's no excuse. I should have understood about love." Tortuga bowed his head reflectively. "Once, many years ago, I was enamored with a lovely turtle myself."

"S was in love with someone? Who?" Reese interrupted impatiently.

The big head nodded. "The Elfman of Breslaw. Strong, tall and emotional for someone of his sort. When he left, her heart was instantly broken, wounded like a bird with one wing. S was no longer the powerful confident sorceress she once was. She was a shell of a nymph, yet I questioned her morals and ignored her pain.

"Why did he leave, Almighty Tortuga?"

"He had more important ones in his life, or at least he thought so."

"And you didn't stop him?"

"I could not. He was determined to do what was right no matter who it hurt."

"And so he left?"

The turtle nodded. "It changed everything for S and for all of us here under the sea. In her sorrow, S wept. Red tears filled our ocean. All the sea creatures suffered and it was my fault for being so rigid. I was wrong. No one should judge others."

"No, Almighty Tortuga! You weren't at fault," protested Tora. "S is evil. She is responsible for ruining the sea. You did nothing wrong."

Reese found this a strange turn of events. He hadn't pegged Sangra as a sentimental type. "You're saying the elf did not love S?"

Tortuga shook his head sadly. "He did. They were soul mates. He was perfect for her." The dark depths of his eyes became misty like a foggy night on the Dartmouth moors. "When the elf came to me for council, he told me he'd never thought to find a love like theirs."

Reese's forehead furrowed. "Then why did he leave?"

The big shadowy eyes fixed on Reese. "He felt guilty."

"Why would he leave S if he was in love?"

The sprite fluttered her wet wings nervously. Water dripped off onto the rocky floor. "Yes, why?"

From the reflected light of the coral cave, Tortuga's shell glittered like a Maharaja's ruby. "I advised him thus."

What a cold-hearted reptile, Reese thought, glaring at the turtle. "You interfered with their lives? They were in love, weren't they?"

Tortuga's eyes were like blotches of black ink. His voice grated. "The elf had a son. He wanted to bond with him. Of course it meant he had to return to the mother of the boy. He stared at Reese challengingly. "You don't know this but the first born boy is always important. Love with a female is but a passing fancy."

"Really? I think both are equal." Reese sat down on a stone and stretched out his legs, eyeing the monstrous reptile. This whole thing was like a trip on mushrooms gone wrong. It was a bad idea to get involved in this drama. Somehow he had to get back to Earth. But, if he was ever to get out of here he had better know more about the characters involved and that would mean this turtle needed to tell all. "And the woman, the mother of this child, who is she?"

From the corner of his eye, Reese noticed that Tora was still as if struck by lightening. She seemed to have gone into a trance. Reese was beginning to think she knew something about this Elf man and whatever she knew scared her.

"She is not important. Do not judge the elf, Son of Earth. Life is different here."

"Of course it is. S has ruined everything," Tora muttered.

"Silence," Tortuga grumbled. "You are a sky sprite and quick to interfere. Know your place. This situation is much more complex than you realize."

"So explain it, Almighty Tortuga." Reese was puzzled by both the turtle's words and Tora's reaction.

"I will think on this."

"But…but…" Tora stuttered. "We are in danger."

"Enough! Tomorrow I will hear your story and then I shall decide what to do with you." The turtle tapped a flipper on the coral and the eel shot out. With a head as big as a giant pumpkin and tiny slits for eyes, science fiction couldn't have created a better monster. That was bad enough but Reese went pale when the gaping mouth opened like a bloody wound to reveal dangerously sharp pointy teeth.

"Morahy, take the Earth man to R7 and the sprite to R1."

Tora flew closer and hovered in front of the turtle's face. "I have something to say."

Before she could go on, the eel interrupted, "You bother the Almighty Tortuga. Come with me."

Even the seemingly fearless sprite knew when to change course. In this case it was obvious the eel would not take no for an answer.

The wall of coral slid open to a tunnel lit by lanterns. Although there was no water, the eel moved smoothly in the air. Strangely, Reese found himself floating through the tunnel following its tail. Beside him, Tora flit her wings rapidly in an effort to keep up with the guard.

Their journey was a silent one, all of them lost in thought or at least two of them since it was hard to discern what the eel was thinking.

***

Stretched out on Francisco's jacket, I was protected from the sharp edges of the tall grasses. My lover cupped my breasts contained in the cotton bra while his sensuous lips softly caressed the valley between. "I love you."

I was confused. It was all so crazy. I didn't know why I had allowed any of this to happen. Francisco was virtually a stranger. Memories clouded my mind. Was he really a man and not a spirit? I was powerless in this journey. The sun had found its match in Francisco, so hot were the kisses that seared my skin.

Sometimes the only thing to do is to give in to what the body craves and in this instance it was Francisco. There was no stopping now. My hands tore at his shirt and the buttons unfastened before he took it and flung it off into the grass. Trousers joined the pile. As I lifted my hips to free myself of the baggy pants I wore, my lover jumped forward to assist.

In slow motion we explored each other, our senses drifting. Our eyes met and I drowned in the bourbon pools. His passion became mine. In a dreamlike state, I pushed away my bra to free my breasts for those full lips. My hands gripped a body lean and solid. I pulled him close.

Peaks perked with each lick of his teasing tongue. I held his head tight to my nipple, needing the firm grip of his mouth. A powerful current coursed through to my core.

***

Lit by flickering torches, the next bend in the tunnel revealed a row of vertical shells that appeared to be doors.

At the first door the eel stopped. He hissed," You will stay here at R1. Refreshments have been provided. There will be no reason for you to leave your accommodation." A flash of sharp yellow teeth made his grin exceptionally sinister.

"So when do I get to speak to the turtle?" The second the eel bent his head towards the fleshy part of her thigh, Tora stuttered, "I...I beg your pardon, I meant to say the Almighty Tortuga."

The creature hunched himself up in what might have been a shrug. "The emperor will come to a decision soon. Who he sees is determined by the ocean cycles." He pushed the door open and jerked his head for Tora to enter.

"What have ocean cycles to do with it?"

The eel's tiny eyes looked incredulously at Reese. "The cycles are powered by the moon and all the creatures here govern their tasks by its phases."

"You mean it's something like astrology? That's what you believe in?"

"Our beliefs are more complex. There are the saints of the sea to guide us. The emperor must commune to find out what is best. It is not possible to go against the wisdom of the ages. After all, he is..."

Tora interrupted the explanation. "Eel, would you ask the Almighty Tortuga if he might speak to me first? It's important."

The eel's head reeled from side to side as his narrow eyes glinted calculatingly. "I have never eaten a sky creature. Are you flavorsome?"

With a whoosh of wings, Tora flew behind Reese.

The eel guffawed loudly. "Probably a less than satisfying appetizer. A fish might be smaller but is guaranteed to be a tastier treat." With his head cocked to one side, he grunted. "Go in now, winged thing. Earth man needs to proceed to his own chamber."

148

By this time, Tora's face had turned a solid salad green. There was no more need to persuade her. She shot in the room, leaving Reese to face the eel alone.

"Follow me," the eel said, as the door shut. With that, he wiggled down a winding corridor off of the main tunnel. Reese jogged to keep up. Softly lit by red glow worms attached to the ceiling, the hallway had the rosy sheen of the interior of a conch. After what seemed endless, the eel came to a standstill and jerked his head at a shell door.

"R7. You will find all the amenities of home."

Was that a wink? No, not possible, Reese thought. The monster hadn't any eyelids.

"Go in."

As Reese entered the chamber, the shell door clicked behind him. Quickly, he sprang to the door but there was no way to open it since it hadn't a knob of any sort.

"Damn!" Reese exclaimed loudly, a little put off by the situation. His only ally was locked away and he was at a loss as to how to escape. He had to wonder how any of this had occurred and why. Nothing in his life had prepared him for an oceanic prison.

The sparkling chamber was eye-popping. With brilliant coral floors and a gleaming pink bed, it could hardly be deemed a regular room. The reflected lights made the ceiling shimmer as powerfully as the crystal clear stalagmites framing the doorway. When he glanced around, he spotted a rectangular table laden with a delightful repast. A while back his stomach had started to rumble and finding food was a welcome surprise. He sat down on a low flat piece of coral and regarded the feast before him.

Seafood of every description—oysters, lobster, and crab were heaped high on a large oval platter, as well as a side of seaweed salad. Next to that was a pitcher of a frothy substance that reminded him of fruity martini. He decided to fill a goblet and try it. It was time to chill. The trip had been a negative experience in the extreme. He deserved this. With a sip, Reese came to the conclusion it was well fortified with something potent yet extremely pleasant, much like a strawberry daiquiri.

But it was the food that he needed. Reese couldn't believe how hungry he was until he sampled the spread. First, he tried the lobster dunked in butter, then the crab and steamed oysters. He couldn't believe how much he could consume. Each oyster was better than the last. At the same time, the mysterious beverage tasted fantastic. He couldn't resist pouring himself another glass. After swallowing the last oyster, Reese stood but to his dismay found he was less than steady. In fact, he was totally wasted.

A cold shower would clear his head but, although the room was large, he didn't spot anything that vaguely resembled a shower. A splashing sound caught his attention. The noise was coming from behind a shell partition in the corner of the room.

A bath would be welcome if a shower wasn't available. With a tug, he pulled off his gitch and threw it down before he made off for the swishing sound of water. On the other side of a five foot shell, a steamy pool glimmered invitingly.

Supplied by a stream that trickled in from the wall, tiny sparkles in the clear water shimmered crimson-gold like a sunset on Lake Huron. He sighed as he slid in. The water was amazingly warm. When his feet didn't touch bottom, he tread in a bicycle motion to keep afloat. Tired at last, he slumped back, holding onto the edge of the pool.

On the top of the water a few feet away, he noticed something that appeared to be red seaweed. Amazingly enough, the plant seemed to grow bigger the longer he watched it. Reese stared in amazement.

Slowly, more and more of it appeared on the surface until suddenly a torrent of salt water splashed up as the red seaweed became the tangled auburn hair of a gorgeous girl. Flowing long locks, a lovely oval face, dark eyes and a pair of perfectly symmetrical bare breasts much like round apples embellished with rosy nipples. Reese was speechless.

"You think I'm beautiful, don't you?" She flashed a perfect set of teeth. "Males always do." She fluttered long dark lashes. "I thought you might like some company, Earth man. My name is Rosalinda. I've heard of the children of the Earth but I had no idea a man would be so desirable."

Reese didn't know how she did it but almost instantaneously she was in front of him giving him a languid kiss before her pink tongue urgently pressed between his lips. With the alcohol whirling in his brain, he thought he was losing his mind.

When he tried to push her away, his hand found a firm round

mound. He felt his body respond.

Rosalinda laughed. The sound was entrancing to Reese's ears. "Cup it. I know you want to."

What man in his right mind wouldn't want to? Reese let his hand glide over the smooth skin.

"That's right, massage my breast. Mm-mm. Yes, roll my nipple like that. Better still, kiss it."

With his hand around her waist, Reese brought her closer for his mouth to clasp the pert nipple. The surge of arousal that coursed through him was incredible. He was so hard he couldn't believe it. But when his package brushed against scales over what should have been a pubic mound, he recoiled, eyes wide in horror.

Rosalinda laughed. "A little bit of an obstacle, right, Earth man? But why not grind on me? Go ahead. That should get you off."

Finding her comment not so funny, Reese shoved the mermaid away. He tried to speak but the words wouldn't come out. Everything became fuzzy. Bringing his hand to his eyes, he rubbed them.

"Are you alright? Oh, now I know. They were counting on you to fall asleep. They must have overestimated the amount of potion needed."

Hot steamy water made Reese sleepy. The mermaid's face became hazy.

The more Reese tried to focus, the faster she faded.

"Wake up!"

Reese heard her but he was exhausted and the water was so relaxing.

"Get out before it's too late!"

His limbs felt limp and his eyes closed. The mermaid was shrouded in white vapor. "Listen to me." Every word she spoke became fainter. "You must pull yourself out of here!"

Reese longed for sweet rest. How good it would feel to sink down into the warmth and let the water envelope him.

13

"Break the door down, Luis. Something is not right."

Gunther laughed. "Why all the drama, Linda? We knocked and they are not answering. It means nothing. Not everyone gets up at dawn as you do. Possibly they are in the throes of passion and do not wish this interruption. It could be they are having makeup sex."

"That is crude, Gunther. Do not speak so. Anise seems like a very nice lady and I was impressed by her talent. She plays guitar like an angel."

"Linda is right, *amigo*." Luis frowned. "There is no need to discuss them in such a base way."

Gunther shrugged, an amused smile on his lips.

Luis glanced at him uncertainly. "Why did you say makeup sex? Did they argue?"

"No, but didn't you see what happened? Lola was making a play for Reese last night."

Luis shook his head. "It was a time of celebration—my birthday party. Of course they were together but Anise was there also. Surely you're not implying something happened with Lola and Reese?"

Gunther snickered. "If you were not so into your beer, you would have noticed that both Reese and the charming Anise were a trifle *loco,* as were the rest of us. The wine was unusually potent, my friend. I had no idea a shiraz could be such an aphrodisiac."

"What do you mean? Luis's face flushed red. "What is it you're not telling me?"

"Lola slept with Reese."

"What!" Linda exclaimed.

Gunther made a face. "She has strong magic. You think I don't know about Lola?" He picked up the statue of the Virgin from the hall table and twirled it, his voice rising in anger. With a clatter, he slammed the statue down on the table. "You are all Santeros and Lola has been taught as a priestess, hasn't she?"

Luis patted his arm consolingly. "Calm down, *amigo*."

"Last night, I wasn't myself. I almost cheated on Clara."

Linda gasped. "You were with another woman?"

"No, not exactly, but I wanted to be. A strange feeling came over me. I was crazy with passion for a woman, like a man possessed." Gunther held up his finger and dabbed it into the air. "I think there was something toxic in the wine."

"Was this woman Anise?" Luis's eyes pierced challengingly at the German.

Before Gunther could reply, one of the bedroom doors opened and a sleepy Clara poked her head out, long dark hair sweeping her shoulders. *"¿Que pasa?"* In a lacy cotton night gown with a low décolleté, Clara shuffled over to the group. "What has happened?"

Luis motioned with his hand. "Nothing to be concerned about, Clara. We are only worried that Anise and Reese are not up yet. Gunther thinks they might have had too much to drink and could possibly be ill."

Clara nodded slowly. "The wine was powerful last night. I was in a deep sleep."

Arms crossed in front of her chest, Linda said slowly, "Luis wanted to take Reese and Anise into the village but they didn't answer when we knocked."

Clara put her ear to the door. "It is very quiet. Have you checked if it is locked?"

"I don't know." Luis clenched his jaw, his eyes darting back to the door. "I wasn't sure if I should try the handle."

A determined look on her face, Linda brushed past Luis and knocked loudly. When there was no answer, Luis shouted, *"Hola!* Reese, Anise, it is I, Luis! If you would rather sleep than go with me into the village, I understand."

They waited but the silence continued from the other side of the room.

"I know you don't like to speak of it, but I am concerned

about the contents of the wine. Neither of those two were acting normal last night," Gunther hoarsely whispered. He glanced at Clara. "I think we need Lola."

Nervously working her jaw, Clara met his eyes.

"She is the cause of all this. Get her up," Gunther growled.

When Luis jerked his chin in the direction of Lola's room, Clara padded over to the next bedroom and knocked. She waited a moment before entering the chamber, then reappeared almost immediately. "Lola's not there. Perhaps she has gone on a walk. Often, she goes down to the river to gather herbs," she said calmly.

"Try the handle, Luis." Gunther said urgently. "I tell you there was something in the wine. They should have answered."

"He's right, Luis." Clara agreed. "I fell asleep immediately and dreamed the most fantastic things."

Linda squeezed Luis's arm. "Lola has been trained."

"I suppose she might have done something." Luis tried the door. "It's locked."

"I have the key." With a worried frown, Linda inserted the key in the door and shoved it open. "Anise? Are you alright?"

The group came close to the edge of the bed as Linda took a limp hand in hers. She turned to the others. "Anise is in a trance."

"And where is Reese?" The German questioned Clara sharply. "Do you think Lola left with him?"

"No. She wouldn't leave without saying good-bye. Besides knowing my sister, she would be proud that she snatched the doctor away from Anise."

"I'll go and check to see if his motorbike is here." At a clipped pace, Linda disappeared down the hallway.

His eyes on Anise, Luis muttered, "There is something terribly wrong with her, Gunther."

***

I heard them speaking about me but I was somewhere else, far away on a tropical riverbank, palm fronds swaying gently in the breeze. I was no longer Anise. I was Sylvie. My memories of that life had returned.

In Francisco's eyes I saw the deep connection between us— revolutionaries fighting for Bolivian rights. Our ideals were the same. My parents would have been proud of their Sylvie. Not only had I started a women's rights group in Cuba but I was the first female to lead a group of guerrilla fighters.

Francisco was gazing soulfully into my eyes as he brought my hand to his lips. Lightly, his mouth brushed my wrist. My pulse raced with excitement.

Our clothes were strewn haphazardly over the tall grass. We were Adam and Eve in paradise. I leaned back against a tree and brought my lover close. The urge to kiss him was irresistible like a bee to a blossom. My mouth pressed softly on his warm full lips. Each caress was returned, releasing a charge of energy. With the tip of my tongue, I skimmed his lips before I entered the steamy fortress.

"Ah-hh, *mi amor*," Francisco murmured, taking my face in his hands. "You do unbelievable things to me." Tender kisses brushed my shoulder. With each caress, I smoldered like dry woods sparked by a raging fire.

From his strong shoulders down to his broad back, my fingers danced. My body molded to his, breathing in his scent. He slid his hand sensuously over the smooth skin of my breast, a finger taking time to circle over an alert nipple before his hand smoothed the silky skin.

My wandering fingers threaded through his silky waves, and I wanted all of him. "Let's make love."

Against me, he became hard in response to my words. Uncontained lust sparked Francisco's eyes, mirroring my own. Hands and lips explored frantically like teenagers in a parked car. Shivers raced down my spine. I melted like butter in the sun.

Francisco dropped to his knees and lightly licked my leg while his hands stroked upwards. Each touch triggered sensations as I shot up high on a euphoric rollercoaster ride. My body trembled. I tugged on his thick hair wishing for release. The breeze suddenly cooled yet my body was still a burning inferno. No longer able to contain myself, I pulled him up on his feet.

Eyes liquid with arousal, he captured my lower lip and sucked while my hands worked their way down to touch him in a way I knew he must want. A quick intake of breath and he groaned like a tortured being.

Against the tree, strong hands tightened on my hips. "Lift your leg," he directed in a voice husky with desire. Strong hands held me up while I gripped his biceps for support. With a tight grip on his shoulders, I waited with anticipation. Swept up in passion, our bodies rigid against each other, he entered and thrust. With his breath in my hair, I squeezed to keep him in tight. We held each other desperately. Our energies collided, slickly wet in our sensuous storm.

Overhead thunder rumbled. A flash of lightning illuminated the ground and trees in white light. Francisco's face was cast in shadow, his expression lost. Drizzling lightly at first, the drops became heavier, drenching us. Rain ran off my eyelashes. I blinked them away. From the intense look in Francisco's coffee eyes I wondered if making love in the storm thrilled him as much as it did me. I licked his lip and my answer was given as his mouth came down hard on mine.

Though the tropical storm had picked up, it was no deterrent. I wanted and needed him. Nothing could quench my thirst for Francisco or drown out the moans that wrenched from the back of my throat. Soaked with rain and sweat, I reached the peak of that pleasurable mountain I'd climbed so rapidly. Consumed with lust, I cried out, wildly clinging to his body before a shuddering wave overcame me.

Francisco jerked inside me, holding on as if his life depended on it. With a last lurch he shuddered and I felt the liquid heat of his explosion. He pressed close. "Sylvie!" he growled into my hair.

Blissfully exhausted, I sank against my lover. He loosened his hold, and my leg was released. When I placed it back on the ground, it was as wobbly as the leg of a newborn foal. A giggle escaped my lips. "That feels better."

Francisco tilted his head and raised an eyebrow. "Disappointed?"

"It was worth every uncomfortable second."

"Really? Then there should be more, shouldn't there?"

"Are you serious?"

"I want to do this with you forever."

"Yes, it bears repeating." I ran my fingers over a dark bruise on his thigh. "It must have been painful. How did you manage?"

Francisco pushed back a damp tendril that had fallen down on my cheek. "I'm your stallion, aren't I?"

I nodded. "Come, sit with me."

Simultaneously we sank into the long wet grass. Francisco threw a muscular arm around my shoulders and I rested against him, comfortable with him near. Sliding my bottom over closer to him, I rested my head on his chest, loving him then even more.

"I think we caused that thunderstorm."

Bourbon lights flickered in his eyes. "Our connection is deep, Sylvie. You are aware of that now. This bond can never be broken."

I nodded, knowing I was caught up in something extraordinarily bizarre. Making love with him was something I had been waiting for all my life.

At twenty-nine, I'd refused to settle. Not many men liked a woman with strong convictions. Women in the workplace were the assistants not the bosses. The *pill* was the latest hope in the women's liberation movement yet fifty per cent of the population had no input in the mechanics of government.

I ran my fingers down his cheek and gazed into intelligent eyes that looked into my soul. This man was different than any man I'd met before. He made me feel extraordinary. Never had I felt so close to a man as I was now.

I leaned my head back on his arm and looked up. The sun was creeping out from the last gray cloud. The clear blue sky was pure and beautiful, just like my love. Warmth filled my center. Perhaps I had his seed in me already and if I did, I wouldn't be ashamed. It would make me proud to carry his child.

"I was so honored you chose me to command the unit."

"You deserved it! No one trained harder than you. And you shoot better than anyone," his lips twitched, "except maybe myself. And more importantly, the men know and respect that."

"Alright." I grinned. "You convinced me. Wonder Woman will lead our men into victory. Have you heard anything from Cuba?"

Francisco frowned. "Unfortunately, no." Looking up into the sky as if searching for answers, he said resignedly, "I suppose we'll have to do it without reinforcements."

"They have abandoned us."

Francisco reached over and squeezed my hand. "But we won't give up, will we?"

I shook my head. "No. We are doing what is right. We are not cowards."

"Victory or death."

There will be no defeat," I said emphatically. "When do we leave?"

"They are waiting for you to return to the campsite. When you return, some of the men will come join me here. Our plan is to travel down the river together. In five days we will meet up. Hopefully, the end is near."

"Francisco, I will think of you always. Each moment of every day I'm away from you."

"And I of you. Ever since the day I met you, I loved you." A furrow creased his forehead. "Stay safe, *mi amor*." He took my face in his hands and kissed me tenderly on the lips. "I shouldn't, but I have a sense of foreboding."

I touched him lightly on the forearm. "Don't worry. There aren't many of us but we believe in our cause. No one will betray us. The deserters are gone. Only the best of us are left."

Francisco bent his head down and planted a kiss on my forehead. "I will always remember the scent of you. Don't worry. I will be with you again. It's a promise."

I reached up and for a moment we clung together.

"You fit like a glove on my hand. You are my dream girl."

"I feel more comfortable with you than I've been with any man. How lucky we met," I whispered, gazing up to those warm liquid brown eyes and then lower to his full shapely lips.

"And I am even luckier now that you remembered everything again. I was so worried, Sylvie."

"It was the fever." I rubbed his hand. "You should know I would never forget you."

Francisco sighed. "I have something. A gift for my lovely Sylvie." From out of his shirt pocket he took a gold medallion with the Virgin embossed in it. "My mama gave it to me and now it will be yours. Something to pledge my love." He undid the clasp. "Turn around. Let me put it on."

I twisted my body away and felt the warmth of his fingers as he slipped the cool gold around my throat. "How sweet of you," I said, holding the chain steady as he fastened it. "But are you sure?" I swiveled back. "Do you think you should?"

He nodded. "Mama would have wanted me to have a love like

this. I think it disappointed her that I constantly chose the wrong women."

"It happens," I said, thinking how nothing ever worked for me. "But I have nothing to give you in return."

Francisco smiled. "Yes you do. Give me your lips. A kiss will remain forever in my heart."

***

"The motorcycle is parked outside," Linda said as Luis reappeared with Lola in tow.

"So she comes around, at last. Poor Anise." Gunther took Lola's arm and steered her to the bed. "The woman is not well. What did you do to her?"

Lola shrugged.

"Don't deny it," Clara said slowly. "You are my sister but I know you. Tell them."

Lips twisted in a grimace, Lola faced the group. "Reese needed a chance to be alone with me. Of course I knew he found me attractive, but," she waved a finger to Anise, "she was in the way."

Luis took her roughly by the shoulders. "What did you do?"

"Watch it, my brother." Lola shook herself loose. "I will renot be bossed about as you do your wife. I am a priestess and as such demand respect."

Linda placed a warning hand on Luis. He let Lola go.

"I am better than all the other Santeros in Havana." Lola puffed herself up. "You know this." With a glance at Anise, she said dismissively, "She will come out of this eventually. But where is Reese?"

The German turned her to face him. "We were all given some drug, weren't we, Lola?"

"Herbs, my friend. Nothing terrible, but where is Reese?" She glanced at Luis. "Did he leave?"

"He's missing."

"And no one is looking for him?" Lola tensed. "I advise we search the area immediately. He could be in danger!"

Luis's jaw clenched. "They were hallucinogenic, weren't they?"

"I already explained why. Linda will stay here with the woman and the rest of us will search for Reese. I think since I just came from the river we need to go to the hot springs.

"Let's go." Gunther took Clara's hand and together they led the way.

For Gunther, it seemed an endless walk. Lola made him sick. She was so different from his sweet Clara. The ancients would say she had the evil eye. He feared for both his friends.

It had been selfish of him to try to seduce Anise. He knew all along she was not his. And Clara was special. Possibly he loved her more than all the other women in his life.

A warm haze of gold filled the morning sky. On the hillside, a cluster of broad-leafed trees swayed with the breeze. Yellow flowers and butterflies flitted in the field by the path. It was beautiful outside but he had a feeling of dread in the pit of his stomach.

When the path veered to the right, a patch of trees obscured the view. On entering the opening, Gunther drew Clara close to shield her but she saw it first.

"*Mira!*" She pointed. "There!" She quickened her pace, pulling him along.

In the pool, the upper part of a man was barely above water. "Quickly," Gunther yelled over his shoulder at Luis, "it's Reese. We need to get him out!"

14

I tried to stare the witch down but the deadly dark eyes wouldn't release me. "Go away."

"Did you hear that, Luis? Anise is talking again!" The man with the accented English squeezed the pretty brunette's hand. "Clara, isn't this wonderful? She must be coming out of it."

My head pounded like a drum solo. Who were these people? It especially bothered me that the witch was making herself at home pulling up a rattan chair to seat herself.

"I hope you're right." The man they called Luis pushed past his burly friend and perched on the bed next to me. "We are very happy you are feeling better, Anise. Please tell me if we can do anything to help?"

"Yes, there is something."

"A doctor? I could call someone. It might take a while."

I met Luis's dark brown eyes. "No, not a doctor. I can't be here any longer. But it is imperative I get back immediately."

"What do you mean? You want to go to your hotel?"

"No, I need to return to my men."

Luis's eyes narrowed. "Lola, what is she saying? Who are these men she is talking about?"

"She is experiencing an altered state of consciousness." Lola's lips twisted. "A hallucination."

These people were causing my head to spin. "Stop it!" I croaked, my throat dry as sawdust. "I've had enough." I drew myself up higher on my pillows. "All of you should leave."

"What the hell?" the bear-like man interrupted, shouting at the priestess. "Why is Anise like this?"

Lola's brow furrowed. "I don't know."

"You don't know? You're the priestess, aren't you?"

"Shut up, you idiot!" Lola glared at the German. "I need time to question her."

"*Por favor*, Gunther. Please, no more arguing." Luis knocked his fist into the palm of his other hand in frustration. "Why would she want to send us away?" He took my hand in his. "*Dios mio!* Listen to me, Anise. You can trust us. You are with friends. We all want you to get better."

"You are mistaken, *señor*. I don't know any of you. And my name is Sylvie."

"Lola!" Luis pleaded. "What is going on with her? Who is Sylvie? You must do something!"

"If everyone left I could question her."

"No way!" Gunther roared. "We can't trust you with this lady. None of this would have happened if it weren't for you."

"Your shouting does not help matters," Lola hissed through her teeth. "If it makes you feel better, let Clara stay with me."

Luis clenched his jaw. "Lola, you must do something."

Gunther nodded in agreement. "If there is some sort of an antidote, use it, woman. Reese is in a similar state in the next room. Both of them like human zombies. You need to fix this." He shook his head as if to rid himself of an annoying insect planted on his face. "I'll try to be generous, for Clara's sake, and give you a chance to right your wrongs." With a hasty fist punch to Luis's shoulder, he added, "Come on, man. Let's see if Linda has made any progress with her patient."

Together, they left me with the two women. Although they spoke in Spanish, I understood them perfectly.

They were both attractive, but one had dark red energy around her while the other woman called Clara had a sky blue aura. This lady's voice was soothingly gentle. "Anise will explain this, Lola. I'm sure of it. Please let me talk to her."

"Alright, go ahead, but remember to stop if she gets agitated. We don't want to send her spirit away."

"Tell me, *amiga,* where do you need to go?" Clara asked in a gentle tone.

"The Grande River. Speak to me in Spanish. It seems somehow to come much easier."

Clara's eyes widened. She looked confused and at the same time relieved to continue the conversation in this way. "Where is this? Near Havana?"

I shook my head. That was crazy. Why did she ask about Havana? A wave of dizziness hit me and I suddenly felt nauseous.

"Are you alright?"

"Water?" I pushed down on my stomach.

From a decanter by the bed, Clara poured water into a glass and handed it to me.

She seemed distraught and uneasy. Why, I wasn't sure. She had a peaceful soul. I knew I'd rather speak to her than to the other woman surrounded with the angry red aura. "Why are you asking me all these questions?"

"You are ill, *amiga*. I'm trying to help. Can you tell me the location of this river you talk about? There are many by that name."

Two years ago I'd helped with the women's group in Cuba. I was wondering if it was possible she had been one of them. I stared into the soft doe-like eyes and sensed the goodness in her heart. "Where did I know you from? Did we meet in Cuba?"

She nodded. "Why do you say it in the past tense?"

"Because I left a year ago."

"*Dios mio*! What place are you in?"

"South America—Bolivia."

Clara's jaw dropped down and her eyes widened.

I gazed at her intently. "Did we meet in Havana?"

"Do you recall the bar, the Mojito? Do you remember? We were together—you, me, Gunther and Reese."

At the mention of the name Reese, a shiver raced down my body. Soap and spice scented the air and I breathed in his essence. An incredible rush filled me with desire.

"Color comes to your cheeks." Clara's dark eyes brightened. "I think you remember?"

"Yes." I suddenly felt alert.

"What?" She squeezed my hand. "Tell me."

"Reese. I know his scent."

Startled, Lola jerked up in her chair.

"Reese does smell nice," Clara agreed. "He is also very handsome."

"Is he?" I was very curious about Reese. Somehow I knew he was important in my life.

"Yes, *muy guapo*. And a doctor. Perhaps you can recollect when you danced with Reese?" She rubbed her forehead. "Unfortunately, I regret to say I had had too much Absinthe to tell you more."

A haze similar to the last rays of sunset filled my mind. A warm orange aura. But those mysterious eyes, vibrant as forest foliage, were what I now recalled. A strong face, with sensuous lips and a high forehead that spoke intelligence, all combined to make him unforgettable. Wavy brown hair flecked with golden lights framed a face that oozed sexuality. This man of my memory must be the one she called Reese.

"Did you enjoy the sites of Havana?" Oddly, Clara addressed me as if I were a tourist. Strange. I'd never had any time for much of anything but work in Cuba. It was there I taught the women in the capital about socialism and equality. Yet, I'd taken time to discover the old part of Havana. I remembered walking in the squares and parks filled with color. "What a lovely city. So European."

"You have been to Europe, *amiga*?"

"Yes, I lived in East Germany. My family moved there after I turned eighteen. I don't know why I thought of Leipzig since it's not really much like Havana. I guess they're both old cities. But Leipzig was bombed terribly and rebuilt in dreary grays and browns. The cities are entirely different." I sighed, suddenly sad.

"Europe must be very interesting. I have never left Cuba." Clara pushed an errant tendril back from her forehead. "Tell me, *amiga*, do you believe you are in Bolivia right now?"

"Yes, of course. I know I am."

"Why not Cuba?"

What was wrong with this woman? "Clearly, we are in Bolivia."

"How do you know?"

"From what I've seen, it's not at all like Cuba. There are swamps and the undergrowth is horrendous. I haven't seen any banana trees or coconut palms, Clara. And there's nothing to eat except nuts and corn. Eating a horse was the last good meal we had."

"Ee-ww! Bolivia sounds awful!"

I laughed. "It is. I can't stand the heat. It's hotter than any day I've ever experienced in Cuba. And the insects are wicked. Naturally, La Paz is different. It's an attractive city. I attended a ball at the president's mansion. Have you ever been there?"

Clara stared.

"I am sorry. How insensitive of me. I didn't mean to sound so full of myself. And I know," I sighed, "it's not very politically correct for me to be in a place like that. The poor suffer while the wealthy party away the night. It's wrong." Feeling suddenly cold, I pulled the sheet up higher. I gazed at Clara. "But I had to go. There had to be someone working on the inside."

"Anise, why are you in Bolivia?"

"I'm on a mission. Clara, I mustn't talk about this. Don't ask me anything more. And I repeat, my name is Sylvie." By now they must be missing me. I hope they won't think I have abandoned them. Would my lover reassure my comrades that I would return? For a second, the thought of Francisco's smile made my heart sing.

"Sylvie," Clara said uncertainly, as if the word was hard to get around her tongue. "Why are they waiting for you?"

"They are there for the good of the people. That's all you need to know."

"Please," Clara took my hand, "I am worried about you. I promise I won't tell anyone."

I lifted an eyebrow at the witch. "What about her?"

"Believe me, Lola is trying to help you."

"If that is true, get me my clothes. I must leave." With a burst of energy, I sat up. The room blurred.

"Anise!" Clara pulled me up into a sitting position. "Drink this water." She pushed a cup to my lips.

After taking a sip, I recovered but was confused remembering why or how I came to be here. With the heavy wood-framed oil paintings on the terracotta walls, oak furnishings and tile flooring, the room was attractive and vaguely familiar. In La Paz, the apartment had not been nearly as fancy as this room. I had a hard time believing this was a clinic.

"Are we in a hospital? Was I injured?" When she didn't answer, I lifted the sheet. My eyes swept down the length of my body but found no sign of a wound.

"No, you are in a house."

Lola shot up from her chair and grabbed Clara's arm. I could make out the whispered words. "Ask her what year it is."

As I watched, the brunette's head distorted grotesquely. I recoiled with horror when it detached itself from the slender body.

"Please, Sylvie," Clara persisted, sitting on the bed. "What year do you think it is?"

As I stared, Lola's head became part of her body once again. "What year?"

"Nineteen sixty-seven."

Clara's face paled. She clutched her sister's hand tightly. "What has happened to Anise?"

Lola's red lips pursed. "She is living in a past life."

***

On the coral throne, Tortuga sat imperiously looking down on the prisoners. "Today is the day of decision."

"And what would that be?" Tora interjected impatiently.

The eel swished forward and opened his humongous mouth, razor-like teeth displayed. "Show respect," he growled.

Tora clamped her lips shut and in her anxiety turned a shade of putrid green.

"If I may continue before I was so rudely interrupted."

"Sorry, Almighty Tortuga. I did not mean to insult your highness."

Had anyone spied this pixie looking so contrite and pretty, they would have assumed she was all sweetness and light. Reese knew differently. On the surface, Tora could be exactly that when she wasn't being impish but there was an irrational side to her. He was beginning to believe that her anger originated from her mysterious relationship with Sangra.

"Let it not happen again or you shall be removed," the turtle grumbled. "Now, I wait for your story, sky sprite. What is your connection to S and why did you choose to bring the Earth man here to me?"

"I thought you could help us. S left the castle with an army to search for Crema's vixens and siren allies. That's when I took the opportunity to free the Earth man."

"Crema is at war with S? I know nothing of this. "

Tinkling laughter filled the air. "You're not the only one," Tora said with bafflement in her tone. "It must have been a surprise to Crema when S started her attack on her castle. But she probably enjoyed gunning down the nymph army."

"And why would S go to war against Crema?"

Tora wiggled her shoulders. "Maybe she believed my story."

"That is wrong, sky sprite."

"It was all for the good of the Earth man."

"How so?"

"He was being held against his will. It wasn't his fault that magic had sent him to Nuncamorir. Poor guy had no way of getting back."

"Why were you helping him?"

Tora giggled. "It was fun to put a wrench in S's plan."

"You seem to have some animosity towards her."

"You got that right."

The turtle glared at the pixie. "And what do you wish me to do?" he said sharply.

"You have the power to bring me where I must go."

"I see." The turtle stared steadily at Tora. "But before we discuss that I would like you to tell me how you came to know S."

Tora gritted her teeth.

But the turtle would not be put off. "I wish the truth."

With an agitated flutter of wings, the pixie settled on the coral and stared straight ahead.

"I need to hear the whole story if I am to help you. Leave nothing unsaid," Tortuga cautioned sternly.

"It is not common knowledge but I am the daughter of S."

It was quiet enough to hear a pin drop.

"What?" Reese couldn't believe this news.

Tora nodded solemnly. "It's true. My father is the Elfman of Breslaw. He is the white-haired elf who now lives with the powerful Crema of Pygmacous. It wasn't until recently that I found this out. But I didn't know why he had left until you told us."

"I see." He turned his massive head. "Does the sky child tell the truth, Earth man?"

"I didn't know Tora was S's daughter. If she is, why would she help me escape her mother?"

The humongous turtle eyed Tora but the little sprite was silent.

"Were you the prisoner of S?" the turtle inquired of Reese. "Is this true?"

"Tora helped me escape." Reese frowned, thinking of the violent way the pixie had dealt with the guards.

The turtle jerked his head forward and peered closely at him. "Do you wish to return to S?"

"No thanks. She is gorgeous but I have a need to get back to a wonderful woman on Earth. There is something fascinating about her. Strangely, I am drawn in by her scent. Don't ask me what this means. I have no idea except that there is a deep connection."

"But perhaps you would grow to love S? The nymph has suffered. I think she needs a male at her side."

With a sigh, Reese sat down on a rounded mound of brain coral. "I'm not sure what to make of S. Could be she is complex and not the evil nymph I had assumed she was but nevertheless, I am not interested."

"I understand your confusion. Love is a complex subject that I no longer understand myself." Flippers reached high to cover the turtle's face as if he needed to block out everything but his thoughts. When he placed them firmly down again on the coral, he said, "I will need council."

From behind the purple fan coral, three angel fish appeared, flimsy fins fluttering and lips puckered as if ready for a kiss. Two had deep wine-red patterns on their oval bodies while the middle one was scarlet with a bright yellow marking on its head.

"What wisdom have you for me?"

Silently, the three fish positioned themselves in a straight line from which the middle one swam out and hovered. Reese couldn't understand how all these creatures survived without water. The very unusual atmosphere was of a consistency somewhere between air and water, enabling all types of species to breathe and swim.

Reese watched with interest as the angels opened their pouty lips. In a lilting melody the three began to sing.

Sky, earth and wood

A woman true
Must focus on you.

(Here the angel with the yellow crown sang solo)
Reese holds the key
Help love to be.
Reese holds the key
Help love to be.

Turtle remember
That S needs
Sweet September.

(At this point the other two joined in)
Sky, earth and wood
Licorice is the taste
Time do not waste
Reese holds the key
Help love to be.
Reese holds the key
Help love to be.

Their voices were so exceptionally sweet, they could have been angels from heaven. Yet how absurd was this? Three fish singing of love? He smiled thinking how ludicrous this all was.

Tortuga was not amused. His displeasure was evident as he rasped, "Stop with the levity, Earth man! You are named Reese, correct?"

"Yes." The doctor glanced at the fish again and grinned.

"This is extremely serious, indeed." He waved his flipper indicating the angel trio. "Did you listen to their song? These balladeers are the keepers of your fate."

Reese lifted an eyebrow. "What? You mean the fish? You must be joking."

"I never joke!" the turtle bellowed. "And you should be hoping they have the solution to your problem."

"You mean their little song has some importance?"

"They are oracle singers. If I can interpret their words I will know what to do with you." He turned to the pixie. "As you are not mentioned in the song, I think we can let you go."

Tora flicked her wings joyfully. "Thank you! But Almighty Tortuga, I have a request."

"What is it, young one?"

Tora settled on the coral, wings bent back. "I have thought of this long and hard. From what you told us yesterday, I need to go to Elfland."

"Why?" Reese asked, confused. She knew how to get him back to Cuba yet she was going to Elfland? What was this all about?

"Gotta visit Daddy," she said, with a smirk.

"Now?" Reese was confused. First, the story of Tora's relationship to Sangra and now her need to see her father. "But weren't you bringing me home?"

Tortuga's heavy lidded eyes studied her solemnly. "Would you like to wait? Perhaps the Earth man needs your assistance?"

Tora scratched her head thoughtfully.

"What would you have me do?" the turtle persisted.

Tora shrugged. "Whatever."

"You mean it does not matter to you?" the turtle's voice boomed.

Reese's eyes shot over to the pixie.

Tora giggled. "I think S will be happy to see him again."

Not quite believing she was serious, Reese leaned over and grabbed her wrist. "You said you'd help me return!"

"Ouch! Let me go!" Emerald eyes narrowed dangerously. Her tiny hand curled up in a fist and firmly walloped the side of his head. Flying up to his other temple, she raised her hand again.

The unexpected sucker punch dazed Reese but he recovered fast enough to push her away before she could make contact again.

At a signal from the turtle, two barracudas zoomed up in front of the prisoners. The sight of a mouthful of pointy teeth was enough to freeze the angry pixie. Reese released Tora's wrist abruptly. "Traitor!"

"Never trust a pixie!" Head thrown back, Tora laughed maniacally and kept it up even while the barracudas nudged her along to the exit. Wings flapping wildly, the tiny feet wriggled in time to a mad salsa beat playing inside her brain.

Left alone with the giant turtle, Reese was not happy. He

wanted to ask what the turtle planned for him. Surely it wasn't to keep him here for Sangra? "Almighty Tortuga?"

The reptile appeared to have gone asleep. At least it seemed that was the case as he lay so quietly sprawled on his throne. From behind a cactus coral, the hideous eel took that opportunity to zip up. His voice was like sandpaper scraping on old paint.

"Silence! The Emperor of the Seas must rest and contemplate your pitiful fate without any further interruption. Come with me, Earth man."

How the hell would he get out of here now?

***

The Bolivian army was close. I had to do something to stop them. Yet here I sat in this bed, immobile, my legs and arms useless. Heat consumed me one minute before I succumbed to chills again.

Clara reached over to the table to bring a glass of water to my lips. "Drink. Soon you will feel much better. Lola has assured me these hot and cold flashes will soon be gone."

"How does she know?" I stammered, teeth chattering.

"Lola is a high priestess of Santeria. She will summon her powers to find out what we must do."

I had heard of Santeria but knew little about the religion. "I want nothing to do with animal sacrifice."

"It won't be a ceremony. We wouldn't do that with a non-believer."

I sank back on the pillow. "I have to return to my troops." I squeezed her hand. "Please. They are depending on me."

Clara shook her head. "You will stay here for now. This reading will tell us what direction to take. Trust me."

A table had been moved next to the bed and Lola had taken the chair on the opposite side. From out of a velvet bag held high, rounded egg-shaped shells dropped on the table. They were bright, orange and brown flecked with white. Some fell upwards with a slit-like opening.

"Pretty, aren't they? See how they resemble the vulva? They are cowry shells. Only a priestess is allowed to do the reading." Clara stopped when Lola shot her a look.

Lola moved the shells in a circle muttering strange words I didn't understand.

"She is calling on our ancestors for their guidance." Clara whispered. "When she gives you the shells, pray to the saints for an answer to your question." She added in an undertone, "I know you don't want to leave Reese. He is in a bad state. He will get better if you help him."

I searched her face but could only see the anxiety there. I remembered my deep connection to Reese. Something existed between us yet there was more we hadn't had a chance to explore. My brain whirled with confusion. There were two men in my life and both needed me.

Clara guided my hands to form a cup, and Lola dropped the tiny shells in my open palms. Questions scrambled in my brain. Francisco with the bourbon eyes and the big wide grin was an unforgettable man. Making love had been special but it was more than that. There was a similarity, a connection in philosophy besides the closeness lovers feel. I felt complete with him.

Yet, Clara had reminded me I knew another man. His aura was warm like the sunset sky. I took a deep breath and smelled soap and spice—Reese. Those hazel eyes with forest green flecks pulled deep into my unconscious. Wavy hair felt unbelievably soft on my skin. Those brief kisses had steamed my body until I was unbelievably wet with desire. Never had I experienced kisses so intense. I didn't know him as I knew Francisco but I sensed that under the gruff exterior he wanted to cure people and help them. The car accident had left him scarred. My psyche told me it was guilt rather than love that caused him to withdraw. He wanted to love me if only he could free himself.

But what about Bolivia? I wanted to return. It was clear Lola felt Francisco and the guerillas were part of a past life. Yet they were all so real. Where was I meant to be? Not altogether sure this was the best possible question to ask, I whispered, "Help me to find my true destiny."

I gave the cowry shells back to Lola who threw them down. Some of them faced up.

"There are two paths." The priestess's eyeballs rolled back and only the whites remained as she intoned, "I see danger...and death."

A whirling wind swept me up and hurled me into the heat of the tropics. Sweat prickled under the short-sleeved denim shirt I wore tucked into loose khaki pants. In my combat boots, I tread carefully on the grassy path, ever on the alert for snakes. A rustling movement stopped me. Before me rose the thick trunk of a broad-leafed tree. This was the very same tree where I had experienced the electricity of Francisco's love-making. I smiled, warm with thoughts of his tongue on my body.

A chattering sound brought my eyes upward. In the thick green foliage, a small brown monkey quickly sprang from branch to branch anxiously chasing another creature—or was he the one being pursued?

The cloth back pack, heavy with supplies, was a burden and the rifle slung over my shoulder made my shoulders ache yet they offered some measure of security from both human and jungle enemies. It was war. My journey was a great deal more uncertain than my feelings of love for Francisco.

As I crept silently through the unruly vegetation, I became aware of voices. I listened, cautiously stepping back into the underbrush. The familiar tones of Miguel's lilting Spanish allowed me to breathe easily once more.

There were several of us from South America. Francisco and I and two others were Argentine, but there were Peruvians and Brazilians, as well as Cubans. One thing was certain: We were united in our struggle to help the country.

Unfortunately, this guerilla warfare was taking a toll on all of us. Everyone suffered from intestinal problems. It was bad enough that we were forced to eat a mule for supper but that was nothing compared to the lack of pure water. At one point, the men drank their own urine in their desperation.

I pursed my lips and whistled. The talking stopped. Again I let out a macaw screech.

"Sonia?" A burly man in combat green pushed the bush apart and peeked out.

"Yes, I'm back. Did you miss me?"

"We partied late into the night toasting you with beer but *capitana*, we did nothing you wouldn't do." His lips pulled back on a gap in an otherwise toothy grin.

"Hard to believe. You are such a wild man." I laughed. "How

is everyone?"

"Juan suffers from his wound which is slow to heal but the rest of us are the same as ever."

"You mean hungry, thirsty and sick?"

Miguel shrugged. "We're okay."

I shook my head. "If only we had gone into that pharmacy and bought some medical supplies."

"I guess Francisco thought we would be at risk."

"It is hard not to be in danger. Why are you all here? I thought I would have to cross the river to find you."

"Yesterday, Francisco said we were to portage across the river and meet with you here. Sorry to have surprised you in this way but apparently this part of the embankment is easier to hike along."

"Where is Francisco?"

Miguel gazed at the sparkling blue of the Rio Grande. "By now he should be five kilometers up the river on the other side. We are to catch up."

"Has everyone packed up to go?"

"Yes. We were told to wait."

We turned at the sounds of voices. Further down the path, a group of men appeared. When they saw us, they waved. I returned the greeting thinking how emaciated they looked. No one could be happy after the hardships they had endured yet the stories these men told managed to make it all sound like a pleasant picnic by the riverbank.

After a brief discussion, we decided to travel a kilometer onwards and cross the river at that point. My heart sang, thinking how close we were to rejoining Francisco and his troops.

It was an exhausting journey with mosquitoes buzzing around our sweaty, tired bodies. At one point, we rested and ate what was left of the peanuts and corn. My stomach churned and cramped until I was forced to rush to the privacy of the bush to relieve myself of the contents.

Miguel patted me on the back. "Poor Sonia. It's been too long since you've had such a hardy supper."

That remark sparked some laughter from the men even though a few were equally green around the gills.

"Come on," I said. "Let's pack up and go. We want to cross before the sun goes down."

The hike zapped everyone of their strength, even though the going was slow. With the sun low in the sky, we came to the access point. Our back packs secured, we headed into the river, our rifles held high over our heads. There was a comforting warmth to the water, much like embryonic fluid is to a small fetus floating inside the womb. The water glinted gold.

Halfway there, Miguel nudged me. "Look over there."

Movement and the flash of metal. "Ready to fire!" I shouted over my shoulder.

As I lowered my M-16 to take aim, bullets blazed from the other side of the river, sharply cracking the air. The chirping and screeching of the birds and monkeys stopped. I gasped. Intense pain shook my body as I gripped Miguel's arm.

"Sonia!"

Ribbons of red soaked through my shirt and I slumped into the river.

15

It was *déjà vu*. The same room as before. Coral floors and a bed that gleamed rosy pink while the reflected lights on the ceilings shimmered as powerfully as the light show over Niagara Falls. Framing the doorway of his prison, glistening stalagmites, multi-faceted cones, reached upwards to almost meet the crystallized icicles hanging from the ceiling. Odd how he hadn't noticed any of this on his last visit. It was beginning to feel more and more like he was involved in something out of his control. He would have considered this more but right now he felt incredibly hungry. Eating was higher on his list than reflecting on his situation.

A shell table was abundantly spread with seafood and a bottle of wine. Without another thought, Reese took a seat on the golden sponge situated at the head of the table, folded his long legs under him, and contemplated the bountiful repast. A gigantic lobster, several crabs, a dish of oysters on one platter and, on another, a seaweed salad strewn with incredibly thick purple worms. When Reese tilted his head to eye the unappetizing dish, an almost imperceptible twitch worked inside the green mess. He recoiled from that vomit-inducing side dish, shoved it away and concentrated on the seafood.

Prepared with care, the pyramid presentation on a silver platter was quite artistic, he thought. What the pottage contained was a bit of mystery but it looked tasty enough. He dabbed a finger in the orange sauce and his lips curled with the spicy tinge. Nice. Thai flavors came to mind. It would be a perfect dip for seafood.

But what of the food? Should he eat it? Yet hunger prevailed over logic. He separated the lobster shell and pulled out a juicy segment to pop into his mouth.

His view of the far corner of the room was blocked by a shell partition. There would be that amazing pool, he remembered vividly.

And what an experience! Intense jets hitting him at all angles. He had been unbelievably horny. Unfortunately, the female in the pool with those fine firmly-shaped breasts had been missing some rather vital womanly parts. The Almighty Tortuga must have cracked up laughing after he'd heard how he nearly succumbed to the mermaid's seduction. Perhaps it was just as well that he'd slipped away into sleep except for the fact that it had almost ended his miserable life. What exactly had happened afterwards was still a puzzle to him. How had he survived?

The food stared at him. Again, he split open another segment and popped it into his mouth. Heavenly, or should he say mouth-watering, considering they were eighty feet below the surface? He couldn't get enough. The next fleshy bit was about to be tossed back when he spied the orange sauce.

Just as he held the piece of lobster over the dip, a voice echoed like a wave through the chamber.

"No-o-o!"

The lobster slipped out of his fingers. Startled, Reese looked up. Spirits? As a man who had never seen pixies or nymphs until very recently, it would be par for the course to see a phantom emerge from the coral wall but instead, he sighted a flash of red through the steamy haze above the pool's surface and Rosalinda's head popped up.

"You can try the sauce if you like but I can guarantee your evening will be spent on the floor."

"Rosalinda? You're here?"

"Mermaids like the element of surprise."

"So what's going on? Tortuga wants to drug me up again?"

She held up a pointer finger to her lips. "Ssh," she whispered.

"But…"

Rosalinda shook her head and gestured for him to come forward.

With a plate of lobster in his hands, Reese trekked over to the pool and sat down on the edge. The mermaid was incredibly gorgeous but his mind wandered to visions of gold energy and the scent of Anise filled the air.

"The walls have ears. We're okay here, away from the stalagmites."

"You mean they're alive?"

"Not really but they have listening devices."

Espionage in an underwater cave? This place was unbelievable! Gnawing guilt had sent him back to this place. He thought that part of his life was over yet here he was. All he wanted was to be back in bed with Anise. Whatever they had started begged to be completed.

She stared at him curiously. "What's up? You look like a love struck teenager. Oh, I see. It's the Earth woman."

Reese shot her a look.

With a grin, Rosalinda tapped his leg. "You think we don't have the sixth sense here? Just as much as you and your lady. She has the sweet scent of anise."

"How did you know that?"

Rosalinda grinned. "Mermaids are tuned into energy. We are highly evolved."

Reese closed his eyes and breathed in. "God you are so right. Her scent is beyond anything I've experienced."

"If you find her so incredible why have you been resisting her?"

"Resisting?" Reese said with disbelief. "I have tried to connect with her ever since I ran her down in the street. This trip to Cuba has been full of bad luck. And now of all things I'm here. I wish I knew why I'm in this fantasy world."

"It's real enough to all of us." Rosalinda rolled her eyes. "How close-minded of you. Other realms do exist. Surely you as a son of Earth must be aware of that?"

"I can't say I ever imagined anything like this."

"There are many worlds in the solar system but I can only vouch for this one." Rosalinda rubbed the tip of her nose thoughtfully. "Beware, Earth man. All of the inhabitants under the sea can read thoughts."

The eel's sharp pointy teeth and terrible aggressive personality came to mind. No wonder he had threatened Tora. "Air, earth and water," he said slowly.

"The oracle song?"

"It was something like that. You know if I could come up with an interpretation that proved it was better for me to return to Earth, he would let me return."

"The Almighty Tortuga would free you?"

"I hope he doesn't decide to give me to Sangra."

Reese picked out a morsel of lobster and offered it to Rosalinda. She parted scarlet lips to receive the treat.

"I know why I ended up here. It has to do with guilt. When Lisa died I felt it was my fault for letting her drive. The absinthe was to numb all my emotions. I suppose I was easy pickings for Sangra. But why do you think Sangra wanted me in particular? Tell me, Rosalinda, what's her game?"

"Sangra uses her magic. First, the absinthe to get you in the right meditational frame of mind. Your guilt was her ace in the hole. But you aren't just anybody. Sangra wanted to reproduce with a Son of Earth, and with you in particular. I think she thought your spirit could merge with hers and she would have peace."

"Why my spirit?"

"You may not know this but you are highly sensitive and so is she."

Reese rubbed his chin. "I have been picking up scents lately. For years I've seen colors around people but I seriously thought there was something wrong with my vision."

Rosalinda smiled. "Auras. I've heard of those. None of us can see them here. Perhaps that's another reason she picked you. You might be a lot like her boyfriend. Elves have the third eye."

"The elf? This has something to do with him?"

"Yes." The mermaid lowered her voice so much Reese had to shove the food aside and lean closer. This afforded an alluring glimpse of perky breasts peeking out from auburn tresses. "She needed to make the elf man jealous so that he would want to come back for her."

Reese picked at the lobster, tugged out a fleshy portion and munched while he thought this over. "That could work but it wouldn't be good for me. I need to return to Earth to see if Anise and I have a love connection."

With a giggle, Rosalinda said, "I think Anise has a thing for you."

"God, I hope so. But now I'm here—again."

"This trip came about through a herbal drug."

"How did you know about that, Rosalinda?"

"After I pulled you out of the pool, I listened in."

"You heard them speak about me? On Earth?"

Rosalinda nodded. "They thought you had drowned."

"But you saved my life?"

"Yes."

"Why?"

Rosalinda beamed. "Just thought you were kind of cute. Besides, I don't need a dead man in my pool."

"Thank you. You don't know how much I appreciate what you did. I've become wiser. Dying is not the solution. Everyone is responsible for their own actions."

"True. I'm glad you are no longer fragile."

Reese gazed at the mermaid. "All of us are fragile at times."

The mermaid squeezed his hand. "But you're getting better?"

"I won't let the demons take control. This dream is about to end." In his head, Reese knew he had to find the pixie before they released her and hopefully, he could persuade the turtle to help him.

"This is where you usually hang?" he asked, with a glance around.

"Whenever I can. A steamy hot pool like this one is better than the red ocean but don't tell the Tortuga you saw me. He wouldn't want me speaking with you."

"So he didn't set me up with you last time? It wasn't him with the twisted sense of humor?"

With a toss of her auburn curls Rosalinda said, "No, I'm afraid not. I wanted a little fun. Life is dreary below the ocean, Change is good. Besides, I was curious to see an Earth man. I'd heard rumors that you were here and thought I'd have a look."

This time it was Reese's turn to flirt. "And what did you think?"

Rosalinda eyed him from beneath long fluttering lashes. "You have sensitive hands and they know how to touch a Mermaid just right."

With a quick glance at his gitch, he was relieved to see he wasn't aroused.

She grinned. "It's too bad your appendages are mutated though. There's nothing like a good healthy tail on a merman."

"I guess I look stupid to you."

A giggle escaped the plump lips of the mermaid. "No, it was interesting to see that earth men have a visible thermometer of their desire. With mermen, it's a guessing game."

Thoughtfully selecting another morsel of crab for his new friend, Reese brought it to her mouth.

"Mm-mm. Thank you, Earth man. Now I won't have to go fishing."

"I'm the one that should be thanking you. This second trip is something I don't understand at all. First Nuncamorir and now Sea World." Reese snatched up a piece of lobster and tossed it back. "You mentioned a herbal induced trip. Do you know how that happened?"

Like a cataract veil shrouding her pupils, Rosalinda's eyes clouded to a filmy gray. Fascinated, Reese watched her pinch an earlobe and once again her eyes became shiny bright.

Rosalinda gazed at him "It was in the wine. A fine gray powder."

"I thought as much. Both Anise and I were behaving oddly, not to mention Gunther. He was like a dog with a bone the way he hit on Anise."

"Hm-mm," the mermaid chuckled, "you mean boner. That man had it bad for your fair lady."

Reese's eyes widened. "You could see that?"

"I saw everything, if in a rather condensed version. Fast and informative. Something like your YouTube."

"So someone drugged us? Who?"

A tendril of hair twisted on the mermaid's finger before she answered. "You know of a woman whose name starts with L?"

Reese was dumbfounded with this information. "Yes, Lola, but why would she do this?"

"You're not a fool, Earth man. Think hard and you will reason it out."

"Alright, but help me with the oracle, please, Rosalinda. If I don't grasp what that's all about the Tortuga might give me to Sangra as a peace offering." Reese snatched a crab leg and handed it to the mermaid. "Eat this. I'm not sure I can remember it all but part of it was about me and love. And there was something about September and Sangra."

"Oo-hh, dear Neptune!" Rosalind gasped. "That was the month the sea turned red."

Reese bit on a lobster tail to crack it. "The turtle admitted he screwed up the situation. He should have told Sangra to find the elf man or at least do something before the fellow left."

"So the Tortuga told the elf man to go? Why?"

"He thought he should preserve the sanctity of his marriage with Crema for the sake of their son."

"And that broke Sangra's heart and made her bitter."

Reese nodded. "She wept red tears."

"And there was nothing to keep those two together in Nuncamorir?"

A tender piece of lobster in his mouth, Reese had a flashback. "Well, there might be. I found something out. The pixie that came with me is Sangra's daughter. She's cute but really whacko."

"What do you mean by that word?"

"A bit warped and deceptively vicious. You wouldn't think so to see her either."

"Pixies are unpredictable but usually nice enough. Do you know why she was like that?"

"It's because the elf man left. I think she blames Sangra. For the life of me I don't understand why those two have so much animosity towards each other."

"Mother-daughter conflict? Not uncommon. The pixie is a teenager, isn't she?"

Reese looked at the steamy vapor rising up from the pool. It was so inviting. Should he? It didn't take much persuading from his ultra-ego. To the astonishment of the mermaid, he whipped off his gitch and jumped in with a splash.

"The drugs sure make you uninhibited, Earth man."

Reese dunked his head in and popped out again. "It's not like you wear any clothes either, Rosalinda. I wouldn't have taken you for a prude."

"Just teasing," she said, perched on the coral rock, arms raised in a stretch arching her back. This position favorably exposed her apple shape breasts to his view, somewhat distracting him. "Mermaids are insane flirts and we use everything we have to entice the male of the species. For your information, I am a princess. The sharks do my bidding as well as the groupers and octopi."

"You seemed to be afraid of the turtle."

"Just being cautious. I shouldn't really be here while these pools are in dispute. Under sea law it's a pink area. Mom rules the Blue Ocean and Tortuga the Red. So, when I heard there was a human in captivity, I had to see for myself and at the same time have some fun in the hot spring pool." She threw a sly look at Reese's powerful upper body. "It was a good decision all round. Too bad you didn't have a tail. I'd have taken you back to Mom."

Reese grinned. "You are a sweetheart, Rosalinda, but you know my heart is with Anise. Now back to serious business. I just remembered something else the angel fish sang."

"Which is?"

"I thought it was strange." Reese hummed the song softly for a moment, trying to remember the exact wording. Finally, it came to him. "Licorice is the taste. Time do not waste."

The mermaid crinkled her nose. "Licorice? Not my favorite although I like the red. What else was there in this oracle tune?"

Arms spread out, Reese leaned back on the edge of the pool. "It went something like this—" he crooned, "Reese has the key. Help love to be."

Rosalinda shook her head. "It's not making sense."

"I know. I've been trying to piece it all together."

"Let me think." In a flash, the mermaid dove into the pool and disappeared into the depths.

Reese started getting worried when she showed no signs of reappearing but it gave him a chance to put the puzzle together. An idea was forming in his brain when Rosalinda burst from the surface.

"I've got a feeling Sangra needs to get the elf man back before I can leave."

The mermaid shook her tresses furiously. "Makes sense."

"If we went to the elf man, do you think we could persuade him to come back to her?"

"Maybe, but you're going there. I'm not going to any fairy land."

"Okay," Reese said, resignedly, "but easier said than done. I have no idea how to get there."

Rosalinda pursed her lips thoughtfully. "But there is still a problem. Even if you get to the elf, what about the elflet?"

"The son?"

"Yes. If the father wants to be part of the little creature's life, how do you persuade him to come back to Sangra?"

"Well, I'm not sure how you deal with divorce in this land, but on Earth there could be a number of solutions."

Rosalinda pulled herself up on the rim of the shell, her tail partially submerged. Absentmindedly, the mermaid tapped him on the arm. "Even if you have a way out for the elf, there are still two problems left."

"Which are?"

"How to get you to the Elfland."

"And?"

Rosalinda smirked. "The taste of licorice—anise."

16

The current hurled me downstream. Intense pain gripped my chest. I swallowed water, coughing up blood.

After what seemed an eternity, the river swept me onto the soft comfort of the muddy shore. Too exhausted to move, I was startled by his touch. A bolt of electricity from his fingers left me with no doubt of his identity.

"No, *mi amor*," he said, gathering me up into his arms. "This cannot be. I know we were meant to be together. Forgive me?"

"Of course I do. I am happier than I've ever been," I murmured, gazing up at his whiskey eyes.

"Please understand. I turned back time and brought you here. I wanted to make sure we had another chance. We needed to feel love, our hearts as one."

I shifted around, uncomfortable with the pain and his words. "What do you mean you brought me here? To Bolivia?"

"When your body was weak from the drugs I took you away from another life to come back to me. Had you stayed you would have been his. I have no doubt. You were getting so close to him."

His chest became my cushion. "There was another man?"

"Yes, unfortunately there is. He would have claimed you, but for the priestess. For reasons of her own, she sent you here." Francisco tilted my chin up. "I had the best of intentions. Truly I did. When we parted before, it took days before I heard you'd been killed. I didn't believe it. With no reinforcement, my troops were ambushed. Our cause died with us."

I nodded. "And now? It isn't any different, is it?"

"At least I'm here for you this time."

"I love you, Francisco." I gripped his upper arm, fingertips digging in as a wave of agony pierced my chest.

"And I will always love you, sweet Sylvie—forever."

My hand slid to my chest, holding in the pain where the bullet burned.

Francisco took my bloody fingers away and kissed them. "Don't leave me."

As cold flowed through my veins, I shook uncontrollably. Words pressed out painfully. "I must. I'm dying."

"No, you cannot! I won't allow it." Francisco's tawny brown eyes drew me in like a moth to a flame. I had met a man who bonded with my soul.

He drew me closer and whispered, "I was wrong to bring you here. Forgive my selfishness. You need to go back and live."

His face blurred. I tried to raise my hand to his cheek but it wouldn't move. "Where?"

"To your other life. You have a chance to love again with a man who needs you. I must send you back."

"No! I don't want to leave you—ever! Let me die joyfully in your arms."

Before he could reply, from behind the trees came shouting followed by a flash of fire. A tremendous blast hit Francisco from behind. He jerked with the impact and collapsed against me. "Love you…"

Everything went misty. I groaned.

Clara looked on with horror as blood seeped between the fingers clasped to my chest. "No, Anise, please!" She swung around. "Lola, she is bleeding!"

Her sister's eyes pierced. "Like the stigmata."

Clara pushed a towel under my fingers. "Press hard." She glared at Lola. "You cannot let her die. For the love of God, help her!"

I fell back on the mud, my lover's head pressed to my chest. As much as I tried, I could hardly breathe. It was as if bricks had been piled on top of me. I gasped words through my pain. "Francisco, my darling, please don't leave me." A coughing spasm shook my body as the blood bubbled out of my mouth.

"What's the matter with you, Lola? See how she suffers. *Dios mio!*" Clara yelled, frustrated. She felt my wrist. "I can hardly find a pulse. You must do something!"

Lola sat immobile in the armchair, her lips tightly drawn.

"Don't you see? You must undo the wrong you have done. Anise has a promising future. She wants to write a book with photographs of Cuba. You must not take away her dreams for your own selfish reasons." Clara grabbed her sister by the shoulders and shook her. "Yours is a noble calling. Don't make me regret my trust in you."

A hazy white tunnel. Floating, I stepped towards the opening in the distance. Warmth like liquid mercury carried me forward. A brilliant beacon summoned. I needed to go into the misty passageway.

Lola sat silently staring ahead.

"Surely you cannot forsake the teaching of our ancestors?"

"Alright," Lola said slowly. "I will try." Unfastening the medallion around her neck, she held it up. "Look at the Madonna!" She took hold of my chin. "Watch the lady. See how she shines so bright? Her light beckons you," she said in a sing-song voice. "Listen to me, little sister. Look at her golden light and come back here to us."

Lightly skimming a cloud, I eased towards the brilliant white light in the tunnel but something distracted me. Another light sparkled with the warmth of tropical sunlight.

Again, in a monotone, Lola repeated, "See how she shines so bright. Her light beckons. You will come back to us."

I heard her yet I wanted to go to the end, to the intense white light. Halfway there the passageway had another light—this one sparkling yellow.

"See how it shines for you. Our lady needs you here. Do you hear her? She is calling for you. Let her light guide you back." The melodic voice spoke softly beside me. "Come to your future."

I hesitated, not knowing how to proceed.

In the bedroom, Lola waved the medallion slowly. "You are needed here, Anise. Leave Sylvie with her lover. Reese is in danger. His love is true. Return to us."

The voice seemed sincere but I was torn. I gazed at the golden maiden in the long robes standing before me in the tunnel. Her smile was pure and angelic. I felt warmth from her energy. As I picked up speed to follow her, she stopped. The willowy lady in the flowing white robes studied me with clear gray eyes. Her weightless hands touched mine. "She is right. You must not go any further. This is not your time." Her voice caressed like a summer breeze. "This place is not for you. Not yet. Take hold of your destiny and return to Cuba."

Gently, she pushed me about and I slowly floated towards the entrance away from the dazzling light. The misty tunnel gave way to a soft glow as the haze cleared away.

I sank into the bed and opened my eyes. Lola was leaning back in an armchair watching me. With my elbows, I pulled myself up into a sitting position and stared at my nemesis. A leopard doesn't change its spots. Whatever she had in mind for me wouldn't be good.

As if reading my thoughts, she laughed brusquely. "I have succeeded once again. You are back with us." She fastened the gold medallion about her neck. The red aura that had unnerved me before now shone more orange than red.

"I welcome you, Anise."

"That is kind of you, Lola, but why?"

"Why what?"

I gazed at her. "This change of attitude. I know you would rather I had stayed in my past life and died. Why would you take me away?"

Lola's jaw tightened. "Clara, would you get Anise something to eat, please?"

"Certainly. Poor one, you must be famished. I shall be right back." She shot a glance at her sister. "You won't let anything happen to her, will you?"

"Of course not!" Lola replied sharply. "Go, quickly. We have much to do."

Clara gave me an encouraging smile before she made her way out.

Although the woman had helped me, I was still suspicious. "I want to know why you sent me to my past life."

"You didn't like the experience? Admittedly, it was difficult but how many of us get the opportunity to go back in time to a past life?"

"One with a rather violent death."

Lola twisted her lips into a smile. "True, but an interesting one. Besides, the lover was very handsome. You were in sexual heaven. Wasn't that pleasant at least?"

"Whether it was or wasn't is none of your concern."

She leaned back in the chair and crossed a leg over her knee. "A revolutionary hero for a lover? An exciting adventure for a Canadian girl at loose ends. Perhaps that is why you came to Cuba. To make contact with the past?"

"I had no idea this would happen."

"But I think you did. You have the sixth sense. You knew your life in Canada was over."

This woman had manipulated my life. I was lucky to be back but everything I had come to believe in was gone. It was difficult to stay calm, yet I bit my lip, contained my composure and let her continue.

"It would seem you wanted what you lost in Cuba forty years ago."

"Really?"

"The cowry shells gave you two possible paths. I could have left you to die in Bolivia."

"But you didn't. Why was that?"

"I suppose I wanted to see what you're made of."

"You don't look too happy that I came back."

"I am so tired of you. It was unfortunate Gunther didn't bed you. It would have been so much easier that way."

Clara overheard her words upon entering the chamber. Nearly dropping the tray she carried, she managed to place it safely on the bedside table. Hands on her hips she stood glaring at Lola. "What are you saying? My Gunther with Anise?" Clara's finger pressed into her chest. "It is I whom he loves. How dare you imply he would look at another woman!"

"Should I tell her or would you like to do the honors?" Lola stared at me challengingly.

"It was the wine, Clara. Your sister has the means to do whatever she wants to manipulate others. I think you know what she is capable of."

Clara's eyes flicked to her sister. "Yes, it is true. I believe you, Anise. The wine was drugged. If Gunther wanted to have sex, it was because he was not himself."

"Your slutty friend here lay bare-breasted with your lover while he fondled her as happily as a kid in a candy store. When Reese and I walked in, she was more than willing."

For a moment Clara stared unseeingly before she slapped her sister—a resounding blow to the cheek. "You are a cruel woman with no sense of loyalty. How dare you take control over our lives!"

Lola brought her hand up to the bright red blotch marring her pale complexion. "Take care, little Clara," she snarled. "If you want Gunther you can not offend those who have power over many."

Her jaw clenched, Clara defiantly snatched up the medallion around Lola's neck and yanked hard. When the necklace came off in her hand, she held it up triumphantly. "This is how you work your magic—with hypnosis. Now leave the room so that Anise can eat and get dressed. Tell Luis we will be in shortly."

While I dressed, Clara proceeded to tell me what had happened to Reese. As she explained, memories flashed in my mind. I realized there were two men in my life but one was dead.

"You are looking worried, Anise."

"I am. I wish I knew how I could help." As I started to eat the sandwich, I noticed Clara's furrowed brow.

"What?"

"Tell me, did you love him?"

"Francisco?"

Clara nodded enthusiastically. "In my head I have this idea of what he looked like." Her eyes looked faraway. "He was handsome, wasn't he?"

An overwhelming sadness came over me. "Yes, but it was more than that. It was so much deeper."

"Perhaps you aren't ready to help Reese? I think he needs you but if your heart is still with—"

"Francisco. They shot him."

"Oh." She leaned over and hugged me to her. "I'm sorry, Sylvie, er, Anise."

The warmth of another person holding me close made me quiver. I felt a tear drop on my cheek and roll off my chin. "You said Reese is in a coma?"

Clara frowned. "Lola tried to bring him back but nothing. Do you remember him? I know you liked each other."

I had a vision of his full lips and those hazel eyes flecked with forest green. "Yes, I do." After I set my plate on the table, I slipped on my sandals. "Let's go."

With a hand on my elbow, Clara helped me down the hallway to the other bedroom. The men were waiting with Lola.

"Thank God you are better, Anise!" the German boomed, getting up on his feet and bringing me over to the armchair. "Come sit down, *liebchen*. You look tired."

I felt more zombie than human. Yet I needed to know how Reese figured in this.

Huddled in the room together, Luis, Linda and Gunther parted to let me through. Tousled sun-kissed hair and the tanned face belied the gravity of the situation. Propped up by pillows, he lay motionless, eyes fixed unseeingly.

I sat myself on the edge of the bed. "Why is he like that?" I asked uneasily.

From behind, Lola spoke up. "He was almost dead when we found him."

"Where?"

"He was partially submerged in the hot springs. Miraculously, he survived. It was as if someone had pushed him out."

Gunther grunted. "Your drugged wine did this."

"It was meant to wear off in an hour or so." Lola gazed at me. "What I didn't realize was the depth of her extrasensory perception or that Reese had it too."

When Gunther looked at her accusingly, her tone turned sharp. "It didn't happen to either you or Clara. You know that." She turned to her brother and Linda. "All of you drank some of the wine and you were just fine, weren't you?"

"Well, it wasn't the usual night." Linda blushed as Luis said, "It was magical. Right, *mi amor*?"

I suppose one good thing had come of the drugged wine. Linda and Luis appeared to be more in love than ever but when I glanced in Clara's direction, she pulled back from her fiancé who was trying to catch her hand.

Sensing something amiss, Gunther cleared his throat.

"No! Not now. We will talk about what happened later," Clara said tightly.

Lola lifted an eyebrow. "I remind everyone we need to focus on Reese."

My mind had been completely tuned into the doctor's dilemma. "So you think he's in this trance because of his sixth sense?"

Lola nodded. "Yes, he is in a dream." The priestess surveyed the room. "Light the candles, Linda. It will purify the air and let the spirits in."

With a tug on Gunther's rolled up shirt sleeve, Luis jerked his head in the direction of the door. "Let's go. The women will help our friend to come back. I am confident of that."

This time the German had nothing to say as he left the room. It was as if his bubble was deflated and he'd lost his spirit. I heard him speak softly to Luis. "I should never have gone after Anise. I love Clara so much."

"Stop, man!" Luis shushed him. "Give her time."

I glanced up to see Clara glare at Gunther's departing back.

The room, which had been somewhat dim, now glowed softly from the candles Linda had placed in the corners. Once she was done, Linda took a seat in one corner as if to give us more space.

With the men gone and the room quiet, once more Lola moved a chair next to the bed. Once she settled in, she motioned to her sister. "I need the locket."

Clara's eyes narrowed.

"Please."

Hesitantly, Clara handed the necklace to Lola.

When Lola lifted the medallion in front of Reese's face, she spoke in a monotone. "See the lady? She shines her golden light. See the sparkle?" The medallion shimmered with an inner flame as it caught the candlelight. "Look at her dance for you."

Something in either her words or the motion of the swinging necklace awakened Reese. His voice was far away, different than I'd ever heard it. "I don't know what to do. The pixie knows but she is most likely gone."

"Go find the pixie," Lola urged.

"I need to get out of here." He slumped back.

Lola stared a challenge at me. "Reese deserves the best woman."

Clara snorted. "And that would be you?"

"Not so unbelievable. Anise has baggage. And let's not forget he made love to me, not Anise."

I hadn't thought I cared for Reese but what she said made me angry. "When did that happen?"

"A few days ago. He enjoyed himself. I know that. We agreed to meet up again."

I couldn't believe Reese was anything but a meal ticket for her. "It was sex. That's all."

Lola's eyes turned into slits of burning coal. "The more he sees me the more he wants me. I can make love happen. I am a priestess," she said smugly. "I have the power to enter his dreams."

"His nightmare is more like it." A purple haze had spread throughout the room. I realized my attraction for this man transcended chemistry. Love defies reason. I was sure of one thing. Reese understood everything I was. With him I could be who I am.

Just then I noticed an oil painting hanging above the bed. The sky was blue and the water shimmered white. Two women, one blonde and the other a redhead swam towards an ivory cliff. On the far shore a figure of a man stood waiting. In the corner of the canvas, a familiar signature was clearly etched—*A Sommerville.* My jaw dropped. Somewhere in my head, my angel guide whispered, *"Trust those that seek the truth. Go forth with courage."*

Lola crossed her arms over her chest. "Reese is gone. He has escaped into another realm. If nothing is done, he will succumb to danger."

Eyes wild, Clara clutched her sister's arm. "Save him! Don't let him die."

"Calm yourself, Clara." Lola stared at me. "If you want to claim him for yourself, you can try."

"What do you mean?"

"You will need to enter his dream."

"How?"

"Use your psychic abilities."

"And what then?"

"You may be able to free him." Lola turned, holding the medallion up to my face. Her voice assumed a monotone as the gold sparkled rhythmically with the swing of her fingers. "See how my lady sparkles? Will you follow her?"

Francisco had thought I would find love here in this life. Was Reese the other half of my soul?

"Do you have the courage to fight for him?"

I nodded. "Yes, but what if I lose?"

"Oh, Anise. It's simple. If you fail—of course you will die!" Lola threw her head back and laughed.

***

The sea sparkled with shades of scarlet beyond anything I had ever seen yet, as I looked up to the surface, the water was clear as a blush wine. I slowly sank in the depths outfitted with a breathing device. Amazingly, there was no pressure on my ears nor did I feel the sting of salt in my eyes. It was a completely painless descent.

In the ocean, fish of all sizes shot through ripples of brilliant red. Humongous coral tinged a deep orange resembled giant hands praying to an unseen god. Perhaps it was my imagination running wild but I seriously began to wonder if I had been hasty in committing myself to this mission. But what sort of woman would I be if I let my traveling companion die? So, a voice in the back of my mind said accusingly, *he is only a companion to you? You know that's a lie. His touch is unforgettable.*

As I neared the ocean bottom, I became aware of an unusual amount of activity. Groupers, grunts and tangs circled around a large opening. Just in time I sensed danger. I shot forward and hid behind the coral.

The thick head of a monstrous eel poked out. I didn't dare breathe in case he noticed air bubbles but luckily, the eel disappeared back into the coral access. Not knowing the status of my air supply, I was worried, but something was obviously clear. I had to get on with it now or abandon my mission.

When a glittery school of barracuda whizzed by I broke off a chunk of coral and threw it down. The sand swirled around the fish for a moment before my missile landed one. If you've ever seen a wasp nest sprayed in daytime, this was the aquatic version.

It was only meant to cause a minor kerfuffle, but barracuda are equipped with short fuses and sharp teeth. The scuffle was so vicious the eel left his post to mediate. I took advantage and eased my way into the entrance. Amazingly, my t-shirt and shorts were as dry as before and there was air to breathe.

I had no idea where I was heading at first but then I picked up a scent—spice and soap. Excitement mounted in me as I realized it was Reese. I floated forward following the scent. Doorways lined up much like a corridor on a hotel floor, each one labeled with letters. As I passed R7, I had an overpowering feeling that this was it. But when I entered the room, it was empty. Platters had been left on a coral table as if a party had ended in haste and the occupants had gone to find fun elsewhere.

The rush of water from the end of the chamber led me to wander further. Curiously, I trekked to the corner. Here, a shell partially hid a hot spring. As I gazed at the steam rising from the surface, my jaw dropped. Out of the steam, a beautiful woman shot to the surface. Long auburn tresses waved on pale shoulders and a mischievous smile played on her full lips. She was naked and uninhibited.

"You should see your face. Bet you've never seen a mermaid before, eh?"

"Mermaid?"

She flipped her red-scaled tail. "Greetings, Earth woman. I am Rosalinda."

I stood there staring, speechless.

"Your name is?"

"Anise," I managed to whisper, coming to my senses.

"Ah-hh. You've come. I was waiting for you."

"You were?"

"You are the lover of the Earth man, are you not?"

A rush of heat flooded my cheeks as I pictured myself in Reese's arms looking into those dynamic eyes. "Have you seen him?"

"Mm-mm. I can see why you have a passion for the man. He is delectable."

I remembered his kiss and shot her a look.

"No, it wasn't like that, although I wouldn't have minded sampling him. Is he a good lover?" the mermaid asked, with a waggle of her index finger.

When I didn't answer, Rosalinda shook her tresses like a wet dog caught in the rain, giggling when water drenched my shirt. Annoyed with her antics, I glanced down and realized I would have been a fine candidate for a wet t-shirt competition. Even my bra was soaked.

The mermaid's eyes widened. "Even though you have a covering on them, I can see you have pretty breasts. And they are quite large," she glanced down, "compared to mine. Do all the Earth women have big ones?"

Her very serious expression made me smile. "All sizes and shapes."

"I am learning all kinds of things with you newcomers visiting our caves. I was particularly interested in the Earth man. He is fascinating."

She had my attention there. "How so?"

"His reproductive tool was long and poker straight."

"You saw it?" I managed to gasp out.

"I felt it on my scales when I pushed up to him." Rosalinda smirked. "You should have seen his expression. I think he thought I was an Earth woman. Did I ever surprise him."

"Reese was in this pool with you and wanted to make love?"

Rosalinda tilted her head thoughtfully. "Yes. I mean he was here but if he wanted sex it was not really his fault. The food was drugged."

"And then?" I said, trying to encourage her.

"I kept telling him to grind on me."

This was not a detail I needed to hear. "And did he?"

She shrugged. "Much too sleepy for that. The Tortuga had given orders he was to be fed with some powerful opiates. He was lucky he didn't die when he slipped into the water."

"They found him on Earth on the edge of a hot spring, passed out."

The mermaid nodded. "I caught him before he drowned."

"And you never saw him again?"

"Ah-hh, but I did."

This was rather confusing. "I don't understand."

"Reese returned to this very chamber later on and I had a chance to speak with him." She smiled. "He not only thinks of you frequently but when he does, something odd happens."

"Oh?"

"Reese told me he gets your scent."

"It's strange. I have his, too." The spice and soap in the air made me feel all mushy inside. "Do you know where he went? I'd like to bring him back."

Rosalinda tilted her head inquiringly.

"I came to save him. He's in a bad way. Can you tell me why he's here?"

The mermaid floated over. "We need to speak quietly." She gestured towards the door. "The stalagmites have ears."

17

"There is a solution to your problem, Almighty Tortuga," Reese announced loud and clear.

"Oh?" The turtle tapped his flipper impatiently. "It is close to my supper time. Perhaps we should convene tomorrow."

"Please. Listen to me."

"Alright, continue, but this better not be a waste of my time."

Reese took a deep breath. "In September, S cried blood red tears and your sea world changed, correct?"

"Yes, for the worse," muttered the gigantic turtle. "Go on."

"There is a way to get it all back."

"How?"

"First, stop the pixie from leaving. I need to go with her."

"And why should I, Earth man? It would be easier to hand you over to S and make her happy. She would forgive me my lack of understanding when she happily has you in her bed."

Reese gritted his teeth. "S will not forgive you. I think you know that."

The Tortuga's eyes narrowed. "She wants a mate." He pointed a flipper. "You. If I help her, she will be grateful and change everything back."

"You don't know that. It's not easy to forget a true love."

The Tortuga stirred restlessly. "What exactly are you proposing?"

Reese got on his feet. "I want to go and find the elf man."

"Crema won't allow you in," the turtle drawled dismissively.

"She will."

From beside the turtle's throne, the eel rasped, "You will be thrown in her dungeon and the piranhas will have you for breakfast."

"I can persuade Crema. I know I can."

An ugly noise rattled the chamber. The eel laughed until the turtle signaled him to stop. "Enough, Morahy!" The massive turtle head swung lower and two dark pools stared at Reese. "Why would she listen to you?"

"On Earth I am considered handsome. And she is a woman, isn't she?"

The corners of the turtle's mouth curled up. Was the reptile smiling? Reese couldn't believe it.

"Alright you have my permission. Morahy will accompany you."

"Is Tora still here?"

"You are in luck. The tiny winged creature is in our tightest security chamber being readied for release." The turtle's mouth tightened. "Be kind to the little one as she is in a difficult place in her young life."

"She certainly is." Reese was not used to teenagers of any species. All he knew was they were a pain in the butt. At this point he didn't trust Tora but he had a feeling that she was vital for this mission.

***

The water was warm near the surface and very red. It was hard to make out the eel in the bits of seaweed whirling in the current. But there was no mistaking his raspy voice when he growled, "I leave you here. Go forth. There is a grouping of three trees. Choose the tallest tree. Follow its six o'clock shadow into the forest. There will be a clearing with a road crossing. Always take the path to the left and you will find the Land of the Elves. Be cautious and keep your wits about you. If you are captured, tell them the Almighty Tortuga has sent you and they will let you live. With those words, the eel dove back down into the depths of the ocean.

Had he just heard that? There was a question as to whether they would survive this journey? Reese was not a coward, but on the other hand, he was not prepared to fight elves with magical powers. If they were anything like Tora, they would be fierce warriors who struck first and asked questions later. Not his idea of a fun time.

Closer to the shore, the red-hued water faded and finally

became crystal clear. Ahead of them was a pristine white beach.

Tora waved in the direction of the forest. "Hey, dude, that might be it."

He followed her gaze. Surprisingly, the forest was a vision in white. A tall conifer twenty meters away from the beach loomed over two neighboring trees.

Once out of the sea, the hot rays of the sun warmed them up. Reese was glad his only garment was his gitch. Although it was a bit embarrassing the way it clung to his junk, it was cotton and would dry quickly. But when Tora gave him odd looks, Reese felt heat rise to his cheeks. She must think he was some sort of pervert to be wearing only a clingy thigh high boxer brief.

"You earth men need to get better outfits," Tora said, with a sniff. "Maybe when we get to Elfland they'll give you something cool. That thing is so gross."

Reese resented the Tora's remark. He was fond of his blue gitch. Didn't cost much at Zenners and fit his goods nicely. "For your information, this gitch is comfortable and I like it. Sorry you don't but it was hardly my fault that I was zapped straight out of my room and into Sangra's bed before I could get dressed. By the way, why didn't you tell me she was your mom?"

The pixie said nothing. She picked up her pace.

"Tora, stop," Reese said, putting his hand in her path.

The pixie's lips twisted. "She hates me and I hate her."

"Yeah?"

"Sangra wouldn't tell me about my father but I suspected who he was for years." Tora shrugged her narrow shoulders. "I found a picture. I think I look like him."

Reese empathized with the pixie's confusion but couldn't understand the violent way she reacted to Sangra's guard or the rudeness she had shown her mother. "Do all of the nymphs know that you're her daughter?"

Tora nodded. "They were given orders to keep me in my room. Sangra told them I'd disobeyed her."

"And had you?"

"I went to a party the dwarves were having. She wasn't keen on me going. When I went anyway she decided on some tough love."

Reese stopped and faced Tora. "There are dwarves in

Nuncamorir?"

Tora giggled. "They're everywhere. You have them on Earth too, but you won't see them easily."

"Oh." Just when he thought he'd heard everything, dwarves entered the equation.

"They transform, just like witches and wizards," Tora continued solemnly.

Reese was sensitive to energy. He grinned, thinking he could be a wizard with all the auras he saw. Black had surrounded Lisa but until now, he hadn't realized the significance of it. She wasn't evil. Reese had been wrong about that. Her number had come up and nothing he could have done would have prevented it.

"You must have seen them?"

"What?"

A pained expression marred the pretty pixie's face. "The dwarves! Have you seen them on Earth?"

Reese laughed, shaking his head. "Nope, not one."

"You think I'm making this up? You'd be surprised where you'll find them." Tora smiled knowingly. "They'll show up right under your nose."

This gave Reese pause for thought. He shook his head. "Tora, I haven't figured out any of this. With all this rushing around there hasn't been time to think it through."

"Yup, it's been wicked. No picnic for me either." Tora pointed to the sun. "From the position of the sun, I'd say we have perfect timing on this."

They had been steadily climbing the hill and were only a few meters away from a sloping Siberian spruce which towered over the pines. On the ground, the tip of a long shadow pointed to the start of a path heading into the forest. It was a no-brainer.

The woods were quiet with only the occasional shrill animal cry. Probably a squirrel or something of that nature—or so he hoped. Reese saw a flicker of white as a bird flit from one branch to another. Its call was a squeak, something like a marker on a whiteboard.

There was a closed-in feeling to the woodland with patches sky brightly shimmering with sunlight hundreds of feet above. The white conifers with their tremendous trunks were remarkably like sequoia, a good twelve feet in diameter. Ivory branches embraced each other at the top while the bottom boughs below were starkly naked, void of all needles. Although there was life here in the forest, it was different from any he had ever seen.

Farther into the woods, the temperature dropped and the mixture of hot beach air and cool current caused a fine mist to rise from the grass, effervescent like a bottle of champagne. A sharp pain in his backside brought him out of his reverie.

"Ha! Gottem!" a deep voice sang out gleefully.

From over his shoulder, Reese eyed the arrow lodged in his butt cheek that was burning worse than a hornet's sting. "Geez, Tora. Get that thing out."

The pixie was fast. With flutter of her silvery wings, she flitted around and tugged the dart out of his aching behind. "See! Didn't I tell you?"

Reese grimaced. "You mean a troll did that?"

"Yup." Tora flung the offending weapon into the grass. "Damn dwarfs."

One of the ugliest little men Reese had ever seen appeared from behind a nearby rock. Beard to his knees and tufts of red hair over a knobby head, which combined with a toad-like face put him at a negative three on the attractiveness scale.

"You didn't say that last week, honeh."

Color rose to the pixie's round cheeks. "I had too much dew juice, Bart. You know that. We all did."

Reese could see now that the dwarf was not old. His skin was smooth as a baby's bottom but his face was one only a mother would love. Still, maybe the pixie protested too much.

"Watcha doin' here?"

Tora drew herself up to her full height. "We're goin' to see my dad."

"You have a dad?"

"Duh-hh!" Tora jeered. "Maybe you don't, but I do. He's an elf."

The red-haired dwarf eyed Reese up and down and stared. "That guy ain't no elf."

Reese resented that remark. Sure, he was in his thirties but he was not old enough to have fathered a sprite who must be sixteen plus.

Tora rolled her eyes. "The Earth man is on a mission to see

Crema. Say," she looked at him speculatively, "I think you could help, Gordo."

The dwarf brought up a chubby hand and stroked Tora's cheek. "Sure, babe. Bart likes to help sexy pixies."

"What's the fastest way to get to Crema's castle?"

"Why go there, babe? We could rock this planet like they've never seen before." He pointed to the dense bushes off the path. "There's some nice soft grass behind that bush and I've got some awesome dew juice in my backpack. I know you'd like it." He nudged her knowingly and winked.

Tora grabbed the dwarf by the shirt and jerked him towards her. "Get serious!"

"Alright—alright. Chill. I'll show you."

With the matter settled, Tora released Bart. "We've got ourselves a guide, Earth man. He'll get us to Crema's castle."

18

The dark red current thrust us into the mouth of a coral cave. At first, I thought the tunnel was unusually dark but with light beaming in from the ceiling, it became apparent that the merging water was not only cooler, but also no longer red. Somehow, this sea had not been touched by Sangra's tears.

Rosalinda took my hand and together we swam for twenty meters until the forty-five degree tilt angled us slowly upwards into a white sea, past stag-horn coral, a school of cream-striped grunt and ivory tang. It was a shock to be in an ocean as white as snow.

Even with Rosalinda's help, finding Reese would be a challenge. Coming out of a past life to enter the doctor's dream was stressful to say the least. If and when I found Reese, would I be able to help him leave?

As we neared the surface, Rosalinda released my hand. My eyes were dazzled by the columns of crystal clear stalagmites reaching up to the stalactites hanging like icicles from the ceiling. The circular limestone cave was whiter and more brilliant than a Hollywood icon's teeth.

"What is this place?" With this intense light I wondered how I'd be able to proceed.

Rosalinda pulled herself onto a rock and motioned for me to join her. As if she had read my thoughts, the mermaid drew out a pair of sunglasses from a pouch at her waist. They looked like knock-off Dior.

"You'll need these, Anise. Crema's palace is an eyesore." She giggled at her witticism before regaining a solemn expression. "Seriously," she said, fitting them carefully over my eyes, "they will keep you invisible." She then took off a ring from her hand and slipped it on my finger. "The rose quartz will help you win love. Turn it three times to guide desire. The longer you wear it the stronger it will become."

Rosalinda pinched my cheek. "Remember to summon your angels for what you want." From around her neck, she removed a silver necklace with a turquoise stone. "As a Sagittarius, this is your stone. It not only protects the wearer, it predicts the future. And don't forget to rely on your instincts, sweetie. You have the sixth sense. We do not have it here. You have an advantage. Remember to visualize and follow your instincts."

With all this information presented so hurriedly, I only partially took it in. The cave sparkled as brilliantly as the finest diamond in Tiffany's. Thankfully, the sunglasses covered my peripheral vision.

"I bid you farewell, Anise. May you have the luck of the mermaids in enticing the man," she smirked, "and the sexual appetite of one, too."

Not knowing what else to say to that remark, I hugged her. "You're a real friend. Before you go, could you tell me where we are exactly, Rosalinda?"

The mermaid's eyes crinkled at the corners. "In the dungeon of Crema's home. The basement, so to speak. Fantastic lighting, wouldn't you say?" She kissed my cheek lightly. "Remember what I told you. Be brave. You can do this." And with a flip of her tail, she dove down deep into the water, disappearing out of sight.

From the ring I felt comforting warmth as I crept through the low archway. It made me feel like I could do anything. I would find Reese and bring him back to Earth in one piece and then, well, *que sera, sera.*

Once inside, I stopped abruptly and gazed upwards. The railing and steps of the spiral staircase were made of some sort of bone resembling the human femur curving alongside the steps. As I climbed higher, eerie vibrations transmitted to my hand. From the walls I sensed the presence of spirits, each one voicing words of caution.

I was more aware than ever that I knew nothing of Crema or of the residents of her kingdom—a question that didn't remain unanswered for long.

A voice boomed out from the landing: "Who goes there?" On an incredibly long neck , a large head swung half-way down the stairs. The animal's coat was impressively vanilla-white but in every other way, it was still a giraffe. Doe-like eyes surrounded by four inch eyelashes peered in my direction. It waved its front hooves directly in front of my face but appeared not to see me. Was the animal blind? Then it occurred to me that the sunglasses had made me invisible. Silently, hanging close to the railing, I crept up to the landing past the giraffe.

"Do not fear, Ani. We will guide you," the spirits whispered in my ear.

At the top, elated by my success, I rushed forward, only to trip over the uneven surface. I stumbled and landed painfully on my forearms.

The giraffe's neck stretched out. "Speak up and let yourself be known."

Stupid, I'm not. While the creature sniffed the ground near the stairway, I got up and ran like the wind down the hall. When the passageway split, I entered the corridor to the left and stood close to the wall. I heard the clippity-clop of hooves before I saw the giraffe. It hesitated only a second before taking the path to the left. I sighed in relief when it journeyed a hundred feet or so and rounded the corner.

Given that lucky break, I took the passageway off to the right. Giraffes are not fierce beasts but they are considerably larger than horses and I wasn't too keen on being trampled.

Not at all certain I was on the right track, I stopped in the hallway and imagined Reese's green eyes as I turned the rose quartz ring. The scent of spice and soap filled the air. I breathed it in with my eyes shut. Sparks of heat shot out of the ring.

The ring transported me into a circular chamber. Everything was as white as snow. From the floor to the ceiling everything was winter white.

On a white couch loaded with pillows, a petite platinum blonde in a cream toga lay legs stretched out while a man with his back to me knelt on the marble floor. When I approached, I saw he was feeding her grapes.

"You are doing well for a novice." Her voice was high and squeaky. As the tune *Winter Wonderland* tinkled from her phone, she reached over and picked up the cell to check the message. Impatiently, she placed it back on the table.

A pixie appeared from behind a filmy curtain. Her silver suit was body hugging all the way to the thigh high boots. Gauzy transparent wings fluttered as she swept into the room.

The blonde frowned. "Did you find the nail polish?"

I had to strain to hear the pixie's quiet reply. "Your favorite shade of eggshell, princess. Give me your hand and I will apply the first coat."

"Excellent. Be careful not to smudge." The blonde offered her tiny hand to the pixie who set about coating her fingernails. "My husband should be here soon."

"You have heard from him?"

"No, not yet." When the phone tinkled again, the blonde sat up abruptly and grabbed the cell, sending the plate of grapes on the table tumbling to the floor.

"Clumsy fool!" she snipped at the man who had been feeding her. "Clean that up." She checked her cell again.

As the man patiently picked up the runaway grapes, I caught a view of a firm rear covered by a short ivory toga. There weren't many men with that build. Reese was now a slave for a rude princess?

A tall white-haired man with the stiff stature of a soldier entered the chamber, jingling the beaded curtain. "Your carriage is in working order. The mechanic has completed all the repairs."

"Good. What took you so long?" she said petulantly. "Our son has been waiting for us to join him. He's anxious to go to the Goblin Fair."

"It's not a good idea. You know how he gets when he doesn't win at games."

The blonde's face flushed with anger. "You are a terrible father. First you go off to the wars and now you refuse to make your only child happy."

"If I didn't go to war, you wouldn't have this luxurious life."

"Fine! Be selfish, Creyente. I am the mother of your child and all that I ask is some joy for our son." She glanced down at the pixie. "This one does nice work but this knave," she said, pointing at Reese, "is not the best."

"My apologies, Princess Crema." Reese inclined his head and stepped forward. "Sir, may I have a word with you?"

The elf man studied him. "Of course. What is it?"

At that moment a sandy-haired boy of about ten tore into the room shouting excitedly. "They started! Come on!" He ran up to his mother and tugged at her hand. "Now that dad's here, I want to try out the games."

Reese held his had in a stop gesture. "A moment of your time, prince?"

"Mom! Dad!" the boy whined.

Crema sprang up. "Whatever this knave wants can hardly be considered as important as your family." She glanced at her slaves. "But perhaps these two should come. They could carry Diamonte's prizes."

"Mom's right, Dad. They should help. I want to win some huge prizes and we'll need some slaves to haul the loot."

From a safe distance, I followed the group down a hallway and outside into a busy courtyard. There were jugglers, magic shows, acrobats, and booths with games. They stopped at the first stall and paid for darts. The boy threw them at the balloons but only one popped.

"Look, Mom, Dad, I won the giant furry elf!"

The proprietor handed the darts over to a waiting teenager.

"Where's my toy?" the boy demanded.

"Sorry, son, you need all three balloons popped before you get something."

Crema patted the boy's arm. "Daddy will get you one." She nudged Creyente. "Pay the man."

As Creyente reached in his pocket, the old goblin shook his head. "Can't sell them. These here go to the winners. Them's the rules."

"Dad!"

The elf took his son's hand to lead him away. "Let's go to another booth, Diamonte."

"No!" protested the boy, his voice pitched higher. "I want one of those. Make him sell one, Dad!"

Reese pointed to a stall. "That game over there has some."

"Good slave!" Diamonte beamed happily. "Come on. Mom, Dad." He jumped up and down in excitement.

At first I was careful not to get near, but as the events got rolling and the crowd thickened, I was forced to move in closer. The first whiff of Reese's scent was so intense, my body responded. My hands trembled. Would the force between us be strong enough to take Reese back, or would I be stuck here in his dream? With new conviction, I combated my way through the crowd. Elbows hammered into my invisible body until I reached Reese's side.

The booth Reese had pointed out was one with a game where balls were thrown into various holes barely large enough to contain them. It was rigged to be difficult. Only a very accurate pitch could win the prize. As I neared the back of the curtained area, I detected movement. Curiously, I lifted the material and was amused to see the pixie at ground level stuffing the holes to make sure no one could win.

I was beginning to feel sorry for Crema and Creyente. Their child was obsessed with furry elf toys and wouldn't go home without one. Reese pulled the child to another game as soon as it became apparent there would be another disappointment. Again Diamonte did no better and when I looked around, I saw the pixie grinning from ear to ear. Reese, on the other hand, looked as frustrated as the parents.

Crema shouted at Creyente. Through the din I could hear her. "Buy him one!"

"The goblins don't want to sell them," Creyente growled. "They have rules for their fairs. I told you Diamonte would cause a scene if he lost. It's time he learns that not everything goes his way."

At that moment, a blast much like the firing of a cannon drowned out all the sounds. A smoky cloud settled on the booths and the people gathered there. On the gate post at the entrance, a black figure was silhouetted against the sun. Arms raised high, lightning blazed from her fingertips, she screamed, "Nuncamorir!"

With a flash, the fair, the booths, and the people disappeared. No one was left except Crema, her family, and the slaves. Both the boy and the pixie had been thrown to the ground by the tremendous wind accompanying the explosion.

The smoke cleared to reveal a female with cascading auburn hair, a pearly complexion, and a long, lean figure in a slinky black dress. Looking every bit as saucy as a Victoria's Secret model, she strode confidently towards us.

"Shit!" exclaimed Reese, while the others froze on the spot.

About to speak, Tora changed her mind, clamping a hand to her rosebud mouth.

I felt Sangra's anger. The mermaid had filled me in but I was not prepared to see the red aura surrounded by pockets of black. A premonition of death came to me. A shiver raced down my spine.

Sangra towered over tiny Princess Crema. Her eyes flicked to Reese. "So-oo, Crema, you got yourself a trophy. And then you thought you could take Nuncamorir."

Creyente's eyes narrowed.

"Him?" Crema pointed at Reese with her index finger. "This slave riled you up so much that you had to come here with your army?"

Sangra's stormy eyes widened in disbelief. "Have you lost your senses? Yesterday you attacked the Nuncamorir borders with the sirens."

"You have a vivid imagination." Crema sniffed. "The sirens might have been there but there was no war."

"I am taking Earth man back. He belongs to me." Sangra glanced sidelong at the elf man. "I need a new mate."

Creyente frowned.

Just then Sangra caught sight of Tora. Color blotched her cheeks. "What are you doing here? You were told to stay in your room for the remainder of the week."

"When the Almighty Tortuga told me who my father was, I had to come. I have every right. You should have told me!" Tora said defiantly.

"Hush. I will not have you speak of family matters here."

"The man should know. You must tell him. It's only fair."

Crema brushed off some ashes from her toga. "Take the Earth man and go, Sangra. No one wants you here." She gazed at the pixie. "If you're part of her clan, I don't want you here, either. Leave."

"There's more going on here, Princess Crema." Reese smiled. "If I were you, I would be a little curious as to why Sangra knows the prince."

Crossing her arms over her chest, Crema glared angrily. "What are you insinuating?"

"Ask him." Reese jerked his head at Creyente.

Sangra jumped out in front of him. "Come along, Reese.

You're mine—baited and hooked. Besides, you feel guilty, remember? Poor Lisa didn't deserve to die, did she?"

"No, she didn't," Reese said slowly.

"And I didn't deserve not knowing, did I, Mama?" the pixie piped up.

Crema rolled her eyes. "Enough of this drama. Leave us."

Sangra reached over and stroked Reese's bicep. "Nice guns."

Shaking her off, Reese protested. "I don't belong in Nuncamorir. I need to go back to Earth. I'm not going with you."

"No?" The sorceress laughed. "I have the power, not you. Besides, you will enjoy your new life, I assure you." She clapped her hands and what appeared to be a rope curled in the air. I watched it drop down on Reese and wrap itself around his body, from toes to neck. The doctor gasped as it tightened. "Now, smile and say you will come willingly and I will remove the snake."

I could stand it no longer. "You are nothing but part of his dream," I pronounced, stepping up.

Everyone looked about puzzled, except Reese whose eyes shot over to where I stood. "Anise, are you here?"

I pushed the sunglasses to perch on the top of my head and watched Sangra's jaw drop. "Take the snake away. Reese is coming with me." As I spoke I turned the rose quartz ring three times, pointing it first at the elf and then at Sangra. When nothing happened, I got a sinking feeling.

The sorceress snickered. "You are an Earth woman. Whatever magic power you have is non existent here. Surely you can see that?"

I had to stall her. "Reese belongs on Earth. Admit it. You don't *really* want him, do you?"

"She knows, Mama. The Earth woman has the sixth sense." The pixie rocked on her heels. "Why don't you tell them the truth?"

"Silence, Tora." Sangra looked me up and down. "Who are you and why do you challenge my power?"

"I am Anise. If you bring Reese back to Nuncamorir, he will die." I glanced over to Reese. "He will never wake up from his dream. I'm here to take him back. Release him!"

The boy jumped up. "The Earth woman is challenging mighty Sangra, Mom. They must fight!"

Gleefully, Crema tapped the elf's arm. "Diamonte is right. At last some real entertainment."

For the first time, I saw concern on Creyente's face. "No, that can't happen. Sangra, reconsider. Let them go back to Earth. You don't want the man. I know that."

Sangra's face became sad. "Yes, I do. I need a male child, an heir to the throne." She turned to me, hands on her hips. "Choose your weapons."

Silently, I clutched the turquoise stone hanging on the silver chain around my neck. *Please angels, help me! I need to win his freedom.* The whispered words sprang to the stone. Energy entered into the edges and grew fiercely hot like a coal in a raging fireplace. In my mind, I visualized dual silver weapons.

Far above in the sunlit sky a lengthy dagger appeared, gleaming like a jewel before it shot into my left hand. I gripped it tightly. Again, from the heavens, a second dagger zipped into the palm of my other hand.

I knew them well. They were sais, a weapon I'd been trained to use. Fingers on the handle below the prongs, I stood my feet shoulder's width apart in the ready position.

Sangra clapped her hands and a pair of sais dropped into her hands.

"The winner takes the Earth man!" Crema shouted.

For a moment Sangra stood still, her eyes narrowed. "You can give up now, Anise. I will accept your surrender. You will not be hurt."

I shook my head and thought about Francisco and his loyalty to me. He would have died for me. His love was strong. And then I remembered how Reese had saved me from drowning with no thought to the danger he'd placed himself in. There was no choice. I would fight for him.

Knees bent slightly, I stood holding the daggers, the points at a forty-five degree angle. "Death over surrender!"

Sangra fixed her eyes on me and screamed before attacking.

With my left foot out, I brought a sai up to check her lunge. Steel against steel. I swung a sai high over my head and jabbed it between the prongs of the other sai, blocking her. Sangra stepped back but not before I nipped her shoulder.

I heard a gasp from Creyente. With blood oozing from the

wound, Sangra's jaw tightened with new resolution. Sais held high, Sangra stepped forward, arms raised. Weapons crossed. With a powerful push she knocked me to the ground. Sangra rushed to spear my chest. I parried and thrust but her sai jabbed into my collar bone. Pain seared my skin before I threw myself forward. Suddenly, Sangra stepped aside and I fell, my arm knocking Crema back. Her tiny body toppled over like a sapling tapped with an axe.

From the corner of my eye I saw Reese wrench the snake off. He held a bloody knife in one hand and a humongous cobra in the other. Encouraged by his victory, I wobbled to my feet.

"Kill the Earth woman, Sangra! Let her feel pain!" Crema screeched as the elf yanked her to her feet.

This dream was turning into a nightmare. I glimpsed Reese's face as he surged between us. With his sword, Creyente blocked the doctor. "Back!" he ordered. "You must not interfere."

When Creyente pressed the tip into his shoulder, Reese twisted around and backhanded the elf. Blood gushed from the elf's nose over the pristine tunic. Creyente froze. Reese took that opportunity to strike his wrist, knocking the sword away before he charged headfirst bringing down his opponent. Together they hit the dirt, punches flying. All the while, Diamonte couldn't stop squealing, the wrestling making him crazier than a crack addict in need of a fix.

Focusing once more on my opponent, I was glad to see Sangra was just as distracted as I was. With the butt end of a sai, I made contact with her stomach. When she gasped I knew I'd hit the spot. I would have taken her down if it weren't for the boy. Like an annoying bug he decided to enter the fight, a toy sword in his hand. I kicked him back into Crema's waiting arms. My chance lost, Sangra struck my elbow with her dagger. My sai slipped out of my hand.

As Sangra moved in for the kill, I blocked her attack at the expense of my forearm. Intense pain shot to my fingers. I called to my angels, *Help me!* Somehow I pivoted my right foot and kicked out at her knee with my left. The sorceress went down, her face contorted in agony. I shot to my feet. With my sai raised over her Sangra's throat, I looked down.

Dark eyes stared up at me in acceptance. "He is yours. You have won. I am ready to die."

Propelling Reese away, Creyente rushed to my side. "No, don't! I love her."

Crema's face paled. "You love Sangra? Have you lost your mind?" She grabbed Diamonte's hand. "I am the mother of your child."

Her jaw set, Tora's eyes were fiery. She pointed at Sangra. "And she is the mother of your child."

Creyente's jaw dropped.

"Yes, it is true. I am your daughter, Tora. Am I less than this male elf?" She glared at Diamonte. "I needed a father. You deserted me when you left Mama."

Creyente was speechless.

"Listen to her. She's telling the truth." Reese stood up. A brilliant orange surrounded him. "Sangra never wanted me. I was a poor substitute for you."

"I don't believe any of this," Crema hissed. "You are all crazy!" She rushed over and grabbed Creyente's sleeve. "Are they telling the truth? Was it during the War of Irons before the Storm of Sorrow?"

"Yes, it was then." He strode over to Sangra and gently helped her up. "I didn't want to fall in love but I did. When you no longer wanted intimacy our love died a slow death." He gazed at Tora. "I had no idea I had a daughter. It matters not that you are female. You are my flesh and blood. I have room in my heart to love both my children. Forgive me but I knew not."

Sangra bowed her head. "It is my fault. I didn't want you to stay with me because I was pregnant. I wanted you to stay for love."

Creyente took her hands. "I've always loved you. I made a mistake leaving you. Had I known about Tora, I would have found a way to make this all work."

A glow lit up Sangra's face and her angry red aura softened to pink. I could no longer see the black jolts of color.

"Perhaps Crema will allow Diamonte to visit you when you live with Sangra," Reese offered.

"I…I…" Princess Crema stuttered, color rushing to her cheeks.

Rapidly, I turned the rose quartz ring.

On the third twist, Crema regained her speech. "I always knew you didn't love me as you should but I was afraid of ruling alone."

The heat from the ring seared my skin. "Let them discover their love. You can see they need your compassion."

Crema laughed derisively. "That is an emotion I do not possess."

Every one of us was covered with blood and dirt except Crema and her son. How they had managed to remain as clean as freshly fallen snow, I couldn't fathom. A dull green haze surrounded them yet at the edge there was a sickly fringe of yellow. Rosalinda had warned me to use my intuition. I knew what the aura meant. The princess was filled with possessiveness and jealousy.

"Your god believes in forgiveness and compassion," I said to Crema. "It is time to open your heart. Do not fear life."

"You know nothing, Earth woman." Crema pulled her son to her, glaring angrily at her husband. "I will not allow you to see him if you leave me."

"He will always need a father to care for him," Creyente protested.

"And what about me?" Crema said in a pitiful voice. "Who will take care of me?"

I stepped up and handed her the ring. "Take strength in this. You must be an adult. It is time to grow up, Princess Crema."

Crema stared at me and then at the ring. "It has power."

"Take it."

On her index finger, the ring sparkled pink. Crema touched it tentatively. "It is beautiful. Thank you." For a moment, Crema remained silent and then she drew herself up. "Creyente, you are no longer my consort. Go to Nuncamorir."

"But," the elf's gray eyes grew misty, "I worry about you."

Crema shook her head. "I will work on regaining my strength." A tear trickled down her cheek as she gazed at the elf man. "Diamonte may visit you in Nuncamorir. I shall rule the empire."

Reese waved his hand to stop her. "In my world, parents can share custody of their children. Your son can share time equally with both of you."

Creyente glanced at Crema. She nodded. "You speak with wisdom. From here on, love will be the power that rules us."

19

A fluffy cloud shaped like a giant seahorse sailed across the cerulean blue sky. With the call of the birds and the rush of the ocean, all my pent up tension released as a tropical breeze brushed my bikini-clad body.

The current was strong today. Surf pounding the rocks shot up a frothy spray before washing over the sandy shore. Dark green coconut palms waved above our heads blocking the intense heat of the midday sun. Our spot at the edge of the beach was like paradise. The tiny cove was secluded, miles from the road.

Fifty feet beyond the water's edge, grass and trees took over. Stone steps led to a Spanish style bungalow perched midway up a hill. From here, the view of the villa was blocked by palms allowing only a glimpse of the white stucco building with the red tile roof.

After we had said our good byes to Luis and his family, we biked north along the coastal road to find Jorge's cousin. The directions were good and we arrived before noon. Just in time as the government auditor was on his way out, heading back to the capital. A jovial sort, he smiled often, his gold tooth flashing, as he spoke words of welcome. Guillermo said he wouldn't be back until the next day and winked meaningfully. It didn't take much persuading for us to agree to stay on.

Restless, I sat up and gazed at the shore. When I leaned forward I felt something brush my shoulder. It was as if someone had touched me but when I looked down I saw Reese lying still, eyes closed.

"He's so sexy. Forget Francisco. He's dead," My Hormone Voice said softly. *"Make love to Reese and be happy."*

A bright blue butterfly fluttered over my head. Butterflies were spirits of the dead. Was Francisco's spirit trying to make contact?

I sensed Reese before he brought a hand up to brush my hair aside. A trail of tiny kisses from my ear to the nape of my neck sent delightful shivers down my spine.

"Stop thinking," he whispered in my ear. "This was meant to be."

"You mean your coma had a purpose?"

Reese laid his hand on my cheek and moved my face towards him. "I was consumed with guilt."

"Did you love her?"

"In the beginning, but, Anise," he stared solemnly into my eyes, "it was never like this." Pulling me close, he nuzzled my ear. "No one smells as good as you, my beautiful temptress." His head tilted up as he breathed in. "I've had your scent every day since I met you. In the Mojito I woke up in the morning smelling your skin even though you were gone. When we arrived in the mountains I would be standing with Luis and suddenly get a whiff of your perfume even though you weren't there. It was strange how I connected with you."

"Not always," I said, running a finger down his cheek. "You were angry at me at first."

"Yes, the accident. I didn't realize what was happening. It was all too incredible." The emerald depths sparkled in his eyes. "But from the moment I saw you, I felt enormous energy." The doctor laughed. "Funny, it was through the dream that I found out how really wonderful you are. You are fearless." He shook his head. "It was amazing how you fought Sangra." From the basket, he pulled out two wine glasses. "Hold these," he said, pouring out a ruby red wine.

"To you," I said, smiling up at Reese.

He shook his head, clicking my glass. "No, to us."

The shiraz was a perfect blend of plums and ripe raspberries. "Good?"

"Better than good. It's soft in the mouth. But Reese, there is something else. A flavor that is so familiar. I'm trying to put my finger on it."

"Yes?"

I closed my eyes a moment and sipped once again, this time holding the nectar on my tongue. "Mm-mm. There's chocolate."

Reese grinned. "You have quite the palate."

Over the brim of the crystal, I watched him tilt his glass back once more. Dark lashes framed the changeable eyes, which saw things no one else could see. A complex man I hardly knew. Yet, there was an intense chemistry that drew me in. All his elements blended with mine. It was increasingly difficult to focus on conversation.

"Ani."

"Why are you calling me that?"

Reese gazed at me. "I heard a female voice saying it in my head."

"My mom's name for me." I frowned. "She called me Ani because of my Oma Ana. Remember how I came here to find out about her?"

"Yes, and we will. There is an old synagogue in Havana. We'll head out there tomorrow."

"Thank you, Reese. I know Oma and Mom were with me on this journey."

"Your spirit guides." The breeze swept his hair onto his forehead. Softly, he said, "They led you to me,"

I had a sudden urge to touch him. His eyes flickered green as I pushed a lock back and threaded my fingers through the sides.

"It's no use." Reese laughed. "My hair has gone wild."

"Oh?" I wove my fingers through his locks. "At least it's only your hair. I've changed so much since I came to Cuba. The woman who left Canada doesn't exist anymore."

Reese tilted my chin up. "You are my magnet." Leaning in, his lips lightly landed on mine.

Electric. I pulled away from the charge.

Reese smiled as if he knew my thoughts. "I wasn't sure the dream would ever end." He stroked his lower lip with a finger. "What I don't understand is how you were in it."

"It's complicated. I wasn't at first. While you were in

Nuncamorir, I regressed into a past life."

"That must have been fantastic. Who were you?"

"I was a socialist from Argentina."

"Is that why you knew the folk music?"

"Mm-mm. It was much later that I became a guerilla involved in the liberation of Bolivia. The regression was intense. Almost too much for me. I died there." Somehow I couldn't bring myself to speak of that other man who I'd loved so deeply. It was almost like being a widow. Francisco was dead but the love I'd had wouldn't die easily. I was beginning to feel guilty for being with another man.

Reese took my hand. "I can see it's painful. When you're ready, I'm a good listener. "

I nodded.

"Anise, this whole thing is a puzzle. Please enlighten me. How did you come to be in Nuncamorir?"

"After Lola brought me back from Bolivia she told me you were in a bad state. I entered your dream."

"How did you find me?"

"Your mermaid was very helpful."

"Rosalinda?"

"She had all sorts of aids."

Reese arched an eyebrow. "Sounds kinky."

I grinned. "No, just magic. The ring I gave to Crema was for her to gain an understanding of love."

"Rosalinda was both kind and perceptive. Did you know she pulled me out of the water?" He frowned. "But she was only a part of a dream. I must have tried to save myself."

"And you did but the drugs were hard on you. Reese, I'm curious…"

"Yes?"

"Rosalinda didn't really exist. Had you thought about mermaids before, I mean, as a fantasy?"

The corners of Reese's mouth curled up. "You mean was Rosalinda a sexual fantasy?" He squeezed my hand. "Don't worry. She had her attributes but a mermaid is missing some of my favorite parts. I prefer a lovely Earth woman."

"Like Lola?"

Reese stared out at the white caps foaming into the shore, his expression grim. "I saw her aura." He took my hand and looked directly at me. "It was the color of dried blood. What do you think that means?

"Anger." I leaned back on my elbows. "With her it was misdirected passion. You remember the herbs and powders? She drugged the wine."

"I thought so."

"That was the cigar she blew."

Reese laughed. "That's one way of putting it. Her cigar was one of those fake ones, filled with dung, not tobacco. Cohibas are known for their smooth chocolate finish."

"True."

A furrow formed in Reese's forehead. "You know that?"

"When Lola sent me to my past life, I was in the jungle, fighting to free the Bolivians. The worst part was the mosquitoes. All of us smoked cigars to keep the bugs away."

"That was about forty years ago?"

"Um-mm."

"Were you happy?

"The fighting was rough but I was with a man I cared for." I felt suddenly sad. I missed Francisco. But as I gazed at Reese, I knew he was special to me. I could trust him to care for my heart.

Reese gave me a hug. "I'm sorry I mentioned it. I can see it's painful. Let's not talk about it. One day when you're ready. Tell me, Anise, why did you choose daggers?"

"I'm a karate student. Sais are my favorite weapon." I drank a last sip of shiraz. "But to actually use them in a fight was surreal."

Reese looked serious. "It seemed real enough when I saw Sangra's sword jab your shoulder. It made me realize how much losing you would mean to me." Tentatively, he touched the spot where the sai had pierced my skin leaving behind an angry red scar. It had stopped hurting days ago and was now slowly healing. "A strange thing when a dream actually leaves you injured." His jaw clenched. "There was something very familiar about Sangra. She reminds me of…"

"Lola?"

He nodded. "This may seem bizarre but I believe she transformed herself to enter my dream."

"Do you think now she'll go after her lover? The married

one?"

"Good chance." He grinned. "Better him than me."

With my index finger, I smoothed his bruised cheek. "Creyente packed a good punch."

"Yeah? So did I," Reese said, lowering full lips to mine.

Energy sparked my core. The heat of his kiss touched a place never explored. I felt compelled to press my lips to his, to let them ride every curve. Lightly, the tip of my tongue stroked the inside of his slightly parted lips. I was caught in a rapturous net. If I were to die right now it would be a delicious death.

Reese broke away with a smile that went straight to his eyes. He held up his glass. "Shall we finish first?"

"Let's," I said, catching my breath, wondering what else he had in mind. Another sip of the full berry flavor with a hint of chocolate and I let out a sigh. "This is wonderful but I wish…"

"Yes, of course." Reese reached behind him into the basket. "Close your eyes, goddess. Good, now keep them shut and open that sexy mouth of yours. Yes—excellent, but wider."

Creamy rich chocolate entered my mouth, releasing succulent flavors as his lips and tongue pushed in the truffle. Ambrosia that would have made Venus quiver with delight. Endorphins escaped. Hot vibrations raced down my body. Warm lips pressed on mine once more and I felt an unbelievable rush of energy. It had been a while since I'd experienced this sensation; in fact, not since my last life.

Yet, I had to consider what was going on. Lust wasn't love. What I'd felt for Francisco had been deep. Reese was extremely sexy and admittedly I've always been attracted to doctors and men in uniforms—but smokin' hot as he was, Reese was not my guerilla lover. How could I be disloyal to that love?

The chirp of my cell interrupted.

"Ignore it," Reese said, his voice husky.

I was tempted to do just that but my senses told me the text was important. Quickly, I opened my bag and tugged out the cell. A strong sense of urgency made me click the screen.

Before I could read it, Reese tore the phone away and tossed it down on the blanket along with my now empty glass. "It can wait. I'm crazy for you."

He dropped down on the blanket and pulled me close. Kisses

seared my shoulder. Through the bathing trunks, I felt him hard on my thigh.

Desire glittered in his eyes. Teasingly, I brought a chocolaty finger to his full lips, tracing the edges. With a quick movement, Reese caught up my finger and sucked it, igniting a fire in my body. Then he released my hand and kissed my throat, blazing a hot trail to the deep valley between my breasts.

Pulsing sensations perked my nipples. As if in answer to my needs, he slipped his hand in my bikini top, cupping a soft mound. Pushing the strap down, he brought his mouth to the peak while his other hand explored its twin, fingers playing with the bud until it too became erect.

I held his head down to my chest, threading through the thick waves, my senses awakened by the silkiness of his hair and the movement of his mouth. In the sunlight, with the crashing of the sea and the essence of this man, I wished it to never to end.

Fire torched my body. Reese broke away, eyes glittering with passion. Impatiently, Reese tugged on the strings of my top, loosening the bow, letting it slide off onto the blanket.

It was my turn. Reaching up to his chest, my fingernails lightly scraped sculpted abs while my lips journeyed down. His quick intake of breath excited me. I let my hands explore over the bathing trunks. With a groan, he whipped them off.

"Let me taste you," he said in a husky voice.

In a quick movement, he lowered himself between my legs. He sensitively stroked my thighs, mingling kisses with his touch, until I shivered with anticipation. Bikini strings came undone and the fabric fell on the blanket. His tongue swept me into a euphoric cloud. Everything blurred as tremors from deep within me fought for release. A scream tore out and I soared high into ecstasy.

When my pulse slowed, I climbed on top and kissed him passionately. As I sank lower, I leaned forward to lick the contours of his ear and moved back and forth until he let out a groan. Reese brought me closer to caress my breasts. With hands tight around my hips, he thrust up. I received him and returned his force. Like a rapid succession of bullets, Reese banged inside me yet there was no pain. I felt a heat so powerful, my only thought was how to get more pleasure. We rocked in rhythm. When I met his eyes, they gleamed differently somehow. I sensed a new energy I didn't understand.

"I want you behind me," I said, stretching cat-like on the blanket. Flush against me, Reese supported his weight with his arms as he entered. The friction from our bodies stirred an already steaming cauldron of lust. Sweat coated our bodies. It was as if oil had been ignited. Reese moved with the frenzied energy of two men until I climaxed wildly, crying out.

"Oh, Anise!" His body froze. "Look at me," he urged.

From behind my shoulder, I gazed into jungle depths. Reese groaned and sank down against me before collapsing on the blanket.

"You had a fever and lost weight. I need to be careful not to crush you," he said with a wide grin.

I recalled how emaciated I was from the hardships in Bolivia. "Why did you say that?" From underneath, I became aware of the cell phone poking into my hip. I removed it and glanced at the text.

I'm here with you, mi amor.

Startled, I gazed at Reese.

Bourbon eyes stared back. With a soft kiss he whispered, "We belong together. That life and this."

I understood at last. "Soul mates—forever."

****

www.AnastasiaAmor.com
Anastasia.Amor@hotmail.com

http://anastasiaamor1.blogspot.ca